ROBERT LEWIS WARING

AS WE SEE IT

By

ROBERT L. WARING

❦

McGrath Publishing Company
College Park, Maryland

Reprint McGrath Publishing Company 1969

Library of Congress Catalog Card Number: 77-76122

Manufactured in the United States of America
by Arno Press, Inc., New York

TO THOSE NEGRO MEN WHO
DARE DEFEND THE WOMAN-
HOOD OF THEIR RACE.
—The Author.

AS WE SEE IT

FORWARD

INASMUCH as the title to this work, "As We See It," may be a little obscure, I offer the following explanation for its adoption:

Books upon books have been written on the Negro question, but none have told the story as "We" see it. By "We" I mean the educated Negroes, those of cultured families of the third and fourth generations, those Negroes who see things as other men of their mental caliber see them, who feel the sting of race prejudice most keenly, and at whom the damnable laws of the South are aimed. In the books that have been written the "Jim Crow Nigger" is always in evidence and is always a welcome and fit companion for those who father the "Jim Crow Law" industry.

This work is intended to reveal two sides of Southern life, which are carefully obscured, intentionally avoided or deliberately misstated my newspaper and magizine writers.

First, in this story we picture that class of Negroes who are doing something, whose lives, homes and successes are the same as those of other men, and who, starting from nothing, have in fifty years accumulated in the aggregate more than two hundred and fifty million dollars worth of property. These people compose that class of American citizens whom the calamity howlers are careful to keep in the background, and whom the Southern press persist in misrepresenting even to the point of malicious lying.

Second, we aim to represent, in their true character, another class, lower, both morally and mentally, than the Negro. These people, the "crackers" of the South, marry in

5

and out of families closely connected,. first cousin to first cousin, great uncle to niece, step-brother to step-sister, brother to brother's wife, father to step-daughter, adult men to thirteen-year-old girls, etc. These marriages may account for their degeneracy more certainly than the newly discovered hook worm. They can boast, and do boast, of being of the fourth and fifth generation of those who can neither read nor write. They have an utter disregard for the property rights or lives of other men, although this is seldom commented upon by writers. This Southern "cracker" is not multiplying as his birth rate would indicate, for his offspring dies in great numbers in early babyhood owing to a lack of intelligent care, and many older children die in large numbers because of the lax enforcement of the child labor laws. These people, the "crackers" of the South, who today hold that section in political thraldom, and whose uplift, through education or the infusion of live blood, is the only possible means left the white people of the South by which they can hope to keep ahead of the progressive Negro, *present the true problem of the South.* So long as the discriminatory laws remain in force in the South, just so long will the Negroes, as a whole, continue to outstrip the whites, as a whole. Every intelligent Negro who is doing something, and who reads of what his brothers are doing, knows that he is leaving the Southern white man far behind. The "cracker" knows this also.

To illustrate: Was there ever a large business of any character, a store, a bank, an insurance company, a school, college, or what not, organized, built up, controlled by a man or woman who sprang from the "cracker" element of this country? Hundreds of such enterprises are owned and controlled by Negroes who were slaves. This non-progressive citizen is, however, held up to the world not in his true light, as a worthless trouble seeker, a veritable cancer eating into the vitals of the body politic by his "God-given right" (?) to vote, but as a poor, struggling white man whose chances for gaining a livelihood are curtailed by the presence of thrifty Negroes who are bent on removing the bar to their manhood, *placed there by the State.*

These things, which should be apparent to all persons educated in American schools, and also to those who observe the trend of American ideas, are ever before the educated Negro. But, even with conditions as they now are, and the Negro moving along the lines he is pursuing, the time is not far distant when a change will come over the land. The popularity of the doctrine of rope and torch for the Negro is on the wane; the apostles of that doctrine have been relegated to the rear. New ideas, more progressive, have taken hold on the popular mind.

In a few more generations the Negro will be a man, thoroughly trained, a true American, ready and willing, as he has ever been, to fight and to die for the flag that now protects him—NOT.

AS WE SEE IT

CHAPTER I.

ABOUT the year eighteen hundred seventy six, in a beautiful section of the old State of Alabama, there sat upon the large and commodious veranda of an old Southern home in the golden twilight of a perfect sunset, two old friends, whose friendship was of life-long standing, who were alike in many respects, but yet essentially different.

One a white man and owner of the place, the other an aged Negro, of the old school, were smoking in perfect harmony, the white man, a meerschaum pipe of queer workmanship and of great age, having been in his family for three generations, the Negro the old corncob pipe so common among Negroes of that day.

"Go to College? What the darn-nation good would that do? Why, the time is not come for 'niggers' to be educated like white men. I tell you, Abe, I shall not agree to any such d— nonsense."

"Yes, sar, dat what you say I guess am true when it comes to ole 'niggers' like us, but what you goin' do wid a boy lek my Abe? Ise hear'n you say when dat boy's no mor'n twelve yeahs ole dat he war de smartes' boy, white or black, dat war ebber on dis hyar place. Ise de fifth Abe Overley, black, dat war bred an' bornd on dis hyar place. Yuse de fifth Abe Overley, white. Yuse seventy-two, Ise seventy-two; yo' Abe's nineteen, mine's nineteen; yo' Abe's de sixth white, my Abe's de sixth black; yo' Abe an' my Abe was teached by the same 'oman at the same time, den de man come an' dey is both ready to go to College. Now, what yo' goin' do? Yo' boy's weak, my boy's strong. You war weak, I war strong. Could you git 'long widouten me? Yo' Abe need my Abe, my Abe need yo' Abe."

"Yes, Abe, but don't you know that these are different times? That your Abe and my Abe cannot get along in College as they do here? White men do not sleep with 'niggers' at the big Colleges. Times have changed."

"Yes, Ise hear'n dat de times am changed, but de hearts ob true men never change. Does yo' think dat Abe Overley, sixth, white, will ever turn his back on Abe Overley, sixth, black? My Abe say he want to go to College to be a lawyer, why he not? He go to Sunday School an' teach dem young 'niggers' ebery Sunday, an' Miss Annie Godly she say dat she can't git 'long widouten him."

"Oh, yes; that is a sure indication he will make a good lawyer. Who is going to pay for his schooling?"

"Why, who pay for his ticket to de Fair las' fall? Sho' yo' Abe he pay for hit."

"H— and damnation! You ole fool, don't you know that it would cost five hundred dollars a year for his schooling? What have you got, or has Abe got, to pay five hundred dollars with?"

"I could sell my ole mule, an' Baldy, dat would bring something."

"Why, Abe, you have no more sense in that old black pate of yours than that d— old kicking mule. Who would buy the beast? I said five hundred dollars, not fifty cents. Do you know the difference? Now, who will pay the money?"

Abe replied with great solemnity:

"When yo' mammy die, she take our hands an' she put dem togedder, an' she say: 'You two Abes mus' al'ays be friends, no matter what de world say.' You say, 'Yes,' I say, 'Yes.' When yo' wife die, she do like Miss Miranda. She say to you an' she say to me, and to yo' Abe an' to my Abe: 'You mus' al'ays be friends an' honor each odder'; dat was mor'n eighteen yeahs ago. Who been yo' Abe's mammy eber since? How many times when yo' Abe, weak an' sick, habe he crowded my Abe from he own mammy's breast? Dey sho' mus' go through dis world togedder.''

"Abe, you are a cunning old 'nigger.' I cannot forget these things. But conditions are not like they were in the old days. The Old Homestead is mortgaged, and the crops are getting worse each year, and every d— 'nigger' on the place is talking about going to College. What am I to do in the next year or two? This dirty sneak, Lashum, holds the mortgage and he wants to live on the place where the hound used to boss the 'niggers,' and I hear that that whelp of his wants to go to College, too. What is this world coming to, 'niggers' and, worse, poor whites, talking of going to College and being lawyers and doctors?''

It was early in the year eighteen seventy-six that these old friends, both of the royal blood, the kind that never knows a friend but as a friend, and never breaks from a friendship but in death, were thus engaged in a warm discussion as to the future of their sons.

A word as to the place where we find these representatives of their respective races, and as to who and what they are.

About the year seventeen hundred and two there came to this country a sturdy Scotch family, consisting of father, mother and three sons, possessing nothing but their vigorous bodies and a strong determination to get along in this new world. After many wanderings and hardships, they selected this spot in Alabama, upon which they settled and built their ancestral home, and upon which we find them. They did not belong to the people who "gloried in the Holy (?) Institution of Slavery,'' but, owning slaves, they made their burdens as light as possible.

When the great War of the Rebellion came on the Overleys were not eager to join their neighbors in their cause; so, as a consequence, they lived under suspicion, and were in constant dread lest they should be assassinated or burned out by the poor whites who were in those days just as they are today, ignorant, idle and vicious.

The Rebellion finally ended, leaving this family with its ancestral home intact, but much reduced in wealth, all of the stock and animals of value having been carried away by bands of patriotic (?) rebels for use at the front.

Abe Overley came of a stock of nature's noblemen. He was tall, straight, broad of shoulder, strong limbed, good featured and very black—a typical African—but the kind of man that inspires trust and confidence at a glance.

Abe's parents for four generations had enjoyed the confidence and esteem of the Overleys. The first Abe was bought by one of the first Overleys at a public auction, he being sold because he was considered an intractable "nigger," having refused to be whipped by the overseer of the plantation upon which he lived. It was said that Abe was stolen and brought to this country and sold in slavery. His wild and independent spirit was never broken.

Overley saw at a glance what the trouble was. As soon as he had closed his bargain he took the manacles off Abe's arms and said: "Abe, you are to be my right-hand man. Can I trust you?" After a long and searching glance, Abe replied: "You can always trust me; but you nor no living man shall whip me."

"Abe, I do not whip my people."

This bond was never broken.

Before the Rebellion the Overleys had an overseer whose name was Lashum, Nick Lashum, a long, gaunt, typical Alabama "cracker," whose father, grandfather and great-grandfather before him were overseers, and who never aspired to anything higher. This man's sole ambition was satisfied when he became known as Malcolm A. Overley's overseer.

When the war came on it soon began to be whispered about the State that Nick Lashum was engaged by the Confederate Government to press animals and stock of all kinds into service, for the good of the cause. There appears to be no doubt that he "pressed the animals into service," but, according to the whisperers, he did not or was not able, owing to the "press of business," to account for hundreds of them. It was even whispered that numerous droves of cattle gathered by him found their way to the Union lines, much to his profit.

However, at the close of the war, this individual found himself so well supplied with ready cash that he concluded to buy a large plantation and settle upon it and live as a capitalist and planter should. What place should he buy? There was but one place in all the State of Alabama which suited him, that was the home of his former employer, Malcolm A. Overley. But this place was not for sale. The adjoining plantation was, however, so he acquired this place and moved upon it.

Mr. Nick Lashum was a man of family, a large and growing family, a growth peculiar to this particular family of "crackers." As the wealth and numbers of this family increased their church-going parties, regaled in all their finery, came to be the sight of the county, a sight that strangers never failed to enjoy. This great man, former overseer, who had grown so wealthy in such a few years, and one of whose sons was clerk of the County Court, and another about to be sent off to College, was looked upon by the "crackers" of his section of the State as the man who was to lead them back to the good old times when a "nigger's" hog was the property of the first "cracker" who could steal it.

How fared the Overleys as the years sped by? Having been left, after the war, without stock to work the plantation— thanks to the disinterestedness (?) of Nick Lashum—on behalf of the cause, and without farm hands to work the crops—saving the strong arm of Old Abe and his family—things had been going back. For some time poor crops, poor cattle, and only a few of them, had been the rule, until, after a family council, it was decided to mortgage the place and raise money enough to stock the plantation as it was in the old days and begin again. After much dickering and many heartaches, it was decided to borrow $5,000 from the Pioneer Savings Bank of A—— County, Alabama, Nick Lashum, Jr., cashier. Never once did Malcolm A. Overley think that Nick Lashum, Sr., would advance the money and hold the mortgage, but after it was all over Malcolm A. Overley had $4,750 and Nick Lashum, his former overseer, held him bound for five years for $5,000 at 8 per cent. This mortgage had eighteen months to run when we find him discussing the advisability of sending his son, together with Old Abe's son, North to College. Old Abe felt that his boy should go to College with the white boy. After long and deep thought Old Abe, with intense feeling, spoke:

"I thought when I stan' by de bedside of yo' mammy, an' she place our han's togedder and she say we war al'ays to stick togedder an' to he'p each odder, an' when yo' boy's mammy die she say de same thing, dat we was to he'p each odder. I thought when dem Yankee sojers come, an' dey say, 'Old man, you kin go,' I say, 'No, I dun promise his mammy to stay an' he'p him through dis life.' I thought when I teach my boy he mus' stay an' he'p; I thought when I tell dem odder 'niggers,' Joe an' he 'oman, Jack an' he 'oman, an' Cleo an' her gals, to stay, dat I was doin' my duty, dat I was keppin' my word to de daid. Ise worked on dis ole plantation well nigh seventy-two yeahs, and Ise good for twenty mo', but never did I tink dat de time would ebber come when de Overley would break he word."

After Old Abe had delivered himself of his speech there was a long, deep silence. Finally it was broken by Malcolm A. Overley, with a voice trembling with emotion:

"Abe, you old black fool, who has broken word with you? I said, I do not see where the money is coming from. That d— hound's mortgage is due in eighteen months, and I haven't the money to pay it. He will surely sell me out.

Now, what shall I do: take this money and send the boys to College or pay this mortgage?''

Old Abe answered solemnly:

''Send de boys to College, an' trus' in de Lawd.''

''Trust in the Lord! That is all you 'niggers' think about. You had better learn to trust in yourselves. However, I have made up my mind that both boys shall go to Oberlin College. You can tell that boy of yours that he can go with my boy when he leaves for College this fall, but I want all the work done on the place before they go.''

''Thank God!'' said Old Abe; ''I know'd dat yo' heart is in de same place dat all de rest of de Overleys is.''

As a fit finale to this discussion, Mammy Cleo blew three shrill blasts on the supper horn.

Soon the field hands are coming in, as is evidenced by the vocal sounds of melody that float soothingly to the ears of the two old friends. First to come through the yard to the great house is a tall youth, with a delicate face, lit up with clear blue eyes, with a well-formed head, covered with thick light hair, which hung about his ears in ringlets, the face, head and carriage of the man of good blood and breeding. This youth was Abe, sixth, white. He took a seat on the floor of the veranda, leaning his back against a post, looked up at his father and laughingly inquired: ''Why, dad, what is the matter? Have you and Uncle Abe been quarreling over the stock or over some passage in the Bible, or what?''

''No, we have not. That old fool thinks I ought to send his Abe to College with you this fall,'' answered the parent.

''Why, dad, I think he is perfectly right. Abe ought to go to College; he certainly deserves it.''

At that moment a tall young Negro of manly appearance, a perfect counterpart of Old Abe, came up to the veranda and sat down. He also observed the faces of the old men.

''Why, dad, what is the matter?'' he exclaimed. ''Have

you and Mr. Overley disagreed again on some point in the Bible, or some point in farming?"

"No, d— your black hide," spoke up Overley, Sr.; "we have disagreed on you."

"Why, what is the matter with me? Have I not done my work well ever since I have been old enough to work?"

"Oh, d— your work! I wish I could find some fault in that line. This old fool insists that I pay $500 a year for your schooling, until you get through College, that is what I mean."

For several moments there was nothing said by any of the four friends. Finally, the younger Overley said:

"Father, if the money is not to be had, let us fix it this way. Let Abe here go the first year, and I will stay home and keep up the place. The next year he will keep up the place and I will go. He can give me the benefit of what he has learned when he comes home."

Abe protests that the white boy is entitled to the first year, but Overley, Sr., cut the discussion short by announcing that he had determined that both boys should go to College together; therefore he didn't want any more "d— talk."

Both boys then moved away to the corn crib, their favorite resort, to talk the matter over.

"Abe," says the black boy, "your father is a mighty good man to spend all that money on me."

"Yes, but you and Uncle Abe have been mighty good to us. What would we have done after the war had your father left us, or had he said to the rest of the people, 'Let us go North?' We would have been left without help or hope. He remembers how Uncle Abe and the rest worked for five years without being paid one penny, and——"

"Yes, but your father has paid us in full, paid every penny," interrupted the black boy.

"Yes, but off of whose labor?"

"No matter, he has paid up. Where in all this State will you find another white man, who, having had twenty-three colored people working for him for five years, without pay, would have paid them one cent? Very, very few. Your father mortgaged his plantation. If he had not paid us he would not have had that to do. No, Abe, he is a mighty good man."

"Yes," says the white boy, "he is a dear old dad;" then adds: "Say, Abe, didn't he cuss—Well! So we are to go to school together?"

"I am sure I do not know; what College are we going to?"

"Oberlin College."

"That is the one College in this country that I want to go through. They say they do not know color there. Just to think of anyone failing to see whether I am white or black!" and both boys laughed heartily.

"Say, Abe," the white boy said, "I hear that Buck Lashum is to go to College this fall."

"What College?"

"I do not know," answered the white boy.

"Well, we must not let him know what College we are going to attend, nor that I am going with you."

"Why, Abe, what difference does that make?"

"Well, I must say that I feel it would be better to keep our plans from him until we are gone, at any rate."

"Abe, you will see what will happen to him if he has anything to say to me about your going. I haven't forgotten the thrashing you gave him when he tried to force himself on my sister Lucy when you drove her to Deaconsville to the camp meeting last fall," laughed the white boy. "His black eyes were such beauties, and they lasted so long. Say, but dad forgot his rheumatism when he was told what happened. When they told him that the sheriff had put you in the cababoose for licking Buck Lashum for insulting Sister Lucy, gee! how he ran to the harness room, and got a saddle and bridle, and ran to the field, and got Old Ben, and such cussing and riding you never heard nor saw. I, on Nell, kept as close to him as I could, but Old Ben seemed to be cussing mad, too, for I never saw that old horse go so fast before. Didn't the whole Lashum family fall back when they saw him coming? And didn't the sheriff get you out of the pen mighty quick? But, poor Buck was a sight, and Mr. Nick Lashum, how he made excuses for Buck. But dad wouldn't listen, and wanted to lick the whole family. Abe, you must have soaked him some good ones. Dad was talking about that fellow to us last night, saying he would just as leave be kicked by Uncle Abe's old mule as for you to hit him. Now, I know that those Lashums, and particularly Buck, do not like you, Abe; but I can't see why we should care. A poor white man, Abe, is no good.''

"Yes, yes,'' says the black boy, "I know that, but you cannot view a poor white man, a 'cracker,' from the same viewpoint that I do. Compared, Abe, with the race of white men that you and your family belong to, the 'cracker' sinks away below any living thing. He is meaner and dirtier than any reptile that creeps on the face of the earth or swims in the water beneath the earth. There is nothing too mean and low for him to do to a Negro—Pshaw! What is the use of discussing a 'cracker,' anyhow? The question that concerns me most just now is what will we need to take with us when we go off to College.''

"I don't know,'' said the white boy; "let us ask father; he has been to College.''

CHAPTER II.

FOR the benefit of my readers who are not familiar with the Alabama "crackers" I will give an historical sketch of the Lashum family, that they may draw their own conclusion. This family dates back to the last years of the war for independence; at least, that is the time of the first record which the State has of its existence. The following can be found in the *Western Bulletin*, Monday, September 12, 1709:

"Nick Lashum, who lives in a log cabin on a small clearing in Foggy Bottom, on Mars Creek, was taken out of his cabin by a Vigilance Committee and given nine and thirty lashes on his bare back.

"It appears that the Indians have been drinking and causing a great deal of trouble lately. The source of their supply of whiskey could not be ascertained. It was at last determined by the Vigilance Committee to search Foggy Bottom, where a few disreputable 'crackers' have squatted. The search revealed the fact that Nick Lashum was making corn whiskey and trading it to the Indians in his neighborhood. The search also revealed the further fact that Nick Lashum was the leader of a gang of moonshiners who were making corn whiskey and trading it to the Indians and Negroes in all the lower counties of the State.

"Nick Lashum and his confederates will be tried at the next Quarter Session of Court and are likely to get long terms in the penitentiary."

Thus the Lashums are ushered into the limelight of history. No mention is made of what finally became of this Nick Lashum, but tradition has it that he came back from the penitentiary to his old haunts and resumed his old habits until the time of his death, which was hastened by a Vigilance Committee after Nick had been caught with some cattle upon which the brand had been changed. This man appears to have been the progenitor of this race of Lashum, many of whom proved to be worthy of their sire.

The Nick Lashum of this sketch was a long, gaunt, lean "cracker" with a thin, sharp face, lit up by a pair of small gray eyes full of low cunning and treachery, that never looked you in the face. His head was topped off by a crop of thin stringy hair, that was entirely unused to care. His garments, which were gray in color, might have been homespun or anything else, and hung in loose flaps about his person, the trousers (?) stuffed into ragged cowhide boots.

This gentleman, a typical "cracker" overseer, having heard that Malcolm A. Overley wanted an overseer, owing to the death of Pete Quickly, who had served the Overleys for twenty-five years, betook himself to the Overley plantation to apply for the position.

With much fear and many misgivings he finally mustered up courage enough to pass the portals of the big gate and make his way to the great house, where he expected to find the master. As Nick neared the house he removed his hat and walked slowly up the gravel path, where he was accosted by Old Abe, who inquired of him who he was, whom he wanted to see, and upon what business.

At first, Nick was inclined to feel insulted and hurt that a big black "nigger" should ask him what he wanted. But, upon second thought, he remembered how near Old Abe was to the "throne," so he answered very civilly that he wanted to see Mr. Overley and wanted the job of overseer.

After some thought Abe concluded he would conduct him to his master. This was done with many misgivings as to the future, should he be selected. Nick was cautioned to keep close to Old Abe, lest the dogs should attack him, as they did not like "no po' white man, nohow," and to keep his hat under his arm, where it belonged; all of which Nick was glad to do; but making a mental vow, however, that he would skin Old Abe if he succeeded in getting the place of overseer.

Turning a sharp bend in the path, Nick, without warning, came suddenly upon Mr. Overley and his family under the shade of a large tree, and the sight seemed to deprive Nick of power of speech. He stood looking at his ragged boots and holding his hands before him. Mr. Overley sprang to his feet, looking first at Old Abe, then at Nick, not seeming to comprehend the meaning of the intrusion. At last he spoke, and demanded of Old Abe what this man had done, and why he had brought him there, the man's demeanor leading him to believe that he had been trespassing. When he was told that the man wanted the position of overseer, Mr. Overley laughed heartily, and the women drew close and examined him very attentively.

Abe said:

"Dis po' white man come up de walk an' say he want to see you 'bout being yo' oberseer. I say he kin see you, but I guess he kin talk for heself, maybe. Say, Mr. Oberseer, dat am Mr. Overley. Kin you talk? You hab to talk mor'n dat to git work outten dem 'niggers' back in de cotton patch.''

Nick, thus goaded by Old Abe, finally said:

"Sah, Mr. Overley, I heah thet Old Pete was gone an' daid, an' that you war in need of a man to look arter yo' 'niggers.' My 'oman she say you mought take me on, in Old Pete's place. I've been hankerin' arter yuse job for a long time, sah.''

"Well,—you have, have you? Where did you work last, and why did you leave?''

"I worked for Mr. Jim Connors, down on the bottom in Grove Neck. He sol' all his 'niggers' an' gone 'way. He never did lek plantation life. He gin me one 'nigger,' but I couldn't feed him, so I took an' sol' him. He was as no count 'nigger' as you ever see; couldn't git him to do nothin'. Sell a bad 'nigger,' sah, same as you sell a bad hoss.''

"I have no bad 'niggers,' neither have I any bad horses; all my people are happy and content. I am afraid you would cause them to become dissatisfied. What do you want per year?''

"Mr. Jim gin me $180 a yeah an' house an' ten acres, the house free. I git along on that very well, sah."

"Well, you can see me in two days."

"Yes, sah; my 'oman she say——"

"That is all, sir; you may see me in two days. Abe, see that the dogs do not molest him."

Nick, with his hat still under his arm, bowed most profoundly and turned to leave by the path through which he came.

Old Abe called to him, saying:

"Come dis way, white man. Dem dorgs will eat you up down dat path by yo'sef. What you go dat way for, nohow? You mus' tink yo' Mars Jim Cornors. De nex' time yo' come heah yo' come in de way I am now showin' yo' out. If dem dorgs had seed yo' fust—well, dey don't like yo' kin' people, nohow."

"It strikes me, Abe, yuse a mighty peart 'nigger.' I suppose yuse is boss heah?"

"Yes, Ise de boss of dis house, an' dem stables, an' dat garden patch, an' all dem chickens an' fowls—yo' dunno dat, does yo'?"

"Oh, I tink it war somethin' like that—yuse welcome."

By this time their walk had led them to the barnyard, out of which a lane ran through the cornfield to the main road. Abe's parting shot was:

"Look out, white man, for dem dorgs when yo' come back through dis corn patch, an' git yo' hat off befo' yo' come through dis gate."

"Abe, you kin do me a good——"

"Dat am all, sah; yo' kin see me in two days," said Old Abe, with the most aggravating composure.

Nick stood for a moment glaring at Old Abe; then he turned and walked hurriedly down the lane toward the main road.

Owing to Abe's thoughtfulness, Nick had about three-fourths of a mile farther to walk to get out to the main road on his way home. Abe watched Nick until he passed out of sight; then he laughed and remarked to himself:

"Dat man goin' raise de debble on dis heah place some day."

Turning to a large brindle hound that watched Nick very closely during his visit, Abe said to the dog:

"Joe, yo' jus' watch fo' dat po' white man day arter tomorrow, an' if he try to open dat gate yo' jes' stop him; dat's all."

The dog seemed to understand what Abe had said, for he gave Nick's direction a contemptuous glance and walked away with Abe.

True to his appointment, Nick appeared at the barnyard gate, hat in hand, but afraid to open it, for there stood Joe looking at him in no uncertain way. Abe was in the harness room cleaning harness when Joe, by his growl, let him know that Nick had arrived. Abe looked through the window and saw Nick at the gate and resumed his work as composedly as if he were not there.

"Dat po' white man am com'; well, he can wait or he can com' in, an' Joe an' de res' of de dorgs will look arter him."

After about three-quarters of an hour Abe appeared at the door of the harness room and said:

"Man alives, is dat yo'? I couldn't 'magine what dat dorg dun saw at de gate. Why yo' not cum in? 'Spec' Mars Abe cumin' to see yo' heah? Man, yo' ain't nebber goin' git 'long on his heah place; yo' too slow."

"I was afeared of that dorg," said Nick.

"Well, dat dorg he don't lek no po' white man, dat sho.' Cum on an' see what Mars Abe goin' say. You sich a noble lookin' critter dat I sho' Massa goin' have you," said Abe, after contemptuously surveying Nick's tattered appearance.

Nick made a mental note of Abe's observation and vowed to get even, if the time ever came.

Nick was engaged by Malcolm A. Overley after a long lecture, in which he was told plainly that he was not to curse nor abuse any person on the place, and that no whipping was allowed. When he could not get work out of the field hands they were to be sent to the great house. Nick did not know at first what to make of that kind of treatment for Negroes, but he soon learned. He quickly discovered that he could get more and better work out of them in that way than he could by the lash. He continued in the service of the Overleys until the War of Rebellion.

CHAPTER III.

THE time finally came for the Overley boys to leave the old place for College. Quite a discussion arose as to the names of these boys, each having been known all his life as Abe Overley, one white, the other black. It was seen by them, and very properly, that they could not be thus distinguished while at College. It was finally decided that one should be Malcolm A. Overley, Jr., and the other Abraham Overley, Jr. It appears that the Negroes had never been called Malcolm. The senior Overley on the day of their departure called both boys into his library for a final word.

He said, with great earnestness:

"You boys are now leaving this place for College. This is the first time either of you has been from home. You will meet with temptations, but I expect you both to overcome them. You will meet them within and without the College walls. I repeat that I expect you to overcome them. You both bear a name that has remained unsullied for a century. I expect it to remain so. I have no fortune as my ancestors had. I have but their name left. I entrust it to your safe-keeping.

"You, Malcolm, must remember your mother's last words, that Abe is your life friend; and Abe, you must remember that Malcolm is the son of your father's best friend. Need I say more?"

Abe extended his hand to the elder Overley, who grasped it heartily. He said:

"I cannot express what I feel, sir, when I consider what you are doing for me. I can but say that you will never regret what you do for me. If I live to get through College I will repay you. I thank you, sir, with all my heart."

"I do not want your thanks; you deserve what I am doing for you. All I want you to do is to get through College and bring my name back as you take it from the old plantation."

25

CHAPTER IV.

THE next morning at sunrise both of the old men met at their usual place on the veranda. They smoked a long time in silence, which was finally broken by a remark from the owner of the place.

"Abe, what do you think those boys will want to do when they get out of College?"

"I guess your boy will want to go to Congress and my boy will he'p dese po' 'niggers' git back som' ob de lan' dat has been tooken from den by dat Lashum fambly."

"That would be a good thing for him to do; but I am afraid his hide would not be worth a picayune when he tries it."

"Ise hearn him say dat, too. Den he say dat he intends to try, so he'p him God, when he cum back. Dat boy, he mean what he say."

"Well, Abe, what do you think of that boy starting a legal fight with these poor whites? They are in control of the county and the Courts and everything else that I know of. Then, Abe, do you think that it is right for a 'nigger' to fight a white man?"

"Well, I tell yo', 'fore de war, when all de 'niggers' 'long to som'body e'se, all dat I hearn am dat de Lawd made a white man fus', an' dat de white man war made specially by de Lawd to own an' boss de 'nigger.' Den I belebe dat de 'nigger' jes' natchuly 'long to de white man. But when dem white sojers cum heah an' lick de debble outen dese white folks an' I see how meek an' humble lek dey cum to dem, den I say, What am dis? Am I right nohow? Is dese white folks what dey is cracked up to be? Den I see dat Lashum fambly puttin' on airs an' silks—the same folks dat I seed 'fore de war in missus' ole work apron. Den I say, What am dis world a cumin' to? But when I see all dem trash fishiatin' 'round 'lection day an' havin' all de say, den I say dat de

debble am de boss arter all, an' dat de po' 'nigger' am de feed
for his fire, an' dat if de men lek you an' Mr. Jim Cornors
an' Mr. Big Joe Wheatly don't took an' do somefin' dis
country ain't goin' to las'. Whoever hear'n of anything
lassin' dat dese po' white trash does? Does I tink dat a
'nigger' oughten fight a white man? Dis is what I was
teached. Dat I was to 'spect a white man an' not answer him
back nor hit him. But dem was slavery days. What de difference now, I dunno.

"I does know dat dem po' white trash on de Neck is a
whole lot wus den me or my people is, an' dat you an' Mr. Jim
an' Mr. Big Joe is a mighty sight better'n dem 'niggers' what
gits drunk all de time an' hangs 'round de cross-roads. But
is I as good as you an' de res' ob yo' friends? Dat keeps me
wake ob nights. My boy he young an' read de books. He
say dat all men is bornd ekil, an' dat a man is what he make
heself. He say dat a man hab no right to say he am as good
as dis one or dat one, because he am a man, but he mus' make
heself a man. He say dat ebry man will find he strata in
'ciety. What he mean by dat?"

"He means his level."

"He say dat a 'nigger' or po' white man dat say he got a
right to cum to yo' house an 'cum in an' set down, widouten
you ax him in, am a fool. Dat what I tink. I don't let dem
trashy 'niggers' cum to my house, nor does yo' 'low dem po'
white trash to cum heah. But den I jes' don't feel dat Ise fit
to mingle wid yo' gess. No, I don't tink so. Now, when dem
boys cum back from College, dey may or dey may not be
chums; but dey will say how dey will treat each odder at dey
own house. It 'pends 'tirely on who dese people is. I tink
dat a 'nigger' oughter fight ebry po' white man dat don't treat
him or he kinfolks right. Dat what yo' an' yo' friends
does."

"That is so, Abe; but I did not think that you felt that way
all together."

After Old Abe had relapsed into silence, Malcolm A. Overley pondered Abe's remarks for a long time.

"What a change a few years have wrought! Old Abe, d— his black hide, feels that he is almost as good as me and my friends! He has doubts on that score. Well, who the h— would have thought it? But he has sense enough not to push himself. He holds himself above the low 'niggers' about here. He is looked up to by all the 'good niggers' far and near. He is right to hold himself above these d— poor trashy whites. I could never understand why these poor whites hated Abe and his boy so. I see now. There is a natural antipathy between the two classes. Abe and his kind represent all that is honest and true, while the poor whites are just the opposite. But can this boy afford to start a fight with these people just at the time he comes out of College and with nothing to live upon? In spite of myself, I can but admire that boy's pluck and spirit.

"Well, I guess I will come in for my share of trouble for sending him off to College. Why, I must be getting babyish. Who the h— will dare to question an Overley as to his reason for doing what he thinks proper?"

Thus he smoked and dreamed for an hour. Suddenly he exclaimed:

"Abe, you have changed somewhat in the past year or so, it seems to me."

"I don't reckon yo' ever axed me dat question befo'. My boy say dat dere am no mo' 'niggers,' but all am 'Merican citizens, free an' ekil befo' de law. Dat what he say. Now, Ise a citizen an' has de rights. What 1 goin' to let dem po' white trash bamboozle me oughten dem fo'?"

"Abe, why do you continually refer to the poor whites? Are they the only people who do not treat you right?"

"Why, man alives," said Abe, with wrath, "don't yo' know dat de po' white trash am de onliest people in dis whole world dat am al'ays hollerin' 'nigger,' 'Jim Crow,' 'social 'quality,' 'nigger marrying white 'oman,' an' de debble knows what—all sich fool talk dat causes trouble? Dem very same trash dat kotches our likely lookin' gals on de road an' drags dem in de bushes. Dem de people dat sees a hard-workin' 'nigger' wid a home, an' a mule, an' a 'fix' to go to church wid, dat gits up de mob an' hollers dat dis 'nigger' is arter he wife or gal. Den dey burn he home, an' barn, an' take he life, an' mule, an' hog, an 'fix' to pay de damage. Dem's de trash dat gemmen lek you an' Mr. Jim an' Mr. Big Joe oughter he'p us for to fight. 'Fore de war when dem same critters did steal hogs an' de lek, yo' all did ride to dere cabins an' take dem out an' flog dem on dere bare backs. Now, dey do de same thing more bold; holler rape, an' de whole country is ridin' an' beatin' ebry 'nigger' dey meet, an' if he owns a good hoss dat is better'n dear'n, dey swops hosses wid him whedder he wants to or no.

"Why, man alives!" said Old Abe, with increasing wrath, "dese things am 'nuff to make a man bus' wide open, an' dey is gettin' wus. When dat drunken Smaly boy kotch my Sally Jane on de road dat night, when you an' Mr. Jim hearn her holler, hit was a good ting dat yo' Abe hide dat gun. I run for de gun fus', but yo' an' Mr. Jim git dere fus'. I sho' would hab killed him.

"But, Lawdy, how my Abe did walk on him! I think sho' dat de padroller would git him. I nebber tol' you dat it war my Abe dat beat him up so. No, sah. I was afraid dat yo' would think dat a 'nigger' oughten lick a white man."

This last sentence was spoken in such a solemn tone that both men laughed heartily.

"Abe, you are a sly old rascal. You know perfectly well that I have abused your boy time and again and told him that he was a coward for allowing that poor white hound to get off without a thrashing. And you would not tell me? You told my boy, though. I can now understand why you three devils always grinned in my face every time I spoke of that case. Told my boy, but would not tell me. Why not me?''

''Well, when dem boys cum to me an' Abe tol' me what he dun done, yo' Abe say dat you better not know 'bout it. I say no, you dun got 'nuff on yo' mind 'thout dat. Dat I war Abe's daddy, an' dat I war de one to bar de trouble. So I say, no, an' dat end it.''

''Well, Abe, that was very kind of you. What you say about those poor white people has long been a source of worry for me and my friends. Only last night we determined to get together and try to put a stop to these deviltries. It will be a hard job. These poor whites are in the saddle now; we have been asleep too long, and they have taken advantage of everything. We are going to try to stop them by fair means; and, if not, then we will try the same method we used on them before the war.''

It appears that the Negro referred to in a previous chapter as belonging to Nick Lashum—he having been given to Lashum by Mr. Jim Connors, and sold by Nick as a worthless 'nigger'—had, after the war, accumulated some property and had a good home, upon which he reared a family of nine children, the eldest of whom was a man of family and taught the County School for colored children. This young man had a wife and three children. He rode a very fine colt to and from his school, which was some distance from his home. There was but one other horse in that end of the State which could hold his own at the County Fairs with this colt, and that horse belonged to young Malcolm A. Overley. This Negro's horse was the envy of every poor white man in that section. Often was the remark made that that horse was too good for a 'nigger,' and that he must have stolen it.

Finally, the man appeared who lost (?) the colt, although it was well known that this colt was sired by Malcolm A.

Overley's horse, "Ben," known all over the State by its color and markings.

One warm July night, while this old Negro and his family were sitting about the front of their home, a party of horsemen were heard coming down the road. Nothing was thought of that until the sound of horses' hoofs was heard coming up the back road toward the rear of the place. Suddenly all sounds ceased; then a pistol shot was heard; then a rush of horses' hoofs; and before one of the astonished Negroes could gather his wits volleys from shotguns and revolvers were fired amongst them, killing and maiming men, women and children alike. The old father, the young schoolmaster and his youngest child, who was asleep on his lap, were killed. The wife, who was about to become a mother, was trampled to death beneath the horses' hoofs, before she could drag herself out of the way. The dwelling and barn were fired in a dozen places at once. Both buildings, together with their contents, save the colt in question, were consumed.

The *Alabama News,* the leading newspaper of the State at that time, had the following conservative account of this tragedy:

"George Burrell, a Desperate Negro, Whose Desperate Deeds Date Back Before the War, and His Son, Who Was Following in His Father's Footsteps, and Two More of His Desperate Family, Wiped Out by Sheriff C. Lashum and a Posse of Citizens.

"It appears that a Deputy Sheriff went earlier in the day to the cabin of George Burrell to replevin the colt that Burrell had stolen. The Deputy Sheriff was met at the door by Burrell and his son, both armed with double-barrelled shotguns, and his life threatened if he dared to serve his papers.

"The Sheriff was notified and the papers were served with the above result. It appears that in the fight which ensued upon the service of the papers the lamp was overturned and the cabin was soon in flames, which, in turn, spread to the barn, both buildings being entirely consumed.

"It is to be regretted that a Negro woman and two small children were trampled upon by horses; but the citizens claim that the horses became unmanageable when the fire started.

"A Coroner's jury, which was empanelled on the spot, exonerated the Sheriff and his Deputies, as it was clearly shown that the Negroes resisted the service of a legal paper.

"It will be well for the Negroes and all concerned when they learn not to resist the law, but to submit to the lawful service of papers as white men do."

This conservative account of a most atrocious and bloody deed was heralded to the outside world as another example of Negro depravity, degeneracy and disregard for the law and its representatives. This paper sent out this account without investigating the case, and based its report upon the statement made by one of the parties who participated in the killing.

The facts are as follows:

The party who sought to replevin the horse well knew that he could not maintain the suit, if it were presented to the Court in the regular way. So it was determined to put the two principal witnesses, the old Negro and his son, out of the way, which was done very successfully. The finding of the Coroner's Jury, which was composed of members of the midnight marauders, empanelled on the spot, was not questioned. The Sheriff was there with his papers, and the Deputy Sheriff who swore that he was at the place earlier in the day and was met by the old Negro father and son with guns in their hands, was also there, although, as a matter of fact, he was not on the place prior to his coming with the mob, who were bent on killing a prosperous Negro and his family. All these things were known to persons in the neighborhood, but the machinery of the law was in the hands of the murderers and nothing could be done. The attention of the Governor of the State was called to the case, together with the fact that what was left of the family had been driven from that section of the country and their property practically confiscated. The Governor was informed by his special agent, Garrington, that the Negroes resisted the lawful service of a legal paper, and that all the killings naturally followed the unlawful acts of the Negroes.

The loss of property and the driving from home of helpless children by the Lashums was not gone into. Everything was regular and according to law.

This outrage is what brought Malcolm A. Overley and his friends together. We shall see later what good was done by this combination of law-abiding white citizens.

CHAPTER V.

BOUT one week after the boys had gone, two letters arrived. Both began:

> "Dear Father: We arrived safe and sound. So did Buck Lashum."

Each father instinctively looked at the other, and read the other's thoughts. Each felt that this announcement meant trouble for his boy.

The letters contained the statements that the boys were through with their examinations; that both had passed with credit, and had been assigned to their respective classes.

They had secured adjoining rooms, but were very much disappointed to learn that Buck Lashum had secured a room on the same floor, across the hall on the front tier, overlooking the campus—one of the rooms sought by the rich boys.

They also spoke of the boys of different nationalities who were attending the College. There were Englishmen, Scotchmen, Italians, Spaniards, Japanese, Chinese, Negroes, Frenchmen, Germans, and one Persian of a noble family.

As all the young men spoken of in the letter met in the chapel at devotional exercises and at the mess table, the Southern boys, led by Buck Lashum, not understanding the sentiment which prevailed at this College, promptly waited upon the President, the grand old Dr. Finley, and requested that the Negroes, also the Japanese, Chinese and the Persians, be seated at a separate table, so that the gentlemen of the South could enjoy their meals without feeling that they were degrading themselves by eating with "niggers."

The President of the College listened very attentively to these students, then asked: "Do you know who these young men are? And what is your objection?"

Mr. Buck Lashum, being the spokesman of the party, and not having had that early education which would have fitted him to act in such a matter, blurted out: "They are niggers."

"Sit down, gentlemen," said the good man; "let me tell you who these gentlemen are."

He then called the Secretary and had the roster of the College brought.

"Now, let me see who these people are to whom you so strenuously object. First, we have the two Japanese, one, the son of Baron Yoshida; the other, a son of Count Nagayana; both old aristocratic families, whose names have been interwoven in the history of the Eastern world for more than a century.

"Next, we have the Chinese, four in number, who are descendants of families, the youngest of which antedates the building of the great Chinese Wall, years before the Christian era.

"The Persian is a prince of the royal blood, brother of the present ruler of Persia, whose family dates back 981 B. C.

"Next, we have the Negroes from Jamaica, whose fathers are British subjects, included among the wealthy, cultured and progressive men on that Island.

"The next five are sons of Afro-Americans, some of whom you gentlemen may have known before you came to this College. I understand that one or two of you—looking at Buck—have personal acquaintance with some of these Afro-Americans.

"Now, I notice among you some native born Southern men, and some who have never been South. What am I to infer? That you young men have gotten together and come to the conclusion, before you have been here long enough to know the sentiment or learn the rules which govern this Institution, that there is something radically wrong in the management of this College, and that all that is needed is just a little care at your hands and all will be set right?

"You young men who come from the South may think you are right because you have been taught these ideas; but you young men who have never been South must have borrowed these ideas, which are no credit to you.

"As President of this College, I will inform you, gentlemen, that the College will continue to stand by its old rules and customs, and live up to the sentiment which has always dominated it, and if in any way the table does not suit you gentlemen, you will be permitted to have a table at which you may enjoy yourselves as your sense of dignity may dictate. These young men are students here in the same sense that you are, entitled to all the rights and consideration to which you are entitled. It is not the policy of this College to humiliate one student at the behest of another. I am rather astonished at this proceeding. You gentlemen have just entered College. You have been here but three weeks, and yet you come to me with a request for me to unsettle a policy which was established forty years ago. Am I to consider you a disturbing element?

"My advice to all of you is, look well to your books; look well to your lectures; look well to yourselves, lest these same boys whom you now hold in such contempt outstrip you when examination day comes, and leave the management of the College to those upon whom that duty devolves."

With these words, spoken in a kindly voice, but in no uncertain way, the President arose and the interview was at an end.

When this delegation was well out of hearing of the President's office, Buck Lashum burst forth with an oath, saying:

"Who would have thought that a white man would have said that a 'nigger' is as good as a white man, and that a white man can eat at a side table if he don't like the 'niggers' being present!

"I, for one, will write home and tell my pappy that I am

sick from eating with 'niggers' and want to come home. He will send for me by the next mail.".

The next speaker was a boy who came from a "copperhead" family of Southern Indiana by the name of Bloxum. This family possesses nothing but a reputation for aping aristocratic people and forming friendships with the newly rich of their neighborhood.

There appeared to be something in Buck Lashum for Bloxum, hence the newly formed friendship.

"Buck, don't do nothing of the sort; stay right here and let's give them h—. These 'niggers' have no business here; we can freeze them out."

"That is right," spoke up the rest; "we can arouse enough sentiment to force the faculty to put them out."

"We can write home and ask our people to write here, saying that the 'nigger' must go," said Bloxum.

Then spoke up young Bucker:

"Well, you fellows can do that if you choose, but I am going to take Dr. Finley at his word and let this thing alone. I didn't want to mix up with this affair in the beginning, anyhow. My father has no money to waste on me fooling with other people's business. I must make my time count while I am in College."

"Just like you," said Bloxum, "afraid of your shadow. Well, I guess we can find enough white men in this College to carry this thing through."

"We will try without you," said the rest.

"That is what you will have to do," replied Bucker.

When this visit to the President became known, and what these young men had attempted to do, the foreigners were astonished. Being of royal blood, they could not understand what was meant by the attitude, and the request preferred, and took just the opposite view, thinking that the common people were afraid to sit with royalty, and, therefore, undertook to explain to Lashum and Bloxum their willingness to waive the point in etiquette so long as they were in school.

When the students learned that the foreigners had condescendingly endeavored to waive this point in etiquette and were willing that these protesting boys should eat at the same table with them, the jibes and shafts of wit and sarcasm thrust at them by the students would have been unbearable to persons of refinement and culture, but were completely lost upon these boys—one the son of a former overseer of six generations of overseers, the other the son of a "copperhead," whose natural characteristic is what the word "copperhead" is meant to imply.

Consequently, in the density of their ignorance and self-conceit they failed utterly to appreciate the ridiculous position in which they had placed themselves. Both Buck and his friend Bloxum failed to pass the examinations which had been passed with credit by the boys whom they presumed to condemn; but they were permitted to go on conditionally.

Buck felt that he was white and that that was all that was necessary.

By the end of the first quarter he had learned better.

CHAPTER VI.

IT IS now Christmas time following the departure of the boys. We find the two Old Abes before the great fireplace smoking and discussing their absent sons. Suddenly Overley changed the conversation by remarking:

"Abe, I am expecting some friends here tonight. Mr. Jim Connors sent me word that he would come over and stay a couple of days; so I have invited some of the old family heads to join us, as I think it a fit time to discuss ways and means to put a stop to these cussed 'crackers' carryings on. Big Joe Wheatly, the Postmaster, Sam Hurry, and the only one left in office who belongs to my circle of friends, Dr. Jack Cushing, the minister, Rev. Dr. Snell, and——"

"The minister?" interrupts Abe. "I hope, sah, dat you will 'member he presence an' not forgit yo' presence ob mine an' say nothin' dat he will feel called on to pray fo' you fo'. You 'member what you done do de las' time he war under dis roof?" (Overley having been guilty of using some very strong language in reference to the Doctor's sentiment on Slavery.)

"Abe, who the h— made you my censor? Who——"

"What dat? Who made me what? What you mean by dem big words? Dat one ting dat I al'ays take count on when I gits right whar you oughter listen; den you go on wid yo' big words, tell somehow I loses count of what Ise goin' to say, an' den you is seen larfin' to yo'se'f lek de debble. Yo'll not be able al'ays to talk outen my sight. I promise you dat."

"Abe, I did not mean to offend you; but you know that I am not sickly and weak like I was seventy years ago. Maybe you have forgotten that I am the head of the family, and that I may talk as I see fit."

"Yes, sah, dat am true 'nuff; but de good Lawd am sholy takin' count ob how de haid ob de house is 'havin' hese'f.

39

Dare am jes' one ting dat de Lawd seem negleckful 'bout, an' dat am yo' soul. Me an' my 'oman has bin axin' de Lord to sho' you de erer ob yo' way for mor'n fifty yeahs, but all to no puppose.

"Let me axe you, what you goin' do, what you goin' say when de great day done cum, an' de rocks an' de mountains hab all fleed 'way, an' de sea shall be as a burnin' flame; when de great Jehover hab done cum to jedg dis world; when de 'corden angul dun gits down to yo' name an' he dun read all dem bad an' awful words dat you dun say an' dat he hab got agin you? What you goin' say? Huh? What you goin' say? It do seem to me sometimes dat yo' is suttenly foolin' wid de Lawd. Duz you 'member Miss Miranda, what she say when she jine our han's togedder jes' befo' de Lawd done took her 'way? I axe you, duz you 'member? She say : 'Cum close to me, I wants to tell you both what de Lawd has done fo' me, kase I has al'ays trusted Him.' Duz you 'member dat she say : 'Oh, Lawd, Thy will be done.' Den her haid drap an' she dun gone to Hebben. Duz you 'member dat you is de onny pusson on dis heah 'hole plantation dat has nebber gib he soul to de Lawd? You is a old man now, sah, an' hab but a few mo' days to linger on dis heah eart'. You is in good mine an' body today, but you don't know what mout be de matter tomorrow. Duz you not feel de lonel'ness ob bein' outen de Lawd? Duz you not feel dat tim' hab done cum fo' you to spoke to de Lawd an' axe Him to forgin you all yo' many sins? Duz you not feel dat a old man is safer in de Lawd's fole dan he is outen it? Duz you tink dat you will be so peaceful an' happy as Miss Miranda when she died— when she smile an' say : 'Lawd, Thy will be done!' "

Abe observed that his friend's eyes were filled with tears and that he was greatly affected by his reference to the past, and asked him if he would not then and there throw himself upon the Lawd. Overley seemed on the point of opening his heart to God, when there was a knock at the door and Lucy

announced Jim Connors and Big Joe Wheatley. As both
men strode into the room Overley stood looking at them with
a tear-stained face, but unembarrassed. Abe observed the
interruption and noted the harm done by their untimely
arrival; but he bowed his head and murmured:

"Lawd, Thy will be done."

To their question as to what ailed him, Overley said quietly
and with great seriousness that Abe had almost persuaded
him to become a Christian. Big Joe Wheatley laughed and
observed that from his appearance Abe must have persuaded
him that he was an infant again. He also wanted to know
how long Abe had been doing missionary work among the
heathen.

Jim Connors took a more serious view of the matter and
wanted to know what Abe had said. Connors had had a very
pious Catholic mother and had never forgotten her last words,
although he had not followed her parting advice. When he
was told what Abe had said of the death-bed scene of Mrs.
Miranda Overley, he, too, was visibly affected. The words
brought back to his memory a similar experience. He sat
silent and thoughtful for a long time. Finally, he broke the
silence, which had become painful, with the remark:

"Malcolm, I remember your mother's death as well as if it
were yesterday, instead of thirty years ago. Of course, I
remember my own mother's death better, although she has
been dead more than thirty odd years. But they were both
good Christian women, and both left us with the request on
their dying lips that we trust in the Lord. Has either of us
done so? I will say that I have not. What have you to
say for yourself?"

"Jim, at times I have considered this question of eternity
very seriously, but have never gotten to the point where I
could reconcile all the various obstacles that have arisen in
my mind. I do honestly wish that I had."

"Yes, yes, Malcolm, I have no doubt that it would have

been better for us both had we followed our mothers' parting advice. We are old men now——''

"Is it too late now?" exclaimed a voice from the hall, and the good minister, Rev. Dr. Snell, came into the room. In the seriousness of the discussion Lucy's announcement of Dr. Snell's arrival had not been noticed. He had heard the latter part of what was said while being relieved of his hat and outer coat.

"I do not feel that it is too late, nor do I feel that there is any particular hurry about the matter. I just cannot get my mind around to the point where I feel that it is necessary for me to become a Christian," answered Overley.

"Doctor, that is also the way I feel concerning the matter," said Jim Connors.

"Oh, brothers, let me tell you what the Lord has done for you. You are poor insects as compared with Him. He could have crushed you out of this life long ago, but He has spared you for some good purpose. You are old men now, well nigh eighty years of age, though still hale and hearty. Have you nothing to be thankful for?"

"Oh, yes, we have our fallen fortunes to be thankful for," said Big Joe Wheatley.

"Oh, my brother, you always strike a bitter chord when you speak of our fallen fortunes. Years back, when the colored people were our bonded servants, we always had the means of raising ready money; but now we have to content ourselves with the crops and rents. Some years are good, but most are bad. God in His wise providence may send the good old days back again."

"God forbid!" said the three men in chorus.

"I was born on a plantation where there were over one hundred slaves. I came into possession of all those men, women and children. I fought to maintain our cause; but, God forbid that those days of bondage may ever come again," was the remark of Jim Connors.

Big Joe Wheatley remarked:

"I, too, was born on a plantation peopled with dozens of slaves. The old place belongs to me now. My former slaves are now my tenants; some few have bought the places on which they live. But I never want to see these people in slavery again. No, I hope that our fair Southland will never again be cursed with human slavery."

"But, Doctor, I do not understand how you can wish for what you call the good old times. You lived North before the war and saw nothing of the slave system, only when you visited your old uncle here at Christmas time. How do you know that those were good old times?"

"I always heard uncle refer to them as the good old times," was the Doctor's hesitating reply.

Old Abe had been seating the guests, a number of whom had arrived. He had also been a close listener to the remarks of the good minister.

Upon leaving the room he mumbled to himself:

"Dat preacher man he beate de debble. He a good man one way. He sho' can 'zort de sinners to tu'n from dey crooked ways; but den he al'ays droppin' sumfin' sly lek 'bout de good slavery day; 'bout de war times; 'bout he wish dat slavery cum agin'; 'bout de Yankee sojers, when he a Yankee hesef. He onny cum heah to lib arter his uncle die an' lebe him dat plantation. My Abe say he a sturdin' element.. Well, nobody in dis heah house wants slavery to cum agin'. I thank God fo' dat."

After Abe had gone, Overley called the attention of his friends to what was done and said at the last meeting.

It was soon agreed that a set of resolutions should be adopted and published as a warning to all persons engaged in these midnight killings.

The resolutions were as follows:

"WHEREAS, Murder, arson, rape, riots and outrages of varying degrees are of frequent occurrence in this county; and

"WHEREAS, It appears that the regularly constituted authorities do not seem able nor willing to cope with the perpetrators of these outrages; therefore, be it

"*Resolved,* That we, the following-named law-abiding citizens, do pledge our support, our purses and our persons individually and collectively, to the county authorities and to EACH OTHER for the suppression of all kinds of lawlessness. It is further

"*Resolved,* That these resolutions be published and posted, in order that all persons may learn them and govern themselves accordingly."

After much discussion it was finally agreed that a contest should be made in an effort to wrest the office of sheriff from the Lashum family. Little Joe Wheatley was named for the office. After an old-fashioned Christmas dinner, enlivened by wit and good-fellowship, the committee adjourned, subject to the call of the newly elected chairman, James Connors.

CHAPTER VII.

WHEN the two boys had started to College, as previously related, they were both shaken by conflicting emotions. Neither had ever been from home before, but both were determined to succeed.

"Abe, suppose I fail in the examination? How could I look father in the face again?" said Malcolm.

"You fail! How could you possibly get that idea in your head? You will never fail," said Abe. "Did you notice those Lashum and Smaly boys at the station? What a nasty look they gave us when we got on the train? Well, they are far behind now, and we have nothing to fear from them. It is awful to live among people whom you have to watch all the time—people that only let you alone because they fear you. Those Smalys are surely going to do me some harm some day. I feel it."

"Abe, you are getting daffy. I have seen those people drive in the ditch to let you pass in the center of the road. Why do you look for trouble from them?"

"That is just it. You don't seem to understand the nature of these 'crackers.' When they show their teeth or obsequiously drive in the ditch to let you pass them on the road, or offer to shake hands when you meet them, look out for yourself; guard your haystacks and barns and keep off the dark roads at night when alone. I have seen the result of so many accidents (?) to haystacks and lone Negroes that my heart grows sick, and it's getting worse."

"Well, Abe," said Malcolm, "do not take the gloomy side of this affair to rest your judgment upon. There are other things to talk about just now. What will we do when we get to Oberlin? I think it a good thing for us to see President Finley as soon as we get there, and ask his advice as to the courses we shall take in school," continued Malcolm.

"I think that is a very good idea, indeed. We certainly should have some definite object in mind. We must explain to President Finley what schooling we have had and what we want to do in the future and let him advise us."

"Well, Abe, we will do that. Abe, there is another thing about which I want to have an understanding with you. You have already said that you would not agree to room with me even if we could get a large room with two beds. I do not blame you for that. We must have adjoining rooms, however. What do you say to that?"

"That has been my desire from the first, but I did not so express myself, because I am not Malcolm A. Overley, Jr. I am simply Abe Overley, Jr., and have no right to make my expenses at College one cent more than is absolutely necessary."

"Well, that is just what I expected you to say. Father told me, and he told you, that you are to have and fare the same as I do. Now, Abe, you know my father and you know me. You know that if you were not to have the same advantages that I enjoy you would never have been sent from home. You will wound my father's feelings very much if you ever let him know that you entertained any such ideas. Now that is settled, there is one other thing. I promise you that I shall join no society, no team, without your knowledge, and I think we should consult before either of us does anything that may affect our relations or our futures. Do you agree to that?"

"I do. I agree most willingly. I suppose you will come to me if you see a girl you like, and say, 'Abe, I am sweet on Miss Silks. Do you think I had better try to win her?'"

"Well, what would you say to that?" asked Malcolm.

"I would ask you for twenty-four hours, and then I would look up her family, and if she had no 'cracker' blood in her I would say, 'Go in and win her.'"

The next day but one after their arrival they were able to get a few minutes with the good President, Dr. Finley. After they had stated who they were and whence they came and the circumstances under which they came to College to the President, he, after some thought, dismissed them with a request that they come to him again.

The boys' story had greatly impressed Dr. Finley, and he was desirous of consulting his friend, George Billings Donewell. As Dr. Finley and Mr. Donewell sat next evening in the Doctor's library their conversation turned to the College and new students.

"Donewell," said the Doctor, "I have two students here this year whom I shall watch with a great deal of interest. They came here together under most peculiar circumstances. First, let me describe them. Both are about six feet tall; one is very white, with curly chestnut brown hair, blue eyes, ruddy complexion; he does not look nor act like a Southern-born boy. The other is as black as the first boy is white; six feet, good features, with curly black hair of a peculiar texture, a perfect specimen of physical manhood. They appear to enjoy each other's confidence to an unusual degree. They gave me their history and how they came to be here. It appears that the white boy's father is of an old family of Alabama as old as the State itself. And the Negro comes from a slave family that has served the white boy's people for generations. It appears, further, that the respective fathers are close friends, and the white father, though reduced in circumstances, with a heavy mortgage hanging upon his home, is sending his black friend's boy here to College with instructions to me that I look after them both and that they are to fare alike. I tell you, Donewell, these Southern people are a puzzle to me."

"Doctor, you do not know them. You know that I have lived and traveled in every State in the South, both before and since the war. I have had an opportunity to study them psychologically and commercially. There are two separate ánd distinct classes of white people in those States, as separate and distinct as if they were not Caucasians. I refer to the old blue blood families and the people who are commonly designated as 'crackers.' The old blue bloods these days are reduced financially, but their blood remains pure. They would not consent to a daughter or a son marrying a 'cracker' any more than they would consent to a marriage with a Negro. This 'cracker' element was, before the war, the overseer class; now they are the policemen and street car people, and men working along those lines. They are non-progressive, always have been and apparently always will be. There are rare exceptions, however, where you will find one of this class possessed of any amount of brains—brains in the broad sense of the word. Men of this class prefer Negro women to their own, and they are entitled to their share of responsibility for the very large number of mulattoes that are found in the Southern States. In traveling through Maryland I heard, in fact, I saw all the parties to the following story: A white man by the name of Scotch lived with an old black woman who bore him several children, two girls among them, the eldest of whom was a large, well-developed country girl, about twenty years of age when I first saw her. This father persuaded his daughter to come to him in a cabin where he lived. The girl was gone from home for two days and nights. The cabin, the girl, the man, all bore evidence of the two days' struggle. This is an extreme case, but it will give some idea of the nature of this race of white men who live south of us, and who are fast coming amongst us, bringing their uncouth and semicivilized manners and customs. The other class, while they will risk life and fortune for a handsome mulatto or octoroon, will also educate their offspring.''

"Yes, but this does not appear to be a case of that kind. This boy is a full-blooded Negro. There must be some tie that binds these people other than that referred to by you. I shall watch this case with great interest. They have asked my advice, which I shall gladly give them. Do you remember having met a man by the name of Lashum—Nicholas Lashum —in A—— County, Alabama?''

"Oh, yes! I met him, or, rather, his family, ten or twelve years ago. One of the family was sheriff of the county, and I think that one of this family has been sheriff of that county ever since the war. It is a very large family and one of whom some of the citizens of A—— County are not very proud. The elder Lashum was notorious in the State during the war. He made his money in some questionable way during that period. I met them in the course of business while in that county. I also met some very fine old Bourbons in that part of the State.

"These young men to whom I refer both came from that county. Overley is the name," said Dr. Finley.

"Why, I remember the Overley plantation very well. I spent two days upon it. I was greatly impressed with the cordial welcome extended to me by the Overleys. I remember the perfect friendship that seemed to exist between Mr. Overley and his former slave, Abe, than whom a more perfect specimen of physical manhood I never saw. The two sons were like their respective fathers, and each seemed to enjoy the complete confidence of the other. I was struck by the simplicity and beauty of the lives of the people on that plantation. There appeared to be only one thing lacking—funds. I sold the Lashums a large bill of goods, but Overley told me frankly that he had no money and could not purchase anything at that time. I offered to send him what he wanted and take his word for the money, explaining to him that I owned the plant and no one would ever push him for payments. After a consultation with his black man, Abe, he refused my offer. I will always remember that home."

"You will have an opportunity to study that family from another point of view. These boys are no doubt the little fellows whom you saw while at their home."

"When you see them again, Doctor, I would like to be present. I want to note what changes ten years have made in them."

Mr. George Billings Donewell was one of those rare characters sometimes found in this selfish world, who have been successful, and who delight in helping others. He advanced a peculiar "code of ethics," as he termed it, based wholly on the Golden Rule, "Do unto others as you would have them do to you." His theory was that all men are born free and equal; but as God, in His wise providence, endows some men in a greater degree than others, that those persons so endowed hold their endowments in trust for their weaker brothers. He believed that Dr. Finley, having been endowed with great mental faculties and the power to comprehend and digest great educational problems, was in duty bound to disseminate his knowledge and to hold it in trust for all mankind. So also with the man endowed with the faculty for accumulating wealth. He believed that he was required to use that wealth for the benefit of mankind. Mr. Donewell argued and lived up to this theory:

First, that a man's duty is to God, who made him.

Second, that a man's duty is to the family that God has given him.

Third, that a man's duty is to his distressed worthy brother. Should a man be successful in this world, financially, his first duty is to provide for his family; but all over and above their wants and needs he holds in trust for mankind.

Many are the young men who have passed through Oberlin College and felt the aid of a helping hand, but never discovered whence this help came, so careful were Dr. Finley and Mr. Donewell that their good offices should not be heralded.

Two days after their first conference with the President, Dr. Finley sent for our Alabama friends and had a long talk with them, at which Mr. Donewell was present. The Doctor advised them as to the courses he thought proper for them to pursue in order to finish their respective educations. The boys departed highly elated over the friendships they had formed. Dr. Finley and Mr. Donewell both had invited them to visit their homes whenever they found it convenient.

"Abe," said Malcolm, while on the way back to their rooms, "who is Mr. Donewell? He says that he remembers us. He certainly has been on the old place, or how could he locate the corn crib, the spring house or the big cherry tree on the hill. Do you remember him?"

"I cannot say that I do, but I shall always remember him now. He appears to be a very fine old man. When shall we visit him at his home?"

"Whenever you say, Abe."

"Well, tomorrow is Saturday; let us join the boys who are going to Black River to fish."

"I will be glad to do that," said Malcolm, "but we must be careful. I have heard that river spoken of as being very dangerous."

CHAPTER VIII.

IN THE early morning following the two boys, together with several other young men, set out for the river. They had gone but half the distance when they were overtaken by a 'bus load of young people, boys and girls, bound for an outing. As the 'bus passed, Malcolm noticed several female classmates whose names he had not yet learned.

"Who is the young lady with the dark hair and eyes? The one on the end of the seat?" asked Malcolm of young Forbes, a resident of Oberlin.

"Why, that is Miss Donewell. She lives on Main Street. Her father is worth a million, but you would not think he had doughnuts if you saw him on the street. The other girls next to her are New Yorkers—sisters—Chiswells—father is a wholesale druggist. They will graduate this year, I believe. I will take you up to see them tomorrow if you desire to be presented."

"Certainly, I will only be too glad to avail myself of the opportunity. But what about my chum, Abe? Will you be as glad to present him as you are to present me?" asked Malcolm.

"Why, of course I will. He is black enough, but appears to be a gentleman."

"What do you think the young ladies will say?" questioned Malcolm.

"You do not seem to realize one thing," answered Forbes. "I have lived here all my life and I know the sentiment of this College. There is a fraternal feeling that prevails here. All students are treated alike. These young ladies will receive him very cordially, take my word for it."

The young men soon arrived at the river. Some busied themselves digging grubworms; others prepared a camp; the others strolled about the banks looking for a good place to cast the lines.

Malcolm and Forbes were amongst those who went up the stream. Just as they turned a bend in the river a short distance from the camp, Abe, who had remained behind, heard Malcolm's voice ring out clear and sharp: "Stop that! Stop that! You are upsetting the boat!"

Abe knew from the ring in Malcolm's voice that something unusual was happening, and he hastened to the bend in the river, as did some of the others, to see what the trouble was.

They observed a boat containing five persons—three girls and two young men—coming down the stream. One of the men stood in the middle of the boat, rocking it violently. The girl who was sitting in the bow of the boat lost her balance and was about to slip overboard. This young man, whose name was Rattles, heard Malcolm's warning; but, in defiance, gave the boat one more violent tilt, which caused it to careen, and when it righted again Miss Donewell fell overboard, dropping head-first into the water. As the boat lost her weight, Mr. Rattles's position caused it to careen violently to the other side, and he was thrown into the water also. When each came to the surface the current had carried the boat out of their reach. Mr. Rattles grasped Miss Donewell about the shoulders and held her head under the water while trying to keep his own above. Malcolm and Forbes both sprang into the water and were soon at the girl's side, but could not loosen Rattles's hold upon her. She was apparently being exhausted by being kept under the water so long. Abe saw the trouble from the shore, and, springing into the water, was soon within reach of them. Without a moment's hesitation he dealt Rattles a blow between the eyes which dazed him. Abe then pushed Rattles's head under the water, which caused him to loosen his hold on the girl and to grasp Abe. Malcolm and Forbes soon got the young lady to the river's bank, which was not more than twenty yards distant. But Abe came near losing his life. Rattles succeeded in getting a hold on him which Abe could not break. Abe's only recourse was to keep under the water and swim toward the bank, which was a trying thing to do with a struggling man hanging to him. A person possessed of less strength and coolness would not have succeeded. When he reached the bank there were willing hands to help him with his burden. Rattles, in his terror, could not be induced for some time to loosen his hold on Abe's arm, not realizing that he was on "terra firma" and away from all danger. The young man in the boat was unable to render any assistance owing to the fact that one oar had fallen overboard. He tried manfully, however, to scull the boat close enough to Abe to enable him to grasp the side, but did not succeed. Miss Donewell was resuscitated by the young ladies, under Malcolm's instructions, and was soon ready to return to the 'bus. The girls at first wanted to walk back, but Malcolm assured them that he and his friend, Abe, could manage the boat and get them to the 'bus much quicker.

Miss Donewell smiled and said:

"You and Mr. Forbes have just pulled me out of the water. I can trust you both to get me back to the 'bus."

"We did not do it all ourselves, Miss Donewell," answered Forbes. "If Mr. Overley, there," pointing to Abe, "had not come to our rescue when he did. I am afraid four of us, including Mr. Rattles, would be at the bottom of that river now."

"Mr. Rattles, what a pity!" said one of the New York girls. He lay on the ground, limp and motionless, staring at the water as if he were afraid that a wave would come and engulf him and carry him back beneath its surface.

When it became known at the College that Rattles had nearly caused Miss Donewell to lose her life, and that Abe had blackened Rattles's eyes in helping to rescue her, there were many and various comments on the occurrence. Most of the boys were inclined to praise Abe for his bravery. But Lashum and Bloxum, true to their natures, sought to stir up strife. They sought out Rattles with a view to poisoning his mind against Abe, Malcolm and Forbes. Rattles was a Western boy of good family, true-hearted, but a little faulty in judgment at times.

"Say, Mr. Rattles," began Buck, "I hear that you were given a wrong turn on Black River last Saturday. That 'nigger,' Abe Overley, is bigger than you are or he would never have dared to do what he did."

"No," said Bloxum, "if I were you I would not stand for such treatment at the hands of a 'nigger.' He is running about now crowing and saying how he smashed you between the eyes. That fellow he came here with makes a fool of him. The idea, taking a 'nigger' to call on a white woman!"

"Why, Mr. Rattles," again urged Buck, "are you going to stand for that? Look at your face! Just think of it! A 'nigger' hit you! Go to the Dean and complain. We will go with you and help you out. This 'nigger' is too free with his fists." Buck evidently remembered his own encounter with Abe.

"Rattles, come and go to the Dean," said Bloxum; "Buck and myself heard him say what he had done and what he expected to do before long."

"What did he say that he had done?" asked Rattles.

"Why, that you are the biggest cur he had ever met, and all he wanted was just one chance at Dr. Finley's son and he would be satisfied."

"Well, that seems strange to me. Abe refused to go with the young ladies that day; but insisted on staying with me.

"He not only stayed with me, but reduced the swelling in my face, smoothed the matter over with the Faculty, and went with me to Mr. Donewell's home when I offered my apologies. In fact, he has acted like a man in the whole affair. He is my friend. He has just left my room. Maybe you gentlemen would like to have me call him? He is with Forbes and two or three others across the hall.

"We don't want him. We don't associate with 'niggers,' " said Buck.

Rattles surprised them both by springing to his feet and opening the door, saying:

"Go! Go, and go quick! Who sent for you? Who asked for your advice? Who asked for your aid? You are both liars. I do not believe one word you have told me. I say this man is my friend. And you dare to come to me with your lies about him. I never want to see your faces in my room again."

The three young men were now in the hallway. Rattles, in his anger, had elevated his voice above the others, and attracted the attention of several of the young men who were in the adjoining rooms, among them being Abe, Malcolm and Forbes.

"What is the matter with Rattles?" asked Forbes.

"He has his Western dander up. He is out on the prairie now, not out on the water," said Hawkins, Rattles's chum. "Oh, he's got it in him. Say, Rattles, old boy, what is the matter?" asked Hawkins.

"These fellows have taken it upon themselves to come to my room to insult my friends," said Rattles. "What do you think of them?"

"Come in my room, fellows," said one of the young men; "we are not permitted to stand in the hallways. Do not leave, gentlemen," he added, noting that Buck and Bloxum were moving away; "you are welcome, and, further, it will be necessary for you to explain the nature of this insult of which Rattles complains."

All the boys, about fifteen in number, crowded into the room, Buck and Bloxum among the number, though they were not very willing to enter.

"Gentlemen," said Hawkins, "an unusual thing has happened. One gentleman has passed the lie to two others. And, further, has ordered those gentlemen never to put their faces in his room again. According to the 'Unwritten Law' of this College, the offending party must apologize or fight. It is also the Law, that a committee hear the case and pass upon it. Now, Mr. Buck Lashum, you are the insulted party; what complaint have you to make?"

"I have nothing to say, nor have I any complaint to make," was Buck's answer.

"Mr. Squealer Bloxum, you are also one of the insulted parties. What complaint have you to make?"

"I think that Mr. Rattles was a little excited when he used the word 'liar' and that he did not mean——"

"That is not for you to say," interrupted Hawkins. "It is no part of your business to make apologies for Mr. Rattles. The lie has been passed. The question is, have we two liars amongst us, or have we two men amongst us who, knowing they are not liars, do not possess the manhood to resent the insult? Now, what have you both to say? I will say further that you gentlemen must either obtain an apology from Mr. Rattles, or fight, or be branded as liars and cowards; that is the Law."

Buck and Bloxum both remained silent, not knowing what to say.

"What is the matter, Lashum?" asked a Tennessee boy. "Are you afraid to talk? Do you forget that you come from the South, where all men are free, and where you only find true manhood?"

"Yes, these fellows are a sample of your Southern manhood," spoke up a long Yankee boy. "I venture they have lied about somebody, and now they are afraid to own it. Just to think of it, a true Southern gentleman afraid of the consequences of his acts!"

This bit of sarcasm was followed by a peal of laughter.

"Gentlemen, let us have no cross-firing," said Hawkins, adding: "Mr. Rattles, you have violated the 'Unwritten Law' of this College inasmuch as you have called fellow students liars.

"What have you to say for yourself?"

"I will simply say that these fellows——"

"Gentlemen," interrupted Hawkins.

"Well, students," said Rattles.

"No, gentlemen," insisted Hawkins.

"Students came to my room," continued Rattles, "and lied to me about my friend, whose name I may not mention. It is enough to say that he is my friend, and that no gentleman of honor will hear his friends slandered behind their backs. In this case I know they lied. I so expressed myself, and I reiterate what I have said before. They are contemptible liars."

"My God! Lashum, are you a Southern man? Have you any blood in your veins? Will you allow your name to be handed down in this College as a contemptible liar?" again urged the Tennessee boy.

"Oh, this is not the first lie he has told, nor will it be the last while at this school," said Rattles."

"Well, fellows, these gentlemen, by their silence, acknowledge that what Mr. Rattles says is true. There can be but one conclusion for you to reach, which is that they have lied on somebody. Who it is does not matter. What will be your decision?"

"That hereafter all honorable students refuse to believe anything they have to say unless corroborated by a third person," spoke up the long Yankee boy.

This decision was mild in form, but severe in operation. No matter what they said, even that the weather was cold, would be met by the retort, "Whom have you to vouch for that statement?"

After the boys had separated, Buck said to Bloxum:

"That 'nigger' always gets the best of us. We will fix him yet."

"Buck, let's go to Elmyra tonight and have some fun," said Bloxum.

"I don't care. We can stay until Sunday night," answered Buck.

Elmyra is a town about eight miles from Oberlin, in another county, where the students of loose habits go for relaxation.

CHAPTER IX.

AFTER the train bearing Malcolm and Abe had left the station and they were off for Oberlin College, Buck and the Smaly boys watched until it disappeared around the curve at Coon's Tree.

"Well, that's the limit," said Buck; " 'niggers' going off to College! Did you hear to what College they were going?"

"Yes, to the Oberling School, or some sich place," said one of the Smalys.

"Is that so? Why, I am going to that school. Who told you that? I'll go home and tell pappy and he will see about 'niggers' going to school with his son. I bet he won't stay there long. Yo'll see," said Buck, as he mounted his horse and left in great haste.

When he reached home he found his father sitting on the fence by the hog sty—the old man not having been able to outgrow his early habits—together with several kindred spirits, discussing the resolutions published by the citizens who had met at the home of Malcolm A. Overley, Sr.

"I say that them people they think that they is goin' to run things to suit theyselves. But as sure as my name be Nick Lashum they is mistook. Ole Mal Overley, he's at the bottom of this heah whole d— business. He's a mighty white man, he is. Sendin' 'niggers' off to College! D— if I don't fix him yeah a'ter nex'. Yo'll see! I'll——"

Just at that moment Buck dashed into the barnyard, his horse almost ready to drop from hard riding.

"What ails yer, boy? What yer ridin' that critter like that fer?"

" 'Nuff ails me. Malcolm Overley has gone to Oberling College with that 'nigger' Abe. Do you think I want to go to school with 'niggers'?" yelled Buck.

"Yes jis' knowed that? Why, I mistook yer haid fer a place fer brains. Yer lettle sister Arabella, she told me that two weeks ago. What yer think I kin do 'bout it now? Go on to College and see what they do with them 'niggers,' then let me know, and I'll settle the whole matter then. That's what yer do."

"Yes, pappy, but that 'nigger' is at the same school, and I——"

"How long yer been runnin' this heah place? Yer better a darn sight do as yer is tole an' not stop to augrify wid yer betters. I know mor'n a minit than yo'll git outen books in a lifetime. Yer rub thet air critter out and see that she don't git stiff 'morrow mornin'. I won't have my critters worked that way. 'Pears to me thet I have sed thet offen 'nuff," said the father with warmth.

Mr. Nick Lashum prided himself on the fact that he was the boss. There was but one person on his place over whom he had no control, and that was an old Negro woman, of uncertain age, the mother of several doubtful looking children of variegated colors, who resembled the Lashum family. This old woman claimed that she had known Nick Lashum since "long 'fore de wah" and that he was bound to take care of her until she died. All of which appears to be true, from the fact that she lived in a cabin within a stone's throw of Nick's wife and children, without doing labor of any kind, and having free access to everything on the place. This old woman, who was known in war times, when she traveled about the State with Nick Lashum, as Black Sue, and who appeared to know a great deal of Nick's innermost affairs, was a character within herself. No person on the place appeared to know exactly where she came from nor on whose place she lived before the war. Suffice it to say, when Nick came into possession of his present home, she came with her six lean, yellow children and took the cabin in which we find her, as her share of Nick's assets, and lived there with her growing family. We shall see something of her later.

Buck, not having gained his point, and only succeeding in arousing the wrath of his parent, took the mare to the stable yard and proceeded to obey his father's injunction—to rub her out.

After Buck's departure, Nick Lashum and his cronies resumed their talk.

"Why, in course, Ole Mal is the bottom of the whole darn thing," said Si Weedles, a citizen of large family and small resources, whose business was cross-road politics and juryman; "and, furdermore, I hear that little Joe Wheatley is to run 'gin Casper Lashum for sheriff."

"The h— yer say, Si," said Nick; "who tol' yer so?"

"Wal, I dunno 'zackly who it war that tol' me, but I hear'n hit today. That's what I camed heah fer—to talk this thing over. I tol' them darn hothead Smalys and Wardemans to let them 'niggers' alone; thet thet hoss was Burrell's, and sich doin's war goin' to make trouble. Now this is only the beginnin'. Yo'll see," said Weedles.

"So, that's what the matter wid them 'big bugs,' is hit? Takin' up fer 'niggers,' hey? Leetle Joe Wheatley? Him's the one they expects to beat Cas fer sheriff? Wal, I mus' say them people is smart. That darn boy's suttenly well thought on in this heah county. Doggon, if Cas an' his pals ain't got to git out an' hustle," said Nick.

"Yes, time fer 'lection on'y nex' mont', and we jus' knowed who is goin' to run 'gin him," said Weedles. "I, fer one, is goin' to git my coat off an' go to woric. All we is got to say is, that they is takin' up fer 'niggers' an' we will beat 'em sho'."

"Si, yer tell all the boys to meet heah Sunday arter nex' on matters of great 'portance," said Nick, as the friends separated.

On the Sunday afternoon, long before the appointed time, the good citizens of the county began to gather at the home of Nick Lashum. The first to arrive was Si Weedles, clad in his best, which consisted of a large hat, a large pair of boots, a large pair of pants, which were suspiciously like a pair that Sheriff Lashum used to pride himself upon owning, a hickory shirt and a large corn-cob pipe. Attired in this outfit, the Alabama statesman appeared early, because his self-imposed duties, as handy man, ex-officio, at all political meetings, were well understood by himself. Soon the big barn loft, an ideal place for an Alabama political council, was well filled. There were great men galore—judges and former judges, clerks of courts and former clerks of courts, sheriffs and former sheriffs, justices of the peace and former justices of the peace, road commissioners, school commissioners, lawyers, doctors, school teachers and plain country gentlemen—all come to see the lights of the Alabama Democracy flash, flutter, glimmer, sputter and finally become extinguished.

The hour soon arrived for business to be proceeded with. Without the formality of the election of a chairman, Nick Lashum, by virtue of the meeting being held 'neath his vine and fig tree,' and by virtue also of his acknowledged superior ability, took upon himself the right to conduct the meeting. He said: ''Gents, we is hyre on a mos' momentous occasion. Dese hyre 'big bugs' is not satis' by the way things is bein' run in this hyre county. If I war not satis' I would move outen the county. I don't give a doggon fer any of them. They is stuck up and has been always.''

''Right! Right!'' came from the crowd.

''Now, they is goin 'to try to beat Cas Lashum fer sheriff. And who is they goin' to run agin' him? Leetle Joe Wheatley. Is he one of us?''

''No! No!'' responded the hearers.

''Wal, we is got to git t'gether an' beat the whole darn bunch. I tell yer, fellers, that if them people ever gits us onct yer will be jus' lek yer war 'fore de war. I knows what I'se talkin' 'bout. I war hyre on the spot at that there time. You boys that has been to school offen yer po' pappy's labor, may snikker an' grin kase yer ain't got no more sense. Now, gents, this whole thing is up to yo'll.''

After a few moments' silence, a young man by the name of Goodrich called out:

"Mr. Chairman, I move that we do now proceed to the election of officers." Silence. "I therefore place in nomination for chairman the Honorable Judge——''

"No yer don't do no sich a darn thing," said Nick; "I'se the cheerman of this hyre meetin', an' Nickolas Lashum, Junior, is the s'c'tay. Ain't that right, fellers?''

"Sho' yer is," spoke up Si Weedles; "an' anybody thet don't lek them officers, we puts out. We don't 'pose ter have this hyre meetin' 'sturbed by nobody.''

Mr. Goodrich relapsed into a discreet silence, but remarked to his companion, "That he'd be d— if he would vote for such people.'' The chairman announced that the coming election was for Sheriff, County Judge, and one Road and School Commissioner each. Whom would they nominate to run for these offices? The all-important matter to Nick and his friends was the office of Sheriff. To bring about Casper's nomination was their determination.

Si Weedles was on his feet at once.

"Mr. Cheerman: I rases to my feet fer the puppus of puttin' in nomination, fer Sheriff, that battled-scarred hero, that patriotic citizen an' farmer, that Alabamy gent an' fi'ancier, that stock raiser an' father, that man of the world an' the Church, him no other than the man that carried the blood-stained banner of Alabama 'mocracy down to victory, him no other than the man that has always kept 'nuff 'niggers' in the chain gang to woric the roads so no white men don't have no woric to do on the roads, him no other than the one that knows how to keep 'niggers' in they places, him no other than

the man thet ain't heppen' no 'niggers' 'gin white men, him
no other than the wise an' provident Casper Lahsum.''

After this flash of eloquence, the yell, so well known,
peculiar to the savages of the West and the ''crackers'' of
the South, was given with such good will that the barn seemed
to vibrate with its volume. Not a voice raised in opposition
to this nomination. Nick declared, as soon as he could be
heard, that the unanimous ''voice'' of the caucus was Casper
Lashum. The hold-over officers, Judge and Commissioners,
were renominated. Nick then adjourned the meeting sine die.
Just twenty-three minutes had elapsed since the meeting was
called to order. The *County Bulletin*, the official organ of the
county, had the following announcement:

''At a convention, attended by hundreds of delegates (self-
appointed) from all parts of the county, held in the large hall
on Mr. Nick Lashum's place, the following persons were named
as candidates for the offices of Sheriff, Judge, Road and School
Commissioners:
Casper Lashum, Sheriff.
Josephus Wiggles, Judge.
William Runeasy, Road Commissioner.
Jackson Contention, School Commissioner.''

Young Goodrich and his friends engaged in a very warm
discussion as they drove away from the Lashum place, declaring they would do all in their power to defeat Casper Lashum
for Sheriff.

CHAPTER X.

YOUNG GOODRICH and his friends, true to their determination, set about to defeat Casper Lashum for Sheriff. Knowing well the strength of the Lashum following, they were compelled to resort to strategy. First, they made a canvass of all the better class of people in the county and obtained their promises to vote for Little Joe Wheatley when the time came; but in the canvass, up to the last day, they were to appear to be staunch followers of the Lashums. Judge Wiggles and his supporters, who had long wished for an opportunity to throw off the Lashum yoke, also promised to come out at the proper time and advocate the election of Wheatley. So well was this game of politics played, so complete was Goodrich's organization, that the Lashums did not suspect that the enthusiasm on the part of the "big bugs" meant defeat for their kinsman.

The evening before the election the *County Bulletin* came out with a burning editorial denunciatory of the Lashum regime, denouncing their methods and charging that for years they had been corrupt in office. So sudden and complete was the attack, coming from so many unlooked-for sources, that Lashum and his followers were at a loss to know how to combat the new issue. Nick Lashum, Casper Lashum, Si Weedles and a few others, among them the Smalys and Wardemans, met at Nick Lashum's, down by the pig sty, Nick's favorite corner, and engaged in a lively discussion. The Smalys were in favor of going immediately to the office of the *County Bulletin*, get the "nigger" who carried the copies of the paper about the county to the subscribers and hang him, as he was responsible for the paper being in the hands of all the white people in the county who could read. After a very lengthy argument, it was finally decided that, should the Lashums lose, the "nigger," the driver of the wagon owned by the publishers of the *County Bulletin*, should be taught a lesson—should be taught not to distribute papers unfavorable to Lashum and his followers. The ownership of the paper, of the horse and wagon and of the paper route, never entered into their thoughts. The "nigger" was responsible, wholly and entirely. They vowed to run him out of the county.

When the votes were counted the following day it was found that Casper Lashum had been defeated by 54 votes, while his associates on the ticket had been elected without a dissenting vote.

Si Weedles reported that great fraud had been practiced, inasmuch as a report had been put in circulation, by Goodrich, that the Lashums were trying to steal the County Court House and that Nick Lashum had a deed already drawn which he would put on file as soon as his brother was re-elected—all of which the "crackers" believed and acted upon.

Little Joe Wheatley's election to the office of Sheriff gave the Negroes great satisfaction. It forecasted, for them, a possible chance of a "square deal."

They were not disappointed.

CHAPTER XI.

AS WE turn our attention again to the boys at Oberlin we find the school year has come to a close. Buck and Bloxum barely passed their examinations, and were severely lectured by the Dean, though they were permitted to go on with their classes. Malcolm and Abe made good marks and were congratulated by the Dean. Each bore a letter from the Dean to his father commending him and urging his return the next school year. Their homecoming was made a time for rejoicing. Each person on the place vied with the other in his endeavor to make them welcome. The parents of the two boys were greatly elated over the record made by their respective sons. The vacation time passed very quickly, and the boys could hardly realize it was over when told to get ready to return to school. Malcolm and Miss Donewell had become great friends, and he had promised to return a few days before the school term began in order that he might spend some time with her in pleasure-seeking.

CHAPTER XII.

WHEN the time for homegoing drew near Buck Lashum extended invitations to several young men whose acquaintance he had made while at the College to be his guests for a week at his father's plantation. Bloxum was the first to accept; but his railroad tickets were not forthcoming and they were stumbling blocks which he set about to remove. He knew that his parents could not spare the money to cover the expense of this trip, nor would they permit him to go South with Buck if they had to make a further sacrifice than they were making in sending him to College. He had, however, another reason for wanting to go. He was aware that he would have to work if he went home for the summer vacation, and he therefore determined that Buck should bear this expense for the trip, and also that he would stay the whole vacation through. Buck and Bloxum had formed the habit of going to Elmyra to spend Saturday night and Sunday in "recreation." On a return trip, after one of these carousals, when Buck was feeling exceptionally good, Bloxum opened the subject by remarking:

"Buck, I am compelled to ask you to withdraw your invitation to me to take that trip down to your plantation."

"No yer don't. What's the matter with yer? Haven't yer passed yer word that yer would come? Haven't yer learned yet that a gentleman never goes back on his words? Didn't I write pappy that yer particular was coming? Now, what yer goin' to back out fer?"

This was just the position Bloxum wanted Buck to take.

"Of course, I know all these things; that is just the reason I am telling you now. I am so sorry. I wanted, above all things, to meet your sister Clemmie. I know she must be a stunning girl—and little Arabella—Oh, well; I guess I must forego all these pleasures."

All this was said solemnly, with a view of impressing Buck.

"Why, Bloxum, what is the matter with yer? Hope nobody ain't daid."

"No, nobody's dead, but the fact of the matter is, we have been burned out; that is, our barn and farm implements have been burned. Father says in his letter, 'Come home and go to work.' "

Then Bloxum soliloquized:

"Just to think of it! Two months rest—Clemmie and Arabella—and nothing to do—with 'niggers' to wait on me! Now, two months work—work from morning till night—all because I lack a few paltry dollars. Father says he cannot possibly send me one cent, but to come home and go to work."

Then he added:

"Why are you grinning? Can you see anything funny in that? I will not see Clemmie nor Arabella for another year."

"I am not laffin' at yer," said Buck. "I am pleased to know that is all. Why, I can fix any moneys all right."

"What you take me fer? Think I am a 'nigger'? Going to let you buy my tickers and——"

"Yer shut up; ain't yer my guest? How yer get down there is not yer business. I'm responsible fer yer 'til nex' year. So that ends it. Yer write yer pappy and tell him that yer is in the hands of Mr. Buck Lashum, of A—— County, Alabamy."

"Buck, you must be a great man down in your county. When you get through College the people of A—— County will see that you go to Congress from your district. I tell you, Buck, you are a wonder."

"Yer can bet I am going to run things when I git out o' College," said Buck.

"Yes; when I come down their electioneering for you, then you can pay my expenses; and you can then present me to Clemmie and Arabella."

"Bloxum, I tell yer I don't want no more fool talk. Yer

goes with me as my guest. Pappy say fer me to bring yer. I will write yer mammy and tell her that I will look after her little boy.'' And Buck laughed at his own cleverness.

When Bloxum left Buck, he laughed long and heartily to himself at his success in obtaining Buck's promise to take him South as his guest.

"Well, that fellow is easy, sure enough. But that gives me an idea. If I can handle him so easy, what may I not do with the whole bunch of 'meadow hogs' in a year or two? What in the world does Clemmie look like? Wonder how she dresses? Old man Lashum must have lots of money. Bet your life I will find out this summer.''

Such thoughts ran through Bloxum's mind until he finally fell asleep. Buck, being of the same state of mind, congratulated himself upon the clever way he had induced Bloxum to accept his hospitality.

"Bloxum is too darn sensitive. But I must take him down there, or pappy will say that I lied when I wrote that I was the leader of all the Southern boys in the College. I don't know about that Tennessee fellow; he is so darn proper and stuck up, he may refuse. Anyway, I can get four or five to go; that will prove what I wrote pappy.''

Buck was much concerned lest the young man from Tennessee and a few others, who belonged to old aristocratic families, should refuse his invitation, as he had written home giving the names of the young men whom his father might expect as his son's guests for one week.

"Well, DeVaux," said the Tennesseean to his Louisiana friend, "I hear that you propose to visit that Lashum fellow at his home this summer for one week?''

"Not guilty," said DeVaux; "what do you take me for? How long since I commenced to take these 'crackers' on terms of 'Social Equality'? I am under obligations to you, since I got the invitation through your friendship for him.''

"Oh, of course, I am responsible for all your ills. Did I also make you acquainted with Miss Donewell? Did I also cause Overley to cut you out?" laughed DeVaux's friend. "But, seriously, DeVaux, you had the lead until Overley and Forbes pulled her out of Black River; then your colors fell. Why did you surrender so quickly?"

"Why? Because the young lady seemed to want somebody else. My pride would not permit me to wait until I was snubbed," answered DeVaux; then added: "What do you intend to do about your invitation to visit Lashum?"

"Visit Lashum? Why I never took the proposition seriously. I have no intentions of accepting an invitation of any kind from him. Who is going to accept?"

"Bloxum, I guess," answered DeVaux; "he has the one chance left. He was saying to me that he thought New Orleans a most beautiful city. When I asked him if he had ever visited that city, he answered by saying that he had not, but would as soon as he got acquainted with some native of the soil. I did not continue the conversation further. You can bet he will go with Lashum."

Their talk drifted into other channels, and Bloxum and Buck were forgotten.

The time soon rolled around for the boys to leave for their respective homes. Bloxum had finally agreed to let Buck do the honors for the summer, and they left the College together. When they reached their destination, they were met by Mr. and Mrs. Nick Lashum, Sr., Clemmie and Arabella. Bloxum was not prepared for the sight that met his gaze. Nick Lashum, Sr., with his large boots and small legs; Mrs. Nick Lashum, Sr., with her plaid shawl and blue skirt; Clemmie— the divine creature—with her bangs and curls, topped by a picture hat of flowers, ribbons and velvet, a yellow gown trimmed in brown, a costume calculated to cause all the girls of her class in A—— County to envy her.

He could not get his eyes off this vision. Was this the girl upon whom he had set his mind, through Buck's description of her? If he had had the means he would have gone back home by the next train. Bloxum, although of a very small nature, was bright and intellectual, and had had the benefit of excellent home training. He was shocked at the sight that presented itself to him; but when Clemmie came down to breakfast next morning in evening dress with rings on all four fingers, Bloxum was astounded.

Arabella, strange as it may seem, was by nature a very handsome child, and seemed to know, instinctively, what she looked well in, and she did look very attractive in a plain white frock. Nick, Sr., was disappointed, because Buck did not bring with him all the friends he had led his father to expect. Buck explained that the boys had been ordered to come home from College and they were to visit him on their way back in the fall.

Bloxum spent most of his time sleeping, when not riding about the country with Arabella. And while thoroughly disappointed and disgusted with his surroundings and the conditions amidst which he found himself in Alabama, conditions so totally different from anything he had ever before seen or heard of, he yet found much to amuse and interest him. Bloxum frankly confessed to himself that he enjoyed the company of Arabella, a creature so entirely different from the rest of that strange brood.

As the time for them to return to College drew near the elder Lashum began to question Buck about his school friends. Buck was sure they would arrive on schedule time, pretending to receive letters to that effect. At the last moment Buck received a telegram requesting him to join the class in Cleveland, Ohio, at a class reunion. This appeared to satisfy the senior Lashum, and he therefore sent Buck and Bloxum north a week earlier than the time set for their departure. Buck and his friend made good use of this time in Cleveland and other places.

CHAPTER XIII.

A FEW days before the time set for the College boys to resume their studies a discussion was precipitated by Buck and Bloxum, in which feeling ran very high.

These boys, not having anything in particular to occupy their minds, soon began to look about for amusement. In the Mess Hall there were six or eight boys who "waited table" to help pay their expenses at College. Among them were two Negroes, one a green Southern boy with all the fears grounded in him that characterize a great many Negro boys from the South.

The other boy was a Westerner, who knew nothing of the environment in which his co-laborer had formerly lived. Buck had time and again addressed the Southern boy as "nigger," and assumed that the other boy could be so addressed. In this he made a mistake, and his mistake cost him one of the worst beatings he had ever received, and this one was particularly humiliating because it came from a despised Negro.

He tried to forget what happened to him at the hands of this boy, but was unable to do so, nor would his fellow students allow him to forget. This encounter led to a discussion of races that brought out the views of nearly every boy in the College.

Bloxum led off in a wordy defense of Buck.

"I tell you, fellers, that I am going to take this case to the Dean. That fellow—he was careful to say fellow—hit Buck for no reason whatever, and hit him when he was not looking. He should be expelled."

"No, he didn't hit your friend when he was not looking," said the long Yankee boy. "I saw the whole mill. Your friend was given time to withdraw the insult, but would not. He got all that was coming to him. I say no advantage was taken of him."

"I tell you there was," Bloxum answered; "and I can prove it. You are a nice white man, taking up for these people all the time."

"I take up for whom I please, and don't you question me about my actions. You saw, as I saw, that those men were facing each other when your friend was slapped. The idea! Let anybody slap him and never hit back! That's Southern blood for you!"

"Well, Southern people feel that it is beneath them to have personal encounters with Negroes," spoke up DeVaux.

"That is a peculiar kind of reasoning—peculiar to Southern people. 'Beneath their dignity' to fight single-handed with a Negro, but not 'beneath their dignity' to insult and ill-treat him and even take his life, when in a company of three and four, or even in a mob of a hundred!" answered the Yankee boy. Then, turning to the Tennessee boy, he said: "Say, my friend, can you explain that side of the Southern blood to me?"

"No, I cannot," was the answer. "But I want you to understand that the picture you draw is not a true one of all the people in the South. Further, I want you to understand that Buck Lashum and Bloxum do not represent me, my family nor my friends. We feel that it is as much beneath us to insult a Negro as it is to fight with him."

"Well, I guess Buck was moved by your high ideals when he permitted his face to be slapped by a Negro," replied the long Yankee boy. "At any rate, he failed to hit back."

"I have never been able to understand why you Southern boys, particularly of a certain class, are always and continually harping on the Negro," said Forbes; "men like you, DeVaux, and your friend from Tennessee, talk of your mammies and your aunties. Overley, over there, speaks of his Negro friend as his chum. Lashum and Bloxum always speak of Negroes as 'd— niggers.' Wherein does the difference lie? Is it in these Negroes, or is it in your people?"

"Well, so far as I am concerned," said the Tennesseean,

"these things don't worry me nor do they worry my family or friends. We work on the principle that a Negro has the same right to live and enjoy life that any other man has. We hire him and pay him for his labor. He goes about his business; we go about ours. When he is trying to do right and we know he is an honest man and he asks our aid, we give it. WE ALWAYS AID A WORTHY NEGRO. When we see that he is being imposed upon, we call a halt.

"No, indeed, my friend, you don't understand the nature of this race of people," continued the Tennessee boy. "They are simple and they are not simple. Simply because they will trust your word implicitly, do thousands of dollars worth of business with your 'taking your word for it,' but remembering every little detail in the transaction for years back. We never break our word given with them. This is the reason that all men of my class in the South have no grievance against the Negro. He understands us and we understand him. Lashum and Bloxum can speak for themselves."

"My pappy says 'niggers' ain't got no right to live," said Lashum, "let alone own plantations and stock."

"Why?" asked a dozen boys at once.

"Because they are 'niggers,' " was the answer.

"What makes them 'niggers'?" asked an English boy.

"Why, their inferior blood, of course," was Buck's answer.

"Well, that may be from your point of view. You are white; your blood is superior. Thomas L. Jones, who graduated from this College last year and who was rated third in his class, was called a 'nigger.' He was whiter than you are. What made him a 'nigger'?"

"Why, his mother's blood, of course," Buck answered.

"His mother's blood?" asked the English boy. "Why, she was a quadroon, as white as you are, and his father was a Caucasian. Do you mean to tell me that the sixteen drops of your superior blood will be overcome by his one drop of inferior blood? Impossible! Your position is ridiculous. You are governed by a blind prejudice. Get rid of it!"

CHAPTER XIV.

SHORTLY after this discussion among the boys concerning the "status" of the "niggers" Malcolm and Abe, after discussing the merits and demerits of the arguments of the various students who engaged in this animated discussion of the "Race Question," continued:

"Abe," said Malcolm suddenly, "you have not lived up to your agreement with me."

"I have not! Why, Malcolm, what can you mean?"

"Well, last year and since we have been back you have steadfastly refused to go with me to Miss Donewell's home, offering one excuse and then another. Now, I want to know what is the trouble. Has Miss Donewell or her father intimated to you that you are not welcome?"

"Oh, no!" exclaimed Abe; "on the contrary, they both have asked me repeatedly to call on them at their home. I have always refused. Why, you ask me. Malcolm, do you think I do not know that we belong to two separate and distinct races, and that the sentiment in the section from which we come is hostile to the free intermingling of the races? I, of course, know that you do not consider the color of my skin; but there are others who do. You know that I do not visit your female friends down at your old home. Why should I do so here? Buck Lashum and his crowd have said more than once that you invite me to the homes of white women. You can resent it; for it is not true.

"Now, as to my reason. Malcolm, I know that I have no better friends, nor will I ever have better friends, than you and your father. I believe that unless something unforeseen intervenes, you and Miss Donewell will some day become man and wife and reside on the old plantation. I know the harm that will be done her should the report precede her to her future home that she took me on 'Social Equality.' I, therefore, ask you to let me have my own way in this matter. You know that I have always insisted that no good could possibly come by the mingling of the races socially. No, Malcolm, no good can possibly come from my accepting these invitations.''

''Yes, Abe, that is true enough; but you are my friend, and I insist on your receiving the same consideration from my friends that I receive.''

''True, you have so insisted; but can you recall any instance when you have received an invitation and I have not? Well, at any rate, it is left to me to accept or refuse. I beg of you not to press me further. I say that I do not feel, and will never feel, that you have deserted me. You would feel out of place in the homes where I visit. I would feel out of place in the homes that you visit. I trust you now understand me,'' said Abe.

''I understand what you say. Your reason may be a good one, but if I see fit to take you with me, who has the right to dispute my right to choose a companion? Father told me that I was to see that you were accorded the same treatment that I receive, and——''

''Yes, yes, Malcolm; but he never meant that you were to take me into the same society with you. He meant school privileges. I am perfectly satisfied with the young ladies whom I visit.''

''Well, Abe, let that pass. Where did you get the idea that I would some day marry Miss Donewell? She has never said that she would marry me.''

''She will, if you are the man I take you to be. Malcolm, if you do not win her—well, our friendship will end. She is certainly the finest woman, save one, that I have ever met.''

''Hello! Abe, have you a girl? You sly dog! You never told me about her. Who is she? You are a nice one. I have been telling you of my hopes and fears, and you have been hiding your lady from me. I do not think you have been treating me square.''

"I have no idea in the world, Malcolm, that the young lady whom I admire ever thinks of me other than as an acquaintance. We have never had a serious talk in our lives. Miss Watson is her name. The young lady who led her class last year. But for the color of their skins you would think she and Miss Donewell were sisters."

"Oh, yes; I have seen her at Miss Donewell's house. ' She has avoided me on more than one occasion. I think you must have put her up to it."

"We have similar ideas along certain lines, Malcolm. But I am sure she never intended to offend you. She simply feels, as I do, that no good can possibly come by the mingling of the races socially."

"Abe, I guess you are right, after all. At any rate, we now understand each other better. Good night, old fellow; from the bottom of my heart I wish you all the succees in the world," said Malcolm, as he left Abe and commenced to prepare himself for a visit to Mr. Donewell's home.

When Abe was left to himself he sat for a long time thinking of what Malcolm had said.

"I wonder," Abe asked himself, "whether he will ever change toward me. I do not believe he will. I feel that no matter what befalls me, Malcolm will still be my friend."

"Abe is a curious fellow," thought Malcolm. "I could not induce him to change his mind. Well, since I have thought the matter over, I cannot see why I insisted on his visiting these young ladies. Mabel is all right; but the rest? I think Abe would stand by me against a regiment of cavalry. He's true blue."

Malcolm was soon on his way to Miss Donewell's home. He had been invited to meet some young ladies who were visiting Miss Donewell and whose home was in New York.

Abe had also received an invitation; but, as we have seen, had refused to accept.

Upon Malcolm's arrival he was asked by the ladies why he had not brought his friend. He made an excuse for Abe by saying a previous engagement or something to that effect had kept him away. The visiting ladies had heard so much of Abe through Miss Donewell and Malcolm that they were curious to see and learn something more about him. They were very much disappointed that he did not accept the invitation. Malcolm was asked by Miss Donewell if he could not suggest some way by which Abe could be induced to visit her guests, as they were very anxious to meet him. After some thought Malcolm suggested that Miss Watson be invited and that she be requested to bring Abe with her, explaining that the visiting ladies and no one else be present. That the ladies wanted to hear Miss Watson and Abe in their famous duet, the two having won the reputation of being very fine singers. One of the visiting ladies was an exceptionally fine pianiste and a delightful musical evening was promised. Next morning Abe reecived a note from Miss Watson inviting him to accompany her to Miss Donewell's home that evening to meet some ladies of the musical world. Abe was very fond of music, and, as Miss Watson was to be there, the two inducements decided him to accept. This was the first note Abe had ever received from Miss Watson, so he hid it away in his pocketbook, little thinking the service it would be to him a few weeks later.

At the appointed time Miss Watson and Abe arrived at the Donewell home, where they found the ladies waiting. After several choice selections, vocal and instrumental, tea was served. Some time was spent in a very spirited conversation, after which Miss Watson and Abe left to join some friends at the home of Miss Watson's friend, Miss Glenn.

"Mabel," exclaimed her friends, all speaking at once. "My! But he is black! He's your——"

"Mabel, his voice is grand and his manners are——"

"Mabel, where was he educated? He acts like he is white; his table manners are——"

"Mabel, I never saw one so black. Why, his skin is just——"

"How unfortunate that he is black," said Mabel, laughingly, "else what a scramble you four girls would make for him. I agree with you girls, he is all you say and more; he is a young man of exceptional habits. Now, Miss Scott, I hope you are satisfied; you have had a birthday treat," added Mabel.

"Yes," said Miss Scott; "I do not remember ever spending a more enjoyable anniversary. I hope to always remember the two hours, 7 to 9 p. m., November 10, 18—."

It is well for Abe, as we shall see later, that Miss Scott made mention of this date and these hours, as they were thereby impressed upon the minds of the other young ladies.

After Malcolm left, Abe sat musing for some moments, after which he walked into Malcolm's room and took up a queer-looking meerschaum pipe, filled it and began to smoke. Soon he remarked to himself that he wanted to see Forbes, and left his room, taking the pipe with him. Not being permitted to smoke in the halls, he pushed the stem of the pipe up his sleeve, holding the bowl in his hand close to his body. With the pipe in this position, apparently hiding it, Abe met Buck, Bloxum and several other boys of that set.

"What you recon' he is hidin' that pipe fer?" said Buck, as Abe passed him.

"Likely as not he is carrying it down the hall to sell it to Forbes," remarked Bloxum.

"You fellows can always see something wrong in everything that Overley does. Why not tell him what you have just told us?" said Sam Bucker.

"Just like you, taking up fer 'niggers.' I remember when we went to see Dr. Finley 'bout 'niggers' eatin' with us you was the first one to back out and have been leaning 'niggerward' ever since," said Buck.

"No, I am not leaning 'nigger-ward,' nor am I taking up for 'niggers.' I think you two ought to be more manly, either to say these things to Overley or leave them unsaid. But you and Bloxum do not seem to understand the position that gentlemen should take in such matters. If you despise Overley, as you claim, the dignified gentleman would ignore him."

"Bucker, you ain't a thing," said Buck. "Ain't we white? Whose got nothin' to do with us when it comes to these 'niggers'?"

"Well," said a boy from North Carolina, "the whole fetched crowd is bad. But Buck and Bloxum do worry too much about them. We've got nothing to do with thatair pipe. Come on, let's have a game. Do something that gentlemen can find some amusement in."

These young men then passed into Buck's room, where they were soon busily engaged in a game of poker.

CHAPTER XV.

WHILE Abe was at the home of Miss Donewell, Malcolm missed his pipe, the meerschaum pipe spoken of in a previous chapter. He searched his own room, and Abe's, but could not find it.

Upon Abe's return he found Malcolm brooding over his loss.

"Malcolm, what is the matter? You look as if you have lost your best friend. Cheer up. I have a message for you from Miss Donewell. She invites you to call tomorrow evening at 7.30 p. m., as her visitors have received an unexpected summons to return to their homes. They will take the midnight train. They also expect you to see them off. Miss Donewell says she is going with them. You will have four full hours with her, Malcolm, and this is your chance, or else she wouldn't have sent for you. I wish you every success."

"Abe, after the way you treated me in your affair, I think you have nerve and plenty, to expect me to talk to you about my case. But you seem so fatherly, I will say that I do intend to avail myself of the first opportunity that presents to learn my fate." After a moment or two Malcolm added: "We have met with a very serious loss, Abe, if you do not know where our pipe is. I have looked all over the place for it. Do you know where it is?"

"Let me see," said Abe; "I think I saw it just before I went out last night."

"Well, it is not here now," said Malcolm, and the gloomy look which Abe noticed when he entered the room again settled upon his face.

"What will I say to father if we don't find it? He values that pipe very highly, because his great-grandfather smoked it. That pipe was never off the old place before and now it is lost."

83

While Malcolm was talking Abe had been searching the room. He looked in every place in which the pipe could possibly be, but to no purpose. It was gone.

"Malcolm, I cannot find it. Think. Have you left it in any boy's room? Let us ask Forbes and the rest of the boys." They then proceeded to Forbes's room, but Forbes had not seen the pipe nor had any of the rest of the boys.

"What shall I do?" asked Malcolm. "This pipe is a family heirloom. My father will never forgive me for losing it."

"Report the loss to the Dean at once," said Rattles. Maybe he can suggest some way by which it can be recovered."

They went immediately to the Dean, and explained the loss and its seriousness. The Dean promised to investigate the matter at once. He first, however, reported to Dr. Finley that the pipe was lost under circumstances that looked as if it were stolen. They then ordered all the boys on that floor before them. Dr. Finley had a short heart-to-heart talk with them, suggesting that he would consider it a personal favor if the boy who knew the whereabouts of the pipe would see that it was returned. He did not ask nor did he desire the students to inform upon one another. He also intimated that he thought the boys on the same floor with Malcolm and Abe knew all about the pipe, thereby practically exonerating the rest of the school. This brought Buck and Bloxum together about a week later.

"Buck, now we've got him," said Bloxum. "Let us go to the Dean and tell him that we are on his floor and do not feel content to live under the suspicion that has been cast upon us simply because we are on this floor. That we saw Abe with the pipe. All the fellows who were with us in the hall will remember how he had the pipe up his coat sleeve. I tell you we've got him this time."

"D— his black hide! I hope we is. Come on, let's go to the Dean," said Buck.

The two then proceeded to the Dean's office and stated to

him that on account of being on the same floor with the Overleys they were very much humiliated because of the suspicion
cast upon them by the loss of Overley's pipe. They very much
disliked to say anything that would reflect upon any student,
but they saw Abe Overley with the pipe half up his coat sleeve
going into Forbes's room on the night of November 10th;
were confident that it was November 10th. They gave the
names of several other students who saw him, together with
the part of the conversation that followed after Buck's remark
about Abe taking the pipe to Forbes.

These young men were so embarrassed that they could not
tell the story at once, and it was only by dint of close question-
ing that the Dean could get a clear idea of what they had seen.
He reported the facts to Dr. Finley, who immediately sent for
the boys whose names were given as witnesses. After ques-
tioning them very closely, the Doctor concluded to send for
Abe. When Abe put in his appearance the Doctor repeated
to him what he had heard, and asked what he had to say for
himself.

"Doctor," said Abe, "I was not in the hall the night in
question between the hours of 6.30 and 11 p. m. I was at the
home of——," Abe stopped short and looked the Doctor full
in the face, and said, "I cannot tell you at whose home I was
that night without the permission of that person."

"Mr. Overley," said the Doctor, "do you realize the position in which you place yourself and the chain of suspicion
that encircles you? Consider well before you decide not to
make a complete statement of your whereabouts the night this
pipe was missed."

"Doctor, I know only too well the danger in which I find
myself. I know the natures of the persons who have come to
you with this story. I know the animus behind the whole
affair. But, Doctor, for all that, I cannot say where I was
that night. It must come from the other person."

"Does your friend Overley know your whereabouts?" asked the Doctor.

"Yes, sir, he does," said Abe.

"Will you say to him that I desire his presence at once. I do not wish you to say one word to him about what has passed between us," said the Doctor, as he arose and extended his hand silently to Abe.

"What does he want, Abe?" asked Malcolm, when the request was delivered.

He said to me, 'I do not wish you to say one word to him (meaning you) about what has passed between us,' so you see where I am at. You must face the lion unprepared," said Abe, laughingly.

"Well, I will soon know," answered Malcolm, as he prepared to leave for the Doctor's office. After Abe's departure the Doctor turned to the Dean and remarked: "These boys are the two strongest characters in the school. They are friends. This white boy feels the loss of his pipe very keenly. Now, we will see what he will say when he learns what these other boys have said about his friend."

Upon Malcolm's arrival the Doctor told him what he had heard, the number of witnesses who saw Abe with the pipe, and, finally, Abe's refusal to say where he was the night the pipe was lost.

"Now, Mr. Overley, your friend says you know where he was that night. Will you tell us?"

"No, sir; if he refused to say where he was, I, of course, cannot betray his confidence," answered Malcolm, simply.

"Well," said the Doctor, as he handed Malcolm an official note, "take this to him. It is a notice of suspension, pending further investigation. I am very sorry that this course must be pursued."

"Do you mean, Doctor, that you believe, upon the statement of this bunch of——"

"Be careful, Mr. Overley. I have expressed no belief in this matter. I am simply pursuing the course that is usual in matters of this kind," the Doctor answered very quickly.

"I will never believe Abe stole that pipe, nor will he steal," said Malcolm, as he left the Doctor's office.

He hastened to Abe with Dr. Finley's note, which follows:

Oberlin, Ohio, November 28, 18—.

Mr. Abraham Overley,

Dear Sir: This is to notify you that you are suspended from further participation in the College exercises or lectures until further notice.

FINLEY, *President.*

"What have I done, Malcolm, to warrant this?" asked Abe, when he had recovered from the surprise caused by his suspension.

"You have refused to tell Doctor Finley where you were on the night the pipe was lost. Why, Abe, you have not even told me where you were that night."

"Have not told you!" exclaimed Abe. "Can it be possible that you, of all persons on this earth, doubt me, too? Why should I tell you that which you already know?"

Malcolm, with his hands deep in his pockets, stood looking at Abe in amazement.

"Abe, do I understand you to say that I knew of your whereabouts upon the night this pipe was stolen? How can you say——"

"My God, Malcolm, you, too, doubt me?" As Abe asked this question he laid his hand on Malcolm's shoulder and looked him in the face, hoping to find there the old look of trust and confidence. Malcolm turned his face away. Abe's hand dropped to his side; his whole attitude changed to one of despair; he seemed to age perceptibly. Abe moved toward the door, then turned to Malcolm with a look which Malcolm never forgot, and simply said:

"And you, too, Malcolm!"

Malcolm met his gaze with a heart full of doubts and fears, but answered Abe calmly, saying:

"Abe, you did not tell me where you were, nor do I know."

"My God!" exclaimed Abe, "he, too, believes me to be a thief!"

Abe passed into his room and cast himself upon his bed, where he remained for the rest of the night and the following day. The morning of the second day, as Abe had not put in his appearance, Malcolm became uneasy about him. Still Abe had not told where he was the night the pipe was stolen. Malcolm, therefore, went to Forbes and Rattles for advice.

"Say, Forbes," said Malcolm, "what shall we do with Abe? He has not left his room for two days. He does nothing but moan all the time."

"Let us go and see him," said Rattles.

When these young men entered Abe's room they found him lying across his bed, where he had been since his talk with Malcolm. Rattles went to him and lifted his head from the bed, bringing his face into the light, at the sight of which, haggard and careworn, Malcolm and Forbes drew back astounded.

"Abe," said Rattles, kindly, "what can I do for you? Come, old man, brace up; you are killing yourself about nothing. This thing will blow over in a day or two."

Abe raised his eyes to Malcolm's face and kept them there in a long, bewildered stare. Malcolm could not endure the gaze and moved away to his own room, followed by Forbes.

"Malcolm," said Forbes, "what is the trouble between you and Abe?" Malcolm hesitated, but Forbes urged him to tell what had come between them.

"Well, the truth is," said Malcolm, "while I will never believe that Abe stole that pipe, nor will he steal, he would not tell Dr. Finley where he was the night of the 10th, nor would he tell me. Why not me? Then he said I knew. But I do not. He told Dr. Finley that I knew, when he must have known that I did not. What has come over Abe that he has so far forgotten himself as to lie?''

''Are you sure of what you say?'' asked Forbes. ''I am loath to believe that Abe will lie.''

At that moment Rattles came into the room with Abe's pocketbook in his hand and walked to the window, remarking that Abe said there was a prescription in it which he wanted filled. Rattles searched the book and pulled forth the note Miss Watson sent Abe asking him to accompany her to Miss Donewell's. It follows:

Oberlin, Ohio, November 10, 18—.
11 a. m.

Mr. Abraham Overley,

Dear Sir: Will you kindly call for me this afternoon at 6.45 to accompany me to a musicale at Miss Donewell's home? We will meet some musical people there from New York City.

Sincerely yours,
NANCY WATSON.

As Rattles began to read——

''Oberlin, Ohio, November 10, 18—, 11 a. m.,'' Malcolm exclaimed:

''What is that? November 10, 18—? Let me see it, Rattles,'' and he grasped the note. As Malcolm read his color changed, his hand trembled; for a moment he seemed to be deprived of the power of speech; he staggered to a chair and sank upon it, still holding the note before him, at which he gazed in blank amazement.

''Why, Overley,'' said Forbes, ''what on earth ails you? Has that note deprived you of your senses? Let me see this scroll from the Magii.''

Forbes read the note, as did Rattles, but neither of them seemed to understand the situation. Forbes again asked Malcolm for an explanation.

"Do you not see that date?" asked Malcolm. "November 10th is the date upon which I lost that pipe. Abe was at Miss Donewell's home with Miss Watson, and, to make matters worse, I KNEW HE WAS THERE. What a thoughtless thing I have done, to let Abe suffer for two days without attempting to console him. Then, I have written to my father and explained the whole affair to him, as I thought. What an injustice I have done Abe! How I could have forgotten that he was at Miss Donewell's, when I told them how to get him there, is more than I can understand. He ought never to forgive me. I will see him at once."

Malcolm went immediately to Abe, who was seated on a chair, where Rattles left him, staring into space. Malcolm extended his hand to him, saying:

"Abe, can you ever forgive me for the pain I have caused you? I understand now what you meant by asking why you should tell me that which I already knew. My friend, I am ashamed to say so, but I forgot all about that engagement of yours with Miss Watson at Miss Donewell's. Abe, I ask you a thousand pardons."

Abe looked up at Malcolm in a half conscious way, apparently not fully understanding all that had been said to him. He took Malcolm's hand, however, in both of his own and said:

"Malcolm, did you think I stole that pipe?"

"Why, no, Abe," said Malcolm; "no such idea crossed my mind. I thought you were not living up to your promise made to me when we first came here, that we would have no secrets from each other. Abe, I shall go immediately to Doctor Finley and explain this wretched affair."

"No, Malcolm; do not do that. I do not want it done. This explanation must come from them. I must insist, my friends, that each of you promise me that you will not say one word of this to a living soul."

"I am sure I do not see the force of your request," said Rattles; "but I will respect your wish."

"Abe, we want to consult on your case," said Forbes, Malcolm and Rattles as they went out of the room. "Malcolm, you are the only person who has the key to this situation. What does Abe mean by not wanting you, nor either of us, to say where he was that night?"

"I do not believe that either of you has ever heard Abe express himself about visiting white women," said Malcolm; "nor do you know that he has never before November 10, visited Miss Donewell. Well, such is the fact. He has always contended that no good could possibly come by the commingling of the races socially. Now, through Miss Watson, he accepted an invitation to meet some ladies at Miss Donewell's home, and while there this pipe was stolen. Abe absolutely refuses to say where he was that night, nor will he permit us to say. He is already suspended and will suffer himself to be expelled before he will divulge his whereabouts the night in question. What can we do about it?"

"I hardly know," said Forbes. "We must certainly respect his wishes. But must we permit him to sacrifice himself upon the altar of his high ideal, which seems to me a bit overdrawn?"

"What can we do?" asked Rattles. "It is Abe's affair. We have no right to 'butt in.' Say, I admire his grit. He is suspended now, and is prepared to be expelled rather than say that he was at a white woman's home. Many a Negro would be crowing about it."

"When I questioned Abe about not accepting invitations to these various places, he answered that his female associates suited him," said Malcolm. "He even said that you could not tell the difference between Miss Donewell and Miss Watson but for the color of their skins. I tell you, fellows, he has ideas of his own."

"As we have no right to divulge Abe's secret," remarked Forbes, "let us advise him to see Doctor Finley himself."

"Abe," said Forbes, "we are your friends and want to advise you. Overley has just explained this whole affair to us. We think you are wrong. Miss Donewell and her father have invited you to their home; so have I invited you to mine. Do you think that they or that I would object to your saying that you accepted the invitations? Abe, you are drawing it too fine."

"Forbes, I appreciate your good intentions," answered Abe; "but you do not understand. You cannot understand the position in which I am. You——"

"Why can't I understand?" asked Forbes.

"Because you are not a Negro," Abe replied, solemnly.

This remark of Abe's stopped all conversation for several moments. The silence was broken by Abe's remarking:

"Fellows, I am in for it. I can but let matters take their course."

"Well, you can take a little exercise, at any rate," said Rattles, and he suggested a turn around the campus. As Abe and his three friends neared the upper end of the campus they came upon a group of boys, which included DeVaux and his friend from Tennessee, together with Bucker and Bloxum. DeVaux was the first to note Abe's approach.

"Why, fellows, there is Abe Overley," he remarked. "Look at him. I don't believe he would steal anything."

"Nor do I," said the Tennesseean. Turning to Abe, he extended his hand very cordially, saying:

"Overley, I hear that you are in trouble—that you are suspended—that you are practically accused of stealing a pipe from your friend Malcolm; all these things coming through statements of persons not above small things. I want to say to you that I do not believe that you are guilty in any sense of the word. If there is anything I can do for you, command me; I am at your service."

"Overley," said DeVaux, after the general handshaking, which was joined by all except Bloxum, who slunk away as soon as the boys began to gather about Abe, "when this thing is cleared up and you are exonerated, as I know you will be, you must do some lambasting."

"D— if I wouldn't commence now," said the Yankee boy, "if I were you. Those fellows need a good thrashing. I tell you, Abe Overley, I can count on my fingers all the boys in this College who believe you guilty. Whenever I think of this trick, I feel like thrashing somebody."

As Bloxum turned to leave the crowd, Bucker called to him, saying earnestly: "Don't leave, Bloxum; don't you hear what these fellows are saying?" Bloxum apparently did not hear what his friend Bucker said, as he kept on, going straight to Buck's room.

"Say, Buck," he said, "don't you know those fellows down on the campus are making a fool of Abe Overley, telling him that they know he is not guilty, and that a 'nigger' won't steal. Well, you should have heard them."

"Bloxum, I don't give a doggon fer the whole bunch," said Buck. "I am going to Elmyra; come on and go."

Bloxum did not need a second invitation; they were soon on the way.

Abe appeared to feel much relieved after being assured by his friends and acquaintances that he had not lost their confidence and still retained their respect. These young men went back to Malcolm's room, where a free and frank exchange of thought was had. Good-fellowship soon held sway once more.

CHAPTER XVI.

AFTER the conversation between Malcolm and Abe, which resulted in the latter's prostration and seclusion for two days, Malcolm felt it his duty to inform his father as to what had taken place. He, therefore, wrote to him as follows:

Oberlin, Ohio, November 15th.

Dear Father:

I can imagine how you and Uncle Abe will feel when this letter reaches you both, but I feel it my duty to write the whole circumstances, that you may form your own opinion.

The meerschaum pipe that I brought from home is the cause of all this trouble. On the night of November 10th last, I missed the pipe from my room. I reported the loss of the pipe to the Dean; he, in turn, reported the loss to Dr. Finley, who called all the boys on our floor together, stating to them that he thought some of the boys on our floor knew where the pipe was. He asked that it be brought back. Later, Buck Lashum and Squealer Bloxum went to the Dean and told him that they, together with several other boys, saw Abe with the pipe, half up his sleeve, going through the hall to Will Forbes's room. The Dean reported to the Doctor, who sent for the boys, and they all agreed that they saw Abe, as Buck and Bloxum stated.

The Doctor then sent for Abe, who denied being in the hall at the time they claimed to have seen him. When asked where he was he absolutely refused to say.

He said, further, that I knew where he was, but I do not. As a result, Abe is suspended, and at this time is in his room, where he has been for two days.

I do not know what to do with him. I do not believe that Abe knows anything about the pipe; but why does he not tell where he was? And why did he say that I knew where he was, when I did not?

Father, what must I do? Tell Uncle Abe to write to him and command him to say where he was. He will obey his father.

These are the circumstances. I hope this will not worry

94

you, but I feel it my duty to let you both know exactly what has happened.

Give my love to the people. I am well, but worried.

Yours,

M. A. O., Jr.

After Malcolm A. Overley, Sr., had read and reread this letter, in Old Abe's hearing, he said:

"Abe, what the h— do you think of that? Just to think of it! Abe suspended under suspicion of having stolen my pipe, that he has been playing with all his life! Such d— rot! That shows what little sense these d— professors have. That boy steal? Why, I should as soon believe that my Abe would steal. But, why don't he tell where he was that night? Abe, d— your black hide, have you nothing to say? Are you going to let them make a thief of that boy? Buck Lashum! He saw Abe hiding that pipe! H— and damnation, man, are you asleep, or are you dumb, or are you such a fool that you don't care what happens to that boy of yours? D— if I don't believe you are glad he is in trouble! Sit there now looking like that d— old kicking mule of yours. Can't you talk?"

"Yes, sar, ob cose I kin talk," said Old Abe; "but yuse been talkin' an' cussin' for mor'n half hour. How kin I talk? How I goin' to git a word in, nohow? My po' boy, he am in all dis heah trouble 'bout dat pipe. I vouch Buck Lashum stole dat pipe. Yes, sar; de Lawd's will mus' be done."

"Yes, the Lord's will must be done. Saddle it on the Lord. That's the plea of every 'nigger' I ever heard of, after he has been caught doing wrong. The Lord's will! According to that doctrine, the Lord wills that you 'niggers' do wrong. It is too foolish for discussion. What are you going to do about that boy of yours?"

"I does not know. I does know dat my Abe won't steal; but why he not say whar he war, I does not know. Dat boy he sho' got a good 'scuse fo' not sayin' whar he at dat night. All I say is dis: 'Lawd, dy will be done.' "

"Well, I be d—! Is that all you have to say?"

Both of these fathers then relapsed into silence, one to brood over the prospect of a disgrace to his name, the other to pray silently to Almighty God that his son may come out of this entanglement with his name untarnished.

Thus we leave them to their own thoughts.

CHAPTER XVII.

WHEN it became known throughout the College that Abe Overley had been suspended, supposedly for the larceny of his friend's meerschaum pipe, upon the statement of Buck Lashum and Bloxum, feeling ran very high.

The Oberlin College *Bulletin* contained the following editorial comment:

"It is with regret we announce the suspension of Mr. Abraham Overley for the supposed larceny of a pipe belonging to his friend and classmate, Mr. Malcolm A. Overley, both of these young men residents of the State of Alabama.

"It appears that Mr. Malcolm Overley was the owner of a very old and valuable meerschaum pipe. This pipe was stolen the night of November 10th.

"It appears further that Mr. Buck Lashum and Mr. Squealer Bloxum saw Mr. Abraham Overley, with the pipe in question half up his coat sleeve, passing through the hall to the room of Mr. William Forbes.

"It also appears that Mr. Abraham Overley, when questioned by Dr. Finley, absolutely refused to state where he was the night of November 10th. Whereupon his suspension followed.

"It does not appear that Mr. Abraham Overley was given a chance to explain his having the pipe in his possession, if he had it, as claimed by the two gentlemen named.

"We feel that a grave mistake has been made and that Mr. Overley has been done a great injustice."

When this issue of the *Bulletin* reached Mr. George Billings Donewell he forwarded a marked copy to his daughter Mabel, which copy caused a sensation among her New York friends.

"Why, Mabel," said one, "who would have thought he could!"

"Oh, I cannot believe him guilty!" exclaimed another.

"Mabel, I thought you said he was such a gentleman?" said a third young lady.

"What can he mean by refusing to say where he was?" asked another friend.

"Why, girls," said Miss Scott, "November 10th is the date of the night he was at Mabel's house with Miss Watson, and sang so lovely."

"Oh! I see the whole thing now," said Miss Mabel Donewell. "He was at my house, and will not say so because he hasn't our permission."

"Of course that is the night, because that was Jennie's birthday."

"What can we do about it?" asked Miss Chiswell.

"Let us see papa," said Miss Mary Chiswell; "show him this paper and ask his advice. We are the cause of his embarrassment."

After Mr. Chiswell had read the editorial and all the surrounding circumstances had been explained to him, he advised that the young ladies go to Oberlin and state the whole case to Dr. Finley. He advised further that they start immediately.

Preparing themselves with incredible speed, we soon find the girls on a train due to arrive in Oberlin at 8.30 p. m. that night. Upon their arrival in Oberlin they hastened to the residence of Dr. Finley, where they found him in consultation with the members of the faculty concerning this very case. When the girls were announced he was at a loss to understand this unusual visit. Miss Mabel Donewell made plain the object, however, stating how she happened to know of this trouble and where she and her friends were when they heard of it.

When she had completed her statement, the Doctor sent for Malcolm.

"Mr. Overley," said the Doctor, "I have just learned that Abraham Overley was at the home of a young lady who has been out of town and that you knew that he was there. Is that a fact?"

"Yes, sir," said Malcolm. "But I have given Abe my word not to mention his whereabouts unless the other party so directs. I hope you will not question me further."

"Mr. Overley, I appreciate your position and will see what I can do to gain you that permission."

Thereupon he instructed his secretary to bring to him the lady who was in waiting. When Malcolm saw Miss Donewell enter the room he started up wtih a look that betrayed his feelings. He extended both hands to her, saying:

"Thank God, you have come! I knew you would. I know now that Abe will soon be reinstated. I am very glad to see you."

Miss Donewell colored very deeply and drew back, as if she feared Malcolm would crush her in his eagerness.

"Miss Donewell," said the Doctor, with a merry twinkle in his eye, "will you give Mr. Overley leave to say where his friend was on the night of November 10th?"

"Of course I will, Doctor. Mr. Overley, you may say that Mr. Abraham Overley was at my home on this night, and all else you may know about this affair that pertains to me."

Malcolm immediately started into a complete recital of the whole story, stating that it was November 9th that Abe had the pipe in the hall; also stating Abe's reason for not saying where he was the night of November 10th, to all of which the Doctor and faculty listened very attentively. After Malcolm had finished the narration, the Doctor instructed him to have Abe come to him at once, and that he would impose the further burden (?) upon him of seeing the young ladies home. The Doctor also instructed his secretary to go for Lashum and Bloxum, telling him to keep them in the library until he sent for them.

He then suggested to the Dean that he thought it advisable to search Lashum's room. The Dean, together with two other members of the faculty, proceeded to make the search, which resulted in finding the pipe at the bottom of Lashum's trunk.

The Dean took the pipe, wrapped very closely, to Dr. Finley's office.

When Abe reached the Doctor's office he expected to hear that he was expelled. His surprise was very great when told that the whole affair had been cleared up, so far as he was concerned, and that the announcement of his reinstatement would be made in the most public manner next morning in the Chapel, just after devotional exercises. The Doctor and other members of the faculty then shook Abe's hand very cordially and bade him good night. The Doctor had been informed as to how and where the Dean had found the pipe, so, after a short discussion, it was thought best to interview Bloxum first. When Bloxum came into the room, the pipe was on the table in full view, and when he saw it he staggered to a chair and dropped upon it. He knew that trouble was in store for him. True to his nature, he resolved to put the blame on Buck. Dr. Finley did not question him at once, but kept looking at the pipe, waiting for Bloxum to be the first to say something concerning it. Bloxum was wary and did not betray himself. Finally, the Doctor turned suddenly to the Dean and said:

"Dean Sternly, where did you say you found this pipe?"

"I found it in Mr. Buck Lashum's trunk," was his response.

"Mr. Bloxum, how came this pipe to be there?" asked the Doctor. "I hope you will see fit to tell me the whole truth about this matter."

"I did not put it there. I told Buck to let it alone," was Bloxum's answer.

"Now, tell us the entire circumstance," said the Doctor.

Bloxum said that he and Lashum and a few others were passing through the hall the night before Buck got the pipe and they saw Abe with it. Buck said: "Let's get that pipe and put it on Abe," but Bloxum advised him to let it alone. Buck insisted. Buck alone did the whole thing. All Bloxum did was to say that he saw Abe with the pipe, which was true.

After this remarkable statement, the Doctor sent for Buck. When Buck saw the pipe on the table he became sullen at once.

"Mr. Lashum, do you know where that pipe was?" asked the Doctor.

"No, I do not," said Buck.

"It was found in your trunk," said the Doctor.

"I didn't put it there," said Buck; "nor do I know how it got there."

"Have a care, Mr. Lashum," said the Doctor; "I have a statement from one who claims to know all about this affair." The Doctor then read the statement made by Bloxum. Buck thought a moment, then concluded that Bloxum must have "squealed" on him.

"Well, I won't say nothin', because I don't know nothin'," said Buck, and moved toward the door.

"Do not be in a hurry, Mr. Lashum," said the Doctor. I want to know whether or not this statement is true."

"No, it ain't true," said Buck.

At a sign from the Doctor, Bloxum was brought in the room again and his statement was read to him.

"Mr. Bloxum," said the Doctor, "is this statement true?"

"Yes, sir, it is true; every word of it," was Bloxum's answer.

Buck glared at him for a moment, then said:

"So you are trying to put this whole thing on me, are you? Well, you won't. Didn't you tell me how to fix that 'nigger'——"

"Mr. Lashum," interrupted the Doctor, "you will use nothing but proper language here. You will withdraw that word."

"Well, Bloxum told me how to get even with Abe. He told me to get the pipe and hide it and say that Abe stole it, and that we saw him with it, and that the boys would not know what night it was. Now, he tries to put the job on me. I ain't afeared to say what I did. I'm white, I am."

After Buck had finished, Bloxum began to remark that Buck knew better; that he advised against the whole thing all the way through; but he was cut short by the Doctor, who said that their cases would be disposed of that night and that the conclusion would be announced next morning at the Chapel exercises.

Dr. Finley, after a prayer next morning, in which he asked Almighty God to watch and protect the school and those in the school who were weighted down with troubles and sorrows, and those who were about to leave the school and who would need His constant care, said he had two duties to perform, one a pleasant, the other a very disagreeable duty.

First, that the faculty, after new facts had come to light, had unanimously agreed to reinstate Mr. Abraham Overley, who had been suspended pending the finding of Mr. Malcolm Overley's pipe and the investigation as to his whereabouts the night the pipe was stolen. He said it gave him great pleasure to state that the investigation disclosed that Mr. Overley was not guilty in any sense of the word. He, therefore, withdrew the suspension and hoped that all the students would understand that no suspicion whatever rested on Mr. Overley. This announcement was met by the yell that only College boys know. Abe was the hero of the hour. The Doctor's manner then changed. He said the investigation also led to the discovery of a case of criminal conspiracy. He stated that it was discovered that two students had conspired to rob another of his good name by lying about him, and gave the complete details of the affair, after which he announced that the faculty had dismissed Mr. Buck Lashum and Mr. Squealer Bloxum. The boys arose to their feet looking for Buck and Bloxum; but they had been notified of the action of the faculty and were not present. These young men were busy packing their belongings, Buck cursing and scoring Bloxum as an ungrateful dog, Bloxum whining and crying, not knowing where to get money to pay his fare home. When the Doctor's announcement was made that Buck and Bloxum were dismissed there was a moment of silence; then there burst forth a perfect volcano of cat calls, hisses and groans. When the noise had ceased, the Doctor dismissed the students. Out on the campus a party surrounded Malcolm and Abe and wanted Abe to tell where he was that night and all about the case, but Abe still refused to say a word about his whereabouts, remarking that if one visit caused all this talk and trouble, what would ten visits cause? As DeVaux and his friend passed out of the Chapel the Tennesseean remarked:

"That was undoubtedly the dirtiest trick I ever heard of."

"DeVaux, what do you think of such people?"

"Well, I am sure I don't know. They just deliberately stole that pipe and accused somebody else of the theft, thereby bringing other people into it as witnesses," answered De Vaux. "These fellows must feel cheap now."

"I am glad they are gone."

The next issue of the College *Bulletin* contained a full account of the affair. Malcolm mailed one to his father and also a letter to Abe's father, asking pardon for causing him unnecessary worry and trouble.

CHAPTER XVIII.

BLOXUM, unlike Buck, had no cash upon which to draw to procure a ticket for his home trip. He was, therefore, compelled to write his father for the necessary funds. What should he write? How was he to explain his expulsion? After much thought, Bloxum concluded he would write his father at length, explaining that he had brought trouble upon himself in an endeavor to protect a Negro by the name of Overley, forgetting that his father received the Oberlin *Bulletin*. In due course Bloxum received the bare amount necessary to procure his ticket, unaccompanied by either letter or comment. He left by a night train, well knowing that no boy in the school would be sorry to see him leave. Bloxum's father concluded to express himself to his son in person.

After writing home that Abe Overley had lied on him, that Abe had stolen a pipe and put it in his (Buck's) trunk, Buck declared that he was coming home. Oberlin was no place for him. A "nigger's" word there is better than a white man's. Buck also forgot that the *Bulletin* was sent to his home; but he was more fortunate than Bloxum. Nick Lashum, Sr., could not read and was kept in ignorance of those things which the family did not desire him to know. Buck concluded he would visit friends in Elmyra and Cleveland before he started home. He found himself stranded in Cleveland, however. Upon receiving a telegram from Buck, his brother immediately telegraphed him the necessary amount to procure a ticket. When Buck arrived home his father wanted to know about the affair that led to his homecoming, inasmuch as his brothers and sisters had been careful not to inform Nick, Sr., that his son had been expelled from College. He, therefore, launched into a long story as to how he happend to be home. In the first place, Oberlin was no place for a white man, anyhow. "Niggers'' were more thought of than white men. "Niggers" had all the privileges of the school; they stood at the head of some of the classes; they went about with white women. A "nigger" was the captain of the College baseball team. "Niggers" sat at the same table with him. Taken on the whole, he could not understand how he managed to live through it all. He, as you may know, had a very sympathetic audience.

After he had finished his narrative, Arabella innocently remarked:

"Buck, it was awful mean of them to expel you just for that."

"What's that?" asked Nick, Sr., with a blaze of wrath. "Why the damnation hain't yer tol' me that 'fore now? What yer mean by not tellin' me what I aughter know? D— if I don't pull yer lyin' tongue outen yer haid!"

Suiting the acts to the words, Nick, Sr., made a move toward his son, but Buck was on the alert and soon put a safe distance between himself and his irate parent.

"Never yer min', yer ungrateful dorg! Jes' yer put yer foot in this hyre house again an—go 'way Arabella, yer leetle hussy, think I'm goin' to let thet air boy run my house? Doggon ef I don't fix him, yo'll see."

Buck, in his haste to get out of his father's reach ran to the cabin of Black Sue, who was sitting before the door smoking a pipe—a habit common among the Negro women among her class.

"Lor', chile, what's de mattah?" she asked, noticing his haste and frightened look. "Sho' yo' pappy's not arter you 'gin so soon?"

"Yes," said Buck, "and he swears he will kill me if he catches me."

Black Sue insisted that he should tell her about the trouble, thinking something had happened which caused him to return before the end of the school year. Negroes of this class could always be depended upon to know all, even to the smallest

details, that transpired at the Big House. Black Sue was no
exception to this rule. After Buck had related his version
of why he was expelled, this virtuous (?) person was consumed
with wrath. She regarded Buck thoughtfully for some
moments, then remarked:

"Chile, I know jes' how to git eben wid dem Overleys. Ole
Mal Overley and Ole Abe and de rest ob dem men is gone to
take dey grain to de boat. Dey won't be back till day arter
'morrow. Yo' kin kotch dat gal ob Ole Abe's what puts on
so many airs jes' kase she kin read and write, and dat ole
mammy ob hern stealin' bacon outen yo' pappy's meat house.
I dun kotch dem onct. Den yo' kin gib dem a good floggin'."

Buck knew only too well the purport of this statement. He
saw very readily that he could rehabilitate himself in the good
graces of his father by this means. He therefore immediately
sent one of Black Sue's boys after the Smalys and Wardemans, upon whom he could depend. It was agreed in the
council that followed that at 11 p. m. the next night they
were to assemble and go quietly to the cabin of the Overleys,
take the two women out and flog them. At the appointed
time these representative citizens met at the place designated
and proceeded to the cabin, where they found these lone
women.

The daughter was engaged in reading the Bible to her
mother, as she had been accustomed to do for years past, just
before retiring. Jack Smaly burst the door open and with an
oath demanded to know where the bacon was they had stolen
from Mr. Lashum's meathouse. The daughter, who was a
very spirited girl, arose to her feet, saying that they knew she
nor her mother had stolen nothing. Jack dealt the girl a blow
with his fist that felled her to the floor. The mother, in trying
to prevent this assault, was knocked down by one of the Wardemans. They were both then seized, bound, and taken back
into the orchard, stripped bare to the waist by these "Alabama
gentlemen" (?), who proceeded to administer with a leather

horse-trace nine and thirty lashes on their bare backs. At the first blow, the mother, old and feeble, fainted and hung by the thongs that bound her to the tree. No thought of pity for her; no hand was raised to stay the sickening blows that fell upon her emaciated body; no word of warning that her life was being taken; nothing but curses and blows were multiplied upon her, until her brutal lynchers stopped from sheer exhaustion. The daughter begged that the mother be spared, but was answered by a blow that loosened several teeth. The trace was applied to the now perfectly nude body of the unfortunate girl, until she, too, hung limp and apparently lifeless, subjected to the vile remarks and jeers of these merciless wretches. At this moment Buck's brother, Nick, Jr., arrived on the scene. He, though a Lashum, did not approve of such deeds. He went at once to the old woman and cut her loose, thinking she would be glad to get away, but she fell to the ground. After bending over her for a moment, he said:

"You fellows have raised h— now, haven't you? You have killed this old woman."

He then went to the daughter and found her almost lifeless. Some of the Negro women from the nearby cabins were called and they took the girl to her cabin, where she died before morning. This drunken mob, now sobered by the realization of the enormity of their crime, began to move away, leaving their victims dead and dying.

Sheriff Joe Wheatley was notified of this tragedy by some of the Negroes and was soon upon the scene. He learned from them that the deed was committed by Buck Lashum's gang. The Sheriff immediately put Buck and his cronies, the Wardemans and the Smalys, under arrest. The Coroner also soon arrived. When he learned that Buck and his friends were under arrest, charged with murder of these women, he impanelled a jury at once, to determine the innocence of these young men. Testimony was adduced from the Negroes that should have been strong enough to hold the prisoners for the

action of the Grand Jury, but three white men, who were late
in arriving at the scene of action, swore they passed the
prisoners five miles back on the road, going in an opposite
direction from the scene of the tragedy at the time of its
occurrence, which testimony was of sufficient weight, in the
opinion of the jury, to justify them in bringing in a verdict
declaring that the women came to their deaths at the hands
of parties unknown to the jury, probably the result of a fight
among the Negroes on the Overley place, Malcolm A. Oberley
not being home to preserve order.   All this in the face of the
fact that these men were in the custody of the Sheriff at the
time the three citizens swore they were on the road.

The ability to reason in a Negro's favor is not an accom-
plishment characteristic of an Alabama jury.   The Coroner
ordered the discharge of the prisoners.

After a consultation with the State's Attorney, Sheriff
Wheatley rearrested Buck and his friends, and they were
held by Judge Wiggles under heavy bond to await the action
of the Grand Jury.

Old Abe and Malcolm A. Overley learned of the double
tragedy before they reached home.   Old Abe, completely prostrated, lay in the bottom of a wagon moaning and praying
to God.   Malcolm A. Overley, as soon as he learned of what
had happened, lashed his horses into a furious gallop and was
soon dashing along the road toward his home like a madman.
As he passed his neighbors they gazed at him in his mad
flight, fearful for his life.   When he finally reached home his
rage was beyond control.

For two days Malcolm A. Overley rode the country with
his gun, looking for some person to shoot who was concerned
in the murder of these women.   But no man came his way,
however, and he was finally persuaded by Big Joe Wheatley
and others to return to his home.   For six weeks following
this old man's soul hovered between its prison and the bound-
less beyond.   When Malcolm A. Overley finally regained his

strength and took his accustomed place with Old Abe on the veranda, where for two generations they were wont to smoke and talk, the altered appearance of each was so noticeable that the old men sat for a long time gazing at each other. Finally, Malcolm A. Oberley said:

"Abe, what the h— are you staring at me that way for? Have you never seen me before? D— your black hide, do you think I am a ghost?"

"Yes, sah, yo' is de ghost of yo'se'f. But, sah, will yo' nebber 'member dat de Lawd is more pow'ful den we is? Will yo' nebber 'member dat His Will mus' be done? My ole 'oman dat's daid an' gone, she say dat she will die happy when she know dat yo' done gin yo' heart to God. Now, she done pass 'way, an' yo' air still outen de Lawd's fold. Yo' jes' come through de Valley ob de Shadow ob Death an' yo' is not changed yet. I dun stop prayin' fo' my ole 'oman an' my gal, kase I know day is in glory. I'se prayin' fo' yo'. When I see how nigh de grave yo'——"

"Why, Abe, who the h— told you how near the grave I am? You old 'niggers' think that you know as much about the Lord's business as He Himself knows. Where did you get the idea that I am nearer the grave than any other man of my age?"

"Hab yo' forgot so soon dat yo' jus' camed outen yo' sick bade? Dat de doctors say yo' mus' die, an'——"

"Oh, d— the doctors! They tried to kill me. Old Cleo, she brought me out. But, Abe, what will we do when my boy and your boy learn the truth?"

"God am my hepper, I dunno. I pray God my Abe may nebber learn de truth."

After Old Abe had expressed himself as not knowing what to do, Malcolm A. Overley seemed lost in thought.

"Abe," he said, "what will the Grand Jury do with those d— beasts? Si Weedles foreman of the Grand Jury! What the h— has this country come to? Poor white trash! A hound like that foreman of the Grand Jury! I tell you, Abe, if that Grand Jury does not indict that bunch of murderers I shall take my gun and kill the whole d— crowd. What are you shaking your head about? D— your black hide, you haven't the courage of a flea. What are you going to do? Let them go scot free? Well, just you wait until that boy of yours comes back here; then you will wake up. D— if he don't fix matters."

"God forbid my po' boy come back heah wid he heart full of murder an' vengeance. No, he mus' nebber know how he po' mudder an' sister done die. I hopes, sah, yo' will nebber tell him."

At this point Big Joe Wheatley, Jim Connors and several more of Malcolm A. Overley's friends, together with the good minister, rode up to the house. Old Abe called some of the boys to look after the horses.

"Malcolm," said Big Joe Wheatley, "tomorrow the Grand Jury will sit on those cases; already they are bragging that it will not indict. I do not think myself that it will. But what can we do? At times I feel like taking my gun and killing the whole crowd."

"I can but feel that that will be the only way in which this thing can ever be settled," said Jim Connors.

"Why, of course, that is the way," replied Malcolm A. Overley. "D— their dirty hides! I have said so all along. I just told Abe that if the Grand Jury did not indict them, I would indict, try and execute them, too. H—! They deserve to die."

"But, my brothers," interposed the good minister, "that would be murder. Two wrongs will not make one right. Still, when one considers the wickedness of this deed, the wanton brutality attending the crime, there may be some excuse. should the passions and desire for revenge, common to all human beings, get beyond control. My brothers——"

"May de good God Almighty keep yo' gemmen from letten'

yo' passions get 'yon' control,'' interrupted Old Abe. "Ef
yo' does 'venge yo'se'f on dese people, an' take dey life, yo'
souls will be los'. Dar will be no 'scuse fo' yo'. I'se de one
dat is most hurted. I dun forgin dese people. Why yo'
gemmen not do de same? God grant dat yo' will not 'pen'
on any 'scuse an' cubber yo' hands wid blood.''

Old Abe made these observations solemnly and with all the
simple eloquence peculiar to his class. Abe's rebuke to this
man of God was apparent to all. It put a stop to all further
discussion along those lines.

Upon the following day the Grand Jury met and considered the case. After hearing the three white men, who tes-
tified before the Coroner's Jury, together with the Negroes
who witnessed the murders, Buck and his friends were discharged, an alibi having been established.

The following was found next day in the *County Bulletin:*

"Messrs. Buck Lashum, Rex and Tom Wardeman, Jack and
Jim Smaly were yesterday discharged by the Grand Jury,
they having been held by Judge Wiggles in $30,000 bond each,
charged with the murder of two 'nigger wenches' on the
Overley plantation. The time has not yet come for white
men to be tried for killing 'niggers'.''

And thus the matter ended.

Malcolm A. Overley and his friends were compelled to bow
to what seemed to be the inevitable. The Grand Jury exonerated the men who killed these women. The *County Bulletin*
had passed editorially on the killings. The case passed into
history. Malcolm A. Overley was called from his bitter
thoughts by a communication notifying him that his mortgage
would be due in thirty days, and that it must be paid in full.
The money was not available. What was he to do? After a
long consultation with his friends it was decided to ask the
bank for eight months' extension of time.

When the proposition was submitted to Nick Lashum he

denounced the ''big bug,'' saying that now he had him and he was going to sell him out. But the officials of the bank were not of Nick's opinion. The time had not come for the mortgage to be foreclosed. They prevailed upon him to withhold his vengeance for a few months. The extension was obtained and it was placed upon record, and thus the matter was settled for the time being.

CHAPTER XIX.

WHEN Nick Lashum, Sr., learned that Buck and his friends had been arrested by Sheriff Wheatley, charged with the murder of the Overley women, his wrath knew no bounds.

"What the h— yer think of them 'big bugs' 'restin' white men fer 'niggers'! D— if I don't git even. Yo'll see. Go they bail? In course I will. I don't kere a d— ef it's a hundred thousand. They is good boys, an' them 'niggers' was stealin' my bacon. Serve 'em right."

Thus commented Nick, Sr., when requested to offer himself as bondsman for the murderers. When Buck was questioned by his father as to his knowledge of the theft of the bacon, he said Black Sue first told him that the women were stealing from the meathouse; in fact, that she had caught them in the very act. He then determined to watch and see for himself, and he and his friends caught the women red-handed. Buck told these lies without a tremor, without a blush. His father, already convinced that a "nigger will steal," only needed to hear such a statement to convince him that the women were guilty of stealing his meat. It mattered not to him that no bacon was missing, nor that the meathouse showed no signs of having been tampered with.

"Wall, boy, youse in a pretty fix, now, ain't you? 'Cused of killin' 'nigger wenches'. Yo' brother he say youse a disgrace to the family. Wall, all I got ter say is, I'se on yer bon', an' no Grand Jury will 'dict yer, an' no harm will come ter yer. Yo' tell Old Sue I wants her ter come hyre; I want ter see her."

Buck was glad of the opportunity to get Old Sue to talk with his father. He hurried to Sue's cabin, where he found her dozing by the door, with her corncob pipe in her lap.

"Sue, pappy wants to see yer. He wants to ask yer about

them Overley 'niggers'. I told him what yer told me and what I see them 'niggers' do myself.''

''Yer tell yo' pappy I'se got no time ter was' wid him. Yo' tell yo' pappy dat I'se to home.''

''But, Sue, pappy says——''

''Go 'long, boy. What I car' what yo' pappy say. Yo' tell him I'se to home.'' And she laughed at her own cleverness.

Buck went back to his father and told him that Sue was sulky, but she would be up to the house in a few minutes. Nick waited more than an hour for Sue, and then went in search of her himself. He found her where Buck had left her, sitting beside her cabin, smoking.

''Sue,'' said Nick, with a great show of wrath, ''why the h— don't yer come when I send fer yer? Do yer——''

''Look out, white man!'' exclaimed Sue, interrupting Nick with kindling anger. ''Dose yer know who yo' is talkin' at? I'se telled yo' fo' now dat I don't 'low no white man ter talk ter me dat way. Yo' jes' mod'rate yo' tune ef yo' wants me ter talk ter yer. Now, what's yo' gwine say?''

''Sue, I wants the facts 'bout them 'niggers' of Overleys,'' said Nick, meekly. ''Buck tells me thet yer caught 'em in my meathouse. Is thet so?''

''Say, man, ef Buck tell yo' dat, what yo' ax me fer; ain't dat 'nough?'' answered Sue, with great dignity.

''Yes; but, Sue, I wants ter know what yer did see. Ain't yer never goin' ter l'arn to act lek a lady? D— ef I ever seed a woman lek yer. Yer never keeps yer word with nobody.''

Nick said this very meekly, careful not to anger Black Sue further.

''Keep my word!'' yelled Sue. ''Yo's a nice one ter tell folks 'bout keepin' dey word. Does yo' 'member dat yo' promised me er greenback mor'n six mon? Yo's a nice one, I swar—— Man, yo' go long. I tells yo' nuttin'.''

After Sue made this speech she lighted her pipe, closed her eyes and seemed to forget that Nick was in existence. Nick observed her for some moments, well knowing that it would be useless to question her further. He took from his pocket a roll of bills, from which he selected a dollar, saying in a very kind voice:

"Sue, I'se glad yer called my min' to that ar' dollar; hyer's hit. Yer's mor'n welcome. I'd er gin hit ter yer 'fore now had yer sade the word."

Sue eyed the money for a moment; then she reached for it with all the eagerness of a vulture swooping down on a carcass of carrion. As soon as she obtained possession of the money she resumed her pipe, and her silence in the most aggravating manner. Nick noted from Sue's attitude that she did not intend to talk, but he thought he would try again.

"Sue, what did yer say 'bout them Overley 'niggers'? I wants ter know."

"Wal, ef yo' wants ter know, yo' knows how ter find out," answered Sue, and she resumed her pipe with the same exasperating indifference.

Nick knew only too well that Sue meant to make him pay her to talk. He thought, however, he would try persuasion.

"Sue," he said, very kindly, "yer is the on'est gal on this whole place thet I kin pen' on. Yer is the on'est one thet ever watches my stuff, thet keers 'nuff 'bout me ter study my interest. I gives yer credit fer thet. An'——"

"Yes, an I'se de onl'est one dat yo' nebber gins nuttin' to; I tells yo' dat. I studies yo' good and gits nuttin' fer hit. I isn't gwine to do it no mo'," interrupted Sue.

"Wall, Sue, did yer ever tell me thet yer felt thet way. Why, in course yer didn't. How's I going ter know thet yer be dissatis' onless yer say so. Say, ole gal, yer tek this," handing her another dollar bill, "an' brace up an' feel lek yer did in them days when I uster buy yer them bright caliker dresses. I tell yer, Sue, in them days yer was the bes' lookin' gal in all the county. Lor', how the bucks uster run arter yer ontil I thought they was too fresh, and then I would make 'em cut lines. Them was good ole days, Sue; now, warn't they?"

"Yes, dey war," answered Sue; "but yo' gin me mor' in a mont' in dem days den yo' gin me now in er yeah. Dat yo' did. What dat yo' ax me now 'bout dem stuck-up 'niggers'?"

"Yer is right, Sue; them is stuck-up 'niggers'. They never did lek yer nor yer pickaninnies. I jes' wants ter know what yer kotch 'em doin'?" said Nick.

"Wall, de trut' am, dat I hain't kotch dem doin' nuttin'. I jes' see dem crossin' de lot down by de smokehouse. Dat am all. Now, I tells dat ter yo' Buck, an' he put de res' ter hit. Dem 'niggers' war stuck up, but dey warn't de kind dat steals. Dem was hones' 'niggers,' dey war."

Black Sue knew the truthfulness of this statement and watched very closely for its effect on Nick. She noticed that he was startled and became nervous.

She remarked that she knew a "heap 'bout what dey war doin' de night of de troubles."

"Sue, ole gal," said Nick, "I wants ter know all 'bout thet d— row. Hyre tek this an' git yerse'f a nice caliker dress," handing her a five-dollar bill, which he did not notice in his excitement; "now, tell me 'bout hit."

"Wall, all I knows is, dat dem boys follow dem 'niggers' to dey cabin an' tek dem outen hit an' say dey had been stealin' yo' bacon. Den dey flog dem and dey die. Dat is de trut. so hep me God."

Nick stood looking at Sue with a mind to strike her, but his good judgment, together with the knowledge of his former experiences, deterred him. He said finally:

"All yer d— 'niggers' is jes' alek," and departed in high dudgeon. Black Sue laughed to herself, remarking that she "warn't goin' ter hab all de 'niggers' arter her an' her chillern on' dey 'count. Dem women my color, an' I'se goin' ter stan' by dem."

As Nick moved off toward the house he soliloquized:

"Wall, thet do beat h—. Thet 'nigger wench'—is clean outen my hearin'?—tek my money an' not tell me nuttin' I'll sho git even. Yo'll see. When thet Grand Jury meets we is got ter 'pend on dem white men an' Ole Si. I dunno what we would do widouten him."

CHAPTER XX.

MALCOLM and Abe had been informed that Abe's mother and sister Lucy had died very suddenly, and that there was trouble on the plantation because of their deaths; also, that it was advisable for them not to come home, as they would arrive too late for their burials. Abe was prostrated. He could not understand why he had not been telegraphed at once. Malcolm, Forbes and Rattles were unusually kind to him, which only augmented his uneasiness. Forbes was careful to keep the newspapers from him. It was soon known about the College, however, that Abe's mother and sister had been lynched and that Buck Lashum and his friends were under arrest, charged with their murder. How to keep the truth from Abe longer was the all-absorbing question before the three friends. While discussing ways and means to keep Abe in ignorance of the manner of his mother's and sister's death, Malcolm, Forbes and Rattles were surprised in Rattles room by Abe, just as Rattles remarked, "I tell you, fellows, Abe should have been told at first."

Abe heard the latter part of this remark as he entered the room,

"I should have been told what, fellows?" he asked.

The three boys were so surprised by Abe's appearance that they betrayed themselves. Abe noticed their confusion.

"Say, fellows, what is this conspiracy? Why, what is the matter?" he asked, as no one appeared to be willing to answer him. Abe observed them carefully, apparently reading their very thoughts. Finally, he sank upon a chair and said:

"Malcolm, tell me about my mother. You fellows know more about her death than I do."

Abe made this request in such a pitiful, heartrending way

that Malcolm turned from him to hied his tears. Rattles remarked:

"Abe, I am afraid you stay in your room too much; come with me to the campus."

Abe permitted himself to be led from the room by Rattles, who said to Forbes: "Tell DeVaux and his friend to meet us down on the campus."

Soon Rattles and Abe were joined by Malcolm and Forbes, together with the other young men. As soon as Abe saw Malcolm, he attempted to take him to one side and ask him about the part of the conversation he had overheard in Rattles's room, feeling that he still had something to learn concerning his mother's death.

Rattles noticed the movement and signaled DeVaux to follow, which he did, remarking: "You fellows shall have no secrets from the rest of us. Overley, tell us about this sad affair."

"No, I cannot," said Malcolm; "your friend here has kept in touch with the case; let him tell you."

Abe was conscious of the solemn manner in which Malcolm spoke; also of the solemn faces about him. He sank upon the ground in an attitude that College boys know well, and said:

"Fellows, I am ready to be crucified."

The Tennesseean began by saying: "Overly, you may be crucified before I have related all that I know of this affair, but you must bear up like a man. We employed a man to go to your home to learn the facts. We learn that during your father's absence your mother and sister were——"

"Lynched!" yelled Abe, as he bounded to his feet and grasped the Tennesseean by the shoulder in a grip that caused him great pain, but which he bore without flinching. Abe's manner and appearance were so changed that his friends feared for his reason. His eyes bulged from their sockets, they seemed to flash fire. He looked a full foot taller. His hands worked convulsively. His neck was swollen. He did not seen to breathe. He looked the very incarnation of the avenging demon. This was a terrible tableau, lasting for several moments. All stood looking at Abe in awe. They were conscious he would wreak a terrible vengeance when his time for vengeance came. Finally, Abe sat down and said:

"Fellows, I will listen, but I see the whole thing now. I know that my mother and my sister were both killed. By whom? Why were they killed? Why was I not told at once? Malcolm, why did you keep this from me all these weeks? Their murderers may have escaped by this time."

"No, they are awaiting the action of the Grand Jury. They are under heavy bonds," said the Tenesseean.

"Who are these people? Who are under bond?" asked Abe.

The Tennesseean answered after a moment's thought: "Buck Lashum, two Wardemans and two Smalys. The Grand Jury will hear their cases tomorrow."

After a long silence, Abe, as if speaking to himself, said: "So, this is done to be avenged on me. Oh, my poor mother! I am the cause of your death! Can there be a just God! Mother, so surely as you are dead, I will avenge you!"

The boys thought it best not to tell Abe, at this time, of the manner in which his mother lost her life. So they slowly returned to their rooms, Abe walking between Malcolm and Rattles like one in a dream. When they reached the hall DeVaux and his friend stopped; each extended a hand to Abe, the Tennesseean remarking:

"Overley, I have said to you before that I am your friend. I am still your friend. My services and my funds are at your disposal; command me and them."

"Abe, I am with you to the same extent that my friend is; command me," said DeVaux.

"I thank you both. Your God alone knows what I may need!" exclaimed Abe.

The two young men then left Abe and his friends, as their rooms were not in the same hall in which Abe's and Malcolm's were; for they, true to their Southern blood, had, when they first came to Oberlin, refused to live under the same roof with Abe and the rest of the Negro students who were in this building. When Abe and his friends reached his room there was a long silence, which was broken by Malcolm saying:

"Abe, we all sympathize with you. What can we do to help you in this matter?"

"I want to go home! I want to see my mother's grave! Malcolm, why did you keep this from me?" he asked, and then added: "Can there be a God? Can there be a just God? Can there be laws to reach such people? Can there be nothing that governs the universe but the avenging demon?"

Abe had now risen to his feet, towering above his friends in his rage. He called out again in his madness:

"If there be a demon; if there be a devil; if there be an imp of hell; if there be a force that will turn blood to gall, love to hate, good to bad—come to me that I may feel thy full force; come to me that I may forget that I am human, until I have avenged this wrong, perpetrated upon my mother and sister! By all the imps of hell, this was done to be avenged on me! Oh, my poor mother! I am the cause of your unnatural death! By the God that made me, and with the aid of the demons of hell, whose help I implore, I will be revenged! You hear me, fellows? I will be revenged!"

The three young men stood looking at Abe, conscious that all that was human in him, all that was good in his nature, had succumbed to the brute instinct of human nature for revenge. Suddenly, Abe turned to Malcolm and demanded, in a tone and with a look that Malcolm had never heard nor seen before:

"Malcolm, why did you fellows keep this from me?"

Rattles, the only one who seemed to be able to cope with the situation, said:

"Abe, stop a moment and consider. See the rage you are in. You cannot govern yourself now. What would you have done at your home when all this excitement was on? You, by yourself? We talked over the matter among ourselves. Malcolm wanted to go home with you. He was ready to place his life at your disposal. He argued that you should avenge your mother's and sister's death. But he was persuaded that the time was not come. Now, Abe, listen. The school year is now nearly over. You and Malcolm will soon be going home. Then you can ferret out the guilty parties. You can do nothing now. From the beginning Malcolm wanted you to know; so do not blame him. Yesterday I talked this matter over with Dr. Finley, and he told me to bring you to him. Will you go? I think Mr. Donewell has also had this matter investigated. Abe, your friends are doing all they can to have those persons indicted; but, as you know, the Grand Jury may fail to indict. Let us go to the Doctor's office.''

''Abe,'' said Malcolm, ''I have felt all along that you should know all about this deed; but the majority of our friends thought it best for you not to know, as you would naturally want to go home, where you could do no good. I was willing to go with you, and I am still willing to go. I will aid you in any way to right this wrong. I hope you do not think, Abe, that I will desert you in your hour of need?''

''Malcolm, I cannot think. I know you and your father are my best friends. I know you and he will aid me. I will need your help.''

The young men clasped hands in a friendly manner. Suddenly Abe said: ''Stay here six weeks? Why, fellows, I am going tonight. How can I study now?''

''Abe, I took the responsibility upon myself to make an engagement for you with Dr. Finley. Will you go to see him before you decide to leave the College?'' asked Rattles.

''Yes, Rattles, we will go,'' was Abe's answer.

When the boys reached Dr. Finley's office the good Doctor met them very pleasantly.

"Doctor," said Rattles, "I have brought Mr. Overley to see you. We have been discussing his bereavement, and——"

"Yes! Yes!" said the Doctor, who seemed to divine Rattles's intentions. "I have been expecting Mr. Overley for some days."

Rattles gave the Doctor a full account of all that had transpired, and also Abe's determination to go home at once. The Doctor took Abe by the hand and drew him to a chair by his side. He invited the boys to listen. He then went over the whole case, dwelling upon the enormity of the crimes, the flimsy excuse for them, and the environment amidst which the people live, who tolerate such crimes in their midst. He finished by asking Abe what he expected to do after he got back home, provided he should go at once.

Abe, who had been quietly listening to the Doctor, arose to his feet, extended his hands toward the heavens, remarking with great bitterness:

"Doctor, I intend to go home and kill! kill! kill! My poor old mother's blood cries for vengeance. I hear it as it falls to the earth. It calls to me drop by drop, as it is drawn from her emaciated body by the brutal hands of her lynchers. Oh, my poor mother! Poor and lowly that you were; slave, but virtuous and true; ignorant, but wise in the duties of life; look down from thy celestial home upon me, thine only son; search my innermost heart, where, if one drop of blood has its resting place, that calls not for vengeance, that falters even for an instant in that purpose, dry it up. Call me not thy son should I not bring down upon the heads of thy murderers a like fate!"

"But, Mr. Overley, consider that to which you are about to commit yourself; consider the great gifts that God has bestowed upon you; consider the life in a higher world to which your ability will surely lead; consider the wishes of your many friends, those who are sacrificing that you may enjoy the benefits of this great College; consider the wishes of

that old father, who is now praying for the hand that
bereaved him, and who, even when he first received the terrible
blow, bowed his head and said, 'Lord, Thy Will be done.' ''

Dr. Finley spoke these words with great earnestness, but
Abe was unmoved.

''Doctor,'' answered Abe; ''I come from a race of men who,
though slaves, were never known to falter in the performance
of a duty. My poor mother's blood calls for vengeance. I
see that blood, as she lies bound and helpless in the hands of
her murderers, drawn drop by drop from her helpless body.
I tell you,'' continued Abe, as he sprang to the middle of the
room, his whole attitude changed from the man to the animal
seeking an object upon which to vent its rage, ''her blood
calls to me; it calls aloud, Abel-like, for vengeance. I care
not what befalls me. I care not what my life in eternity may
be. Aye, I care not what your God may demand. My poor
mother's blood cries to me for vengeance, and I will answer
that call. All I ask is that the demons of hell may lend me
their strength; that I may possess myself of the bitterness,
gall and hatred—the kind which possessed the murderers of
my poor mother—in order that I may wreak a vengeance suitable to their crime.''

Dr. Finley realized it would be useless to argue further
with Abe, and therefore remarked, without answering Abe's
last outburst of passion, that he hoped Abe would see Mr.
Donewell and Miss Watson before he concluded to leave the
College. After some general remarks the boys took their
leave.

''Abe,'' said Rattles, ''are you thinking about leaving the
College without first asking Miss Watson's permission? I
thought you were more gallant than that. Do you want her
to follow you, seeking an apology?''

Rattles said this with a view to relieving the strain under
which they were laboring. Abe did not answer Rattles, but

he seemed to be in deep thought. He seemed not to have noticed Rattles' little pleasantry.

Suddnly Abe remarked: "That is so; I did not think of her. Well, I can see her tomorrow."

This gave Rattles an idea. He determined to see Miss Watson before Abe saw her. He went next morning to the young lady's home and explained to her Abe's intention to leave the College and go home to revenge himself upon the murderers of his mother. He asked her good offices in persuading Abe to remain until the end of the school year, which she promised to use.

CHAPTER XXI.

AFTER the departure of Abe and his friends, Mr. Donewell came into the Doctor's office in company with Dean Sternly and several of the College professors. "Gentlemen," said the Doctor, "you have come too late. I have just had a most interesting interview with the young Negro, Overley from Alabama. His friends brought him to me. They wished me to talk to him, to try to calm him, and, if possible, to persuade him to stay in the College until the end of the school year. I did my best, but only succeeded in arousing all the animal in him. I suggested——"

"That was very easy to do, was it not, Doctor?" interrupted Professor Smirchum.

"I do not understand you, Professor," answered the Doctor.

"Well, these Negroes have a great deal of animal in them and it only requires a slight offense to arouse them to a point at which they become dangerous," answered the Professor.

"I do not agree with you, Professor," said Dean Sternly; "your statement is too broad. We have thirty Negroes in the College, who are subject to slurs and insults from the Southern boys; but we have only one case of disorder resulting from a Negro's resenting these insults. In that case a Southern boy, after provoking an assault, was slapped in the face, but did not retaliate. No, Professor, you are too hasty in your judgment. You do not judge these boys as you do the other students. Why assume that they are carried away by the same animal instincts that governed their forebears? They are several generations removed from them."

"You gentlemen interrupted Dr. Finley," said Dr. Donewell. "He was about to tell us what he suggested to this young man. I am very much interested in this student and want to hear the Doctor's story."

"Well, I will continue," said the Doctor. "This young man has just lost his mother and sister, who were lynched, as you may know. He has about made up his mind to leave the College at once. I tried to persuade him to remain until the end of the school year. I talked to him like a father. I told him of the enormity of these crimes, of the punishment that would overtake the murderers, of his intellectual gifts, of his bright future, of the old father who was praying for him. I suggested all I could to him. He sat silent while I talked, but when I asked him what he would do, should he go home at once, he bounded to the middle of the room with a cry that startled me, and said: 'Doctor, I shall go home and kill! kill! kill!' His words were not spoken in a loud tone of voice, but with an intensity, a force, that made them cut like steel. He stood towering above us, with his hands extended to the heavens, his eyes emitting the most peculiar flame, his whole being suggesting the incarnation of the evil one. Gentlemen, when he said, 'Doctor, I shall go home and kill! kill! kill!' his wrath was something terrible. Then he moaned, 'Oh, my poor mother! I am the cause of your unnatural death! Thy blood calls for vengeance, and I will answer that call.' His agony was as deep and heartrending as his wrath was bitter and uncontrollable. Gentlemen, I would that all of you had witnessed these outbursts. What will this young man do when he reaches his home? I do not hesitate to say that he will keep his vow. He will surely kill those who participated in the lynching of his mother. He, in his blind fury, can see but the one way to avenge his wrong. I predict for him a carnival of blood."

"Doctor, do you think that what you have just said is possible in a Negro?" asked Professor Smirchum.

"Professor, your question is not quite clear to me. Explain more fully," said Dr. Finley.

"Well, we all know that the Negro is an inferior being. That——"

"You state your conclusion, Professor, and reason back to your premises," said Dean Sternly. "You will pardon me for saying that this is a most unusual manner of reasoning, and one to which you resort only when you have the Negro under discussion. Why say, 'we all know the Negro is thus and so,' when the facts before us are just to the contrary? In your class report of last year you say, to use your own words, 'Overley is an exceptional Negro; I may say an exceptional man.' I did not know then what you meant, nor do I know now. I can simply guess. How a student can be exceptional, and be less than a man, is a point upon which I beg you to enlarge. But this 'exceptional Negro' is the one under discussion, not the race to which he belongs. Will he adhere to his vow? I agree with Dr. Finley, that he will surely kill the murderers of his mother.

"He has been educated, developed, I may say, up to the point that has been reached by our civilization, where men take the lives of one another in revenge for the lives of their kindred or for wrongs perpetrated upon their women. How is it possible for a Negro, or a man of any race, to live amongst us, be educated in our schools, take on our civilization, and differ from us in this respect? I grant that there is a class of Negroes who have been taught that it is a crime against God, for which there is no forgiveness, for them to take the life of a white man. I may add that they think it is even wrong to strike one; but this Negro, Overley, is not of that type, and that old type is now the exception rather than the rule. No, Professor, your conclusion is not tenable. Pardon me, you reason backward. This Negro is a white man, in the sense that his ambitions and his desires for the good things of this world are identical with yours. He loved his mother and he loves his home. His feelings are outraged by the manner of his mother's taking off. He says her blood calls for vengeance. He sees her bound and helpless, being lashed to death. He sees no difference between a white murderer and a black one. He has never been taught that a white man's person is sacred. He resolves to kill. What else can you expect? What would a white man do? What would you do? I am almost prepared to acquiesce in his resolution and bid him Godspeed. But I remember 'Thou shalt not kill.' Were I this young man, placed as he is, could I withstand the desire for revenge that is born in every human being? Would the Mosaic Law deter me? With all the avenues of justice through the courts cut off, compelled to combat a sentiment which sanctions such atrocities, living in a community that bids him be silent, because his mother deserved to die, and that it was fit and proper for those young brutes to take her life—I repeat, placed in his stead, could I, could you, resist the impulse to avenge her death? Would you not avenge your mother's murder? Would you do your mother justice not to avenge her? I do not condemn the man who seeks vengeance. I leave these matters for each person to decide according to his personal feelings.''

"Dean Sternly," said Professor Narrows, "do you consider your doctrine of revenge a sound one? Is it one that should be inculcated into the minds of these Negroes?"

"I have no doctrine of revenge, nor have I said to inculcate any such doctrine into their minds," answered Dean Sternly, hotly. "I have said that the desire for revenge is an attribute of human nature, controlled only by the will of the individual. In the case under discussion, and in all similar cases, the only remedy, the only means of eradicating this terrible evil, is to teach the lynchers, by example, that they will meet like fates. Men who gather in mobs and kill are not of the class who will face death individually. Men who are brave in mobs, when attacking a single person, will not even attack that person with a mob when they know that retribution will certainly follow them. You gentlemen have a certain code of ethics along those lines for yourself and a different one for these Negroes. You say that he must not look at your women, but at the same time his women are not safe from you. That for which he is lynched you simply smile at in one of yourselves. Still, you are educating him along your lines. When you place him in classes along with your sons and daughters he outstrips them frequently in intellectual power; and I cannot conceive how men can be so blind as to think that an educated Negro will be any less the man than any other human being that has taken on your education and civilization.

"You take the Chinaman, the Japanese, all the darker races, in fact, even the native African, and educate and civilize them, and then you point with pride to your work. With open arms this product of your labor is received into the body politic. But the American-born Negro—it matters not what his early environment, the social status of his parents, nor that he has passed through with highest praise the courses here prescribed by you, and brought credit to your school—you consider him with a specially constructed code of reasoning, both illogical and unjust, and force him outside of your consideration and social institutions. No hand is extended to him, unless it brandishes a cudgel; no door is opened to enable him to gain an honest livelihood, no matter how proficient he is in the branches from which you have graduated him. The American Negro possesses a something, I suppose, which you cannot tolerate—a something that no other man nor race of men, not even his forebears, possessed. How came he by this undefinable something? Does he get it by contact with this dominant race of ours? Yes. Examine yourselves and you will find the source of the trouble. Why, you are unwilling to accord him the same privileges, the same chance to earn a living and enjoy life which you accord other men, is a question which I have long pondered. You gentlemen, possibly, can give me the solution."

"Well, for my part," answered Professor Narrows, "the foreigner acts differently from the American Negro. You always know the foreign Negro; but the American Negro has an air about him that makes him objectionable. He likes to rub against one too much. Oh, he presumes to be one's equal. I don't like him for that."

"Yes, that is very true," answered Dean Sternly. "That is the secret of the whole matter. You invite the Chinaman, out of whom you can never educate his opium; the Japanese, out of whom you can never educate his idolatry; the Malays, Hindoos, Moors, Africans, and all other foreign races of men, you invite to come to you. The people who never take on your civilization you bid come. You repulse the American Negro who has taken on your civilization. Can you not see that that of which you complain is but the American idea? How can the Negro come in contact with you and your institutions and not be Americanized? Why do you teach him? You educate him, then ostracise him, apparently for taking on your teachings. This state of affairs must certainly be embarrassing to the Negro. Professor, if you are not willing to live up to the result of your work, you should not be a party to the tragedy which you are helping to enact. I was born and reared in the South, and I know that your theory and comments are all wrong."

"Gentlemen," said Dr. Finley, "a discussion of this question was had over forty years ago. At the time, the founders of this College concluded that there were no white men, no black men, no yellow men, no red men, but that all men were alike before God, and, further, that this idea should dominate the policy of this College. From this ideal it has never deviated, and so long as I remain President it never shall. This brings us back to this young man, Overley. Can he justify himself before God, should he keep his vow? We read, 'the avenger of the blood himself shall slay the murderer: the murderer shall surely be put to death.' We would infer from this charge to Moses that the great God Almighty contemplated an avenger of the blood. Would you consider it strange that this young man feels, in the absence of courts and juries, that he should avenge his mother's and sister's deaths? I, as a minister of the Gospel, do not advise deeds of violence, but in this contemplated deed I am almost persuaded that this young man is right in his determination to avenge his mother's death. When I think of this atrocious crime, the wanton brutality of the whole proceeding, I bow my head in shame that such crimes are perpetrated and countenanced by the race to which I belong. Can this nation of ours stand with this thirst for blood growing upon us? There will surely come a day of reckoning.''

CHAPTER XXII.

THE afternoon of the following day Abe called upon Miss Watson with the avowed intention of bidding her good-bye. She greeted him very cordially, remarking: "You may come in, sir, but I want you to give an account of yourself. Where have you been for the past six weeks? Do you remember, sir, that you promised me that you would sing at our song services last Sunday? I am greatly aggrieved at your unaccountable conduct. I shall accept nothing but the most abject apology. Now, sir, I am ready to listen."

Abe stood looking at her in bewilderment. He finally said: "Miss Watson, my mind has been so paralyzed by my bereavement; the weight of my burden has been——"

"Mr. Overley, why did you not come to me and permit me to share your burden? Do you not know that by staying away from your friends at such times you not only burden yourself, but put a burden upon them, unnecessarily? I have waited all this time for an opportunity to express my sympathy for you. I am very sorry, Mr. Overley, that you have not seen fit to see me sooner. Do you think that I cannot feel the terrible blow that has befallen you? Do you not know that I am aware that no Negro, man, woman or child, is safe in the land of your birth from the kind of assaults that has resulted in your mother's death? Would I be safe there? If I was not subject to one kind of assault I would be to another. And so you have come to say good-bye?"

"Miss Watson, if you will permit me to explain, I know you will agree with me that it is imperative that I go home. My father is an old man, very old—seventy-four years of age. Mr. Overley is of the same age. They are both too old to think of ferreting out the persons concerned in the deaths of my mother and sister, and for them to avenge their

deaths is out of the question. I say 'them.' I, of course, do
not expect Mr. Overley to avenge them; but I know him so
well that I know he will aid me. I am going home for no
other purpose than to take the lives of those who killed my
mother and sister. I am going to kill—kill every man that
has my mother's blood on his hands. I have determined to
devote my life to the wreaking of vengeance. I have come to
make this confession to you. I have come to confess that I
am a murderer at heart and soon will be one in fact. I am
going to ask whether, after I have stained my hands in the
blood of my mother's murderers, which I surely will do, will
you still want to see me? Will you answer me now or shall
I leave you to consider the matter?"

"Mr. Overley, I have already considered," was her answer.
"I have been taught 'thou shalt not kill'—'love thy neighbor
as thyself.' I have also read, 'an eye for an eye and a tooth
for a tooth.' As God is my guide and my helper, I know not
how to advise you. But, were I a man, nay, woman that I am,
should my mother meet the cruel death at the hands of brutal
lynchers that your mother met, I would leave no path
unsearched, no stone unturned; I would delve into the very
bowels of the earth; I would skirt the fires of hell; aye, cross
them, in my endeavor to wreak a suitable vengeance upon such
brutes; nor would I feel, until the last murderer was slain,
that I had done my duty to my dead. Will I care to see you?
Mr. Overley, I feel this outrage upon Negro womanhood most
keenly. I feel that it calls for a terrible retribution. I thank
God that I am permitted to call my friend the one Negro man
who will devote his life to the punishment of the perpetrators
of this crime. Will I care to see you?" again she asked, her
eyes flashing, her slender figure swaying, as the panther sways
when about to leap upon its prey. "Go, and when you have
wreaked the vengeance for which your mother's blood calls,
be it one month, one year, nay, be it Eternity, I will wait for
you!"

As Miss Watson, who was known for her passive Christian spirit, finished this declaration she extended her hand to Abe, who raised it to his lips with the remark: "Miss Watson, I was afraid you would not understand my motives. I am pleased that you take the view of this matter which I do. I am more than proud to know that the one woman now left to me in this world approves of my determination. Miss Watson—may I say Nancy? I am proud of you. I love you. I have always loved you. I loved you before I ever met you, or else how would our souls have joined at sight? Nancy, you say you will wait for me? Wait for me to commit these terrible crimes—for crimes they will be? Oh, Nancy, you have not said you loved me!"

As Abe said this he held out both hands to her. She came close to him, permitting him to put his arms around her and implant a solemn kiss upon her forehead. Suddenly she drew away and asked what his plans were.

Abe said he would go home at once, to which she objected.

"Abe, do not go home immediately; wait until the end of the school year; then go home quietly as if nothing had happened. Learn all you can about this deed, who committed it, and how it was done, why it was committed, if there be a reason. Then you will know what vengeance to wreak and upon whom. Be cautious. Ingratiate yourself into the good graces of all, until you know the whole truth. It matters not if it takes one year or two years. Success is to be your object. To avenge the death of two outraged women is to be your undertaking. I shall expect you to write me as your hunt progresses. Do you think that a good plan?"

"Yes, Nancy, that is a very good plan, and I shall act upon it," said Abe, as he arose to leave.

"Mr. Overley," said Miss Watson, "haven't you forgotten something?"

Abe did not seem to comprehend her meaning.

"Forgotten what, Nancy?" he asked.

"Why, my father, of course; you have forgotten that I am a minor," was her laughing reply.

"Oh, I will never forget that; all girls are minors up to a certain time in their lives," answered Abe.

"That will do, sir; I will call father," and Miss Watson left the room.

Mr. Watson was a substantial citizen, who had conducted a grocery business in Oberlin for a number of years. He was very fond of his only daughter Nancy.

"Mr. Watson," said Abe, "you have been sent for that I may make two confessions to you. You have, no doubt, heard of the terrible deaths of my poor mother and sister. Well, sir, I have vowed to avenge them. I shall go home and kill every man who was concerned in their taking off. I confess this to you, that you may know the next time we meet, if meet we do, that I have the blood of one or more persons on my hands. Further, when we *do* meet, I shall ask you to give me your daughter in marriage."

Mr. Watson arose to his feet, taking a turn across the room. He stopped, looked Abe full in the face, and asked: "Would you give *your* daughter to a murderer—a double murderer, maybe?"

Abe answered solemnly: "Mr. Watson, should your daughter Nancy be foully murdered—lynched—what would you do?"

After a long silence, the old man faltering as to his decision, said, as he extended his hand to Abe: "I will consult my wife and daughter."

Abe then left the house and returned to his room.

CHAPTER XXIII.

SOON the day of his departure came, and Abe, with Malcolm, took leave of the College. When Abe arrived home he found his father broken and apparently twenty years nearer the end of his life's journey.

The old man greeted his son without a word, but with a long, clinging grasp of the hand. In his eyes was a mute appeal, felt only by the two souls that had been stricken by the same blow. The father led the way to two newly made graves, by which Abe kneeled, raised his eyes to heaven, and in a voice choking with emotion pleaded with the Ruler of the Universe for strength to bear his burden.

Abe's father listened, thinking that perhaps after all his son had accepted the situation and would not seek revenge. The young man fell across his mother's grave, where he remained seemingly lifeless, while the father watched and waited, hoping that Abe would soon leave the graves and go with him to the house to greet Mr. Overley. The old man finally concluded to call Mr. Overley and ask him to try and persuade Abe to go to the house. Mr. Overley, accompanied by Malcolm, came to the quiet burying plot, where he found Abe still prostrate on his mother's grave. Abe's father pointed to his son with a silent request for help.

Mr. Overley knelt by him, taking his sand, saying: "Abe, my boy, come to the house with me; I am anxious to hear something of your success at school. You cannot help matters by grieving over what is already done. Boy, I feel for you. This thing is the most hellish crime that has ever been perpetrated on woman in this country. But what can you do? H— and damnation! What can you do, I say?"

Abe arose slowly and stood looking first at one and then the other. Finally, he asked in a solemn voice: "What can I do? By the gods! Ask me what will I not do?"

He again fell upon his mother's grave, where he remained some moments in silence, which was broken by his father saying to him:

"My boy, yo' po' mudder am in hebben. She am now lookin' down from dem stars on yo'. She am sayin' to yo', to belebe in de Lawd. Dat de Lawd's will be done. Oh, my boy! Look to de Lawd fo' he'p in dis matter."

Abe arose to his feet, extended his hand to his father, saying: "Dad, I appreciate what you say, but I feel that I must avenge my mother's death. Oh, my mother! Oh, my poor mother!" Again Abe, in a frenzy of despair, threw himself upon his mother's grave, where he lay supine and quivering, moaning that the great God Almighty had forsaken him and his.

He extended his hands toward the heavens, and in the stillness of the night, in the presence of his father and their old friend, called upon the God that made him to register his vow. He said: "By the God that made me, by that silent breast that nurtured me, by the sister of my childhood, by all that I hold dear in this world, I will be avenged! Mother, may I ever be accursed in your sight if I do not avenge you!"

Turning to his friend, he said: "Mr. Overley, would you not consider me less than a man should I permit these murderers to go unpunished? I swear to you that so surely as there is a God, so surely as this brutal deed is recorded in heaven, so surely as there is an eternity, so surely as there is a hell, so surely as the perpetrators of this crime are watched for in the hell into which I shall plunge them, just so surely shall I avenge this murder."

Finding it impossible to induce Abe to leave his mother's grave and go with them, Mr. Oberley and Abe's father reluctantly left him there and returned in silence to the great house. When they had gone Abe again raised his hands to the heavens and exclaimed: "Mother! Oh, my poor mother!

Look down upon thy son! Let me feel thy presence! Mother,
I devote my life to the wreaking of vengeance upon thy murderers!'' As Abe uttered these words he sank once more upon
his mother's grave, where he remained in silence until morning.

CHAPTER XXIV

IT SOON became known throughout the county that Abe had returned to his home. Speculation was rife as to what he would do to avenge his mother's death. He gave no sign, however, as to what his intentions or feelings were, but set about quietly, though diligently, to glean the facts in the case. He soon learned that Black Sue had planted the germ which led to the deaths that bereaved him. He also learned that the crime had been committed by Buck Lashum, the Smalys and the Wardevans, and that they had used a leather horse trace to accomplish the horrible deed. The trace, he discovered, had been cut in pieces by the five men and the pieces taken to their respective homes to be kept as souvenirs of this great performance, thus perpetuating in their families the fame of having participated in such a laudable (?) undertaking. Abe concluded that he would possess himself of the pieces of trace, splice them together, and make this reconstructed trace the instrument of his revenge. After some thought he concluded to take Malcolm into his confidence.

"Malcolm," said Abe, one evening as they sat in their favorite haunt, the corn crib, "I want to tell you something, and then I want your advice. First, I have discovered by whom and just how my mother and sister were killed. Second, I have determined how these lynchers shall be punished. My poor mother was beaten to death with a horse trace. Just think of it! Seventy years old, and to meet such a death! And my sister, nude, was beaten to death amid the jeers and curses of those drunken brutes!"

As Abe recited these details the tears of rage rolled down his cheeks, his head dropped upon his breast, and he remained silent for a long time. Malcolm, respecting his grief, waited for him to recover. Abe finally resumed, saying: "I have also learned that each archdemon in this horrible crime has a piece of this trace at his home, as a keepsake. I propose to possess myself of those pieces, make a whole trace of them, and then let that gang beware! I shall take them one by one, tie them to a tree, and when I have finished with them all there will be five new graves somewhere in this county. I shall begin with Buck Lashum. There is but one thing, Malcolm, that deters me. I may be compelled to enter the homes of these people, especially Buck's, and steal those pieces."

After a long silence Malcolm said: "Abe, I do not think you should let that stop you. I will go with you and help you get them. Then you will need someone to help handle these fellows. You cannot do the whole thing yourself. And, more, I want the pleasure of laying the strap on Buck. Jim Wheatley and Jack Connors both told me to tell you they would be glad to help you in any way you might suggest. What do you say?"

"No, Malcolm," said Abe; "I alone must do this deed. You and your friends will make this State and county your homes. I have no home. If blood must be shed, I must shed it. There will be a price on my head. No, it will never do for you to be drawn into this affair in that way; you can help me in other ways."

When Abe had finished he arose to his feet, looked out of the door, and remarked: "Well, the moon has gone down; I shall now go on my errand of stealth. My friends who work at the Smalys and Wardemans will be waiting for me with the different pieces. I hope I will have only Buck's house to enter, and I know exactly where to find the piece he has. I hope he will sleep soundly; for if he awakens he will face his Maker sooner than he anticipates. When I return in the morning I will have the five pieces."

With this speech ringing in his ears, Malcolm watched Abe as he disappeared in the gloom.

Abe went to the Wardeman place, where he found the pieces imbedded in the earth on the left side of the left post of the

big gate at the main road. At the Smalys he found the
pieces sticking through a crack in the barn, six boards from
the east corner next to the spring. Then, going to Buck
Lahsum's home, he entered by a back window, which he found
open, and went straight to Buck's room, where he had been
told the piece of trace was tied to a picture which hung over
the head of Buck's bed. These instructions flashed through
Abe's mind as he passed into Buck's room, all the while asking himself what should he do if discovered. He was not
discovered, however, and reached home without accident.
Next morning, when Malcolm came to the harness room, he
found Abe busily engaged splicing the pieces of trace.

"Hello, Abe!" exclaimed Malcolm. "You are a successful
pilferer, I see. Tell me, did you have any trouble?"

"Not a bit," answered Abe. "I found everything just as
I expected—down by the big gate at the Wardemans, sticking
out of a crack in the barn at the Smalys, and Buck had his
piece hanging over his bed. When I looked upon that brute
sleeping so peacefully, the vision of his crime came upon me.
I stood over him, hoping he would awaken, that I might
strangle him. I did not feel capable of striking him down
in his sleep. He slept on, but with a look of terror on his
evil countenance. He felt my very presence, even in his
slumbers. His God was merciful to him. Had he opened
his eyes, had he indicated to me in any way that he was aware
of my presence—well——"

Malcolm watched Abe for some time in silence, then asked:
"What will you do next, Abe?"

"I have been told by friends that Buck is going to ride in
the tournament down on the Neck next Wednesday. That he
will be gone from home two days. He is sending his traps
around the road, and will ride across the country. Now,
there is but one path for him to travel after he leaves the
back end of his place, and that leads through the Gut north
of the swamp. You know where the solid ground narrows

to a neck of ten feet in width? Well, there I shall set a trap
for his horse which will cause the animal to throw him. I will
do the rest. This place is six miles from Buck's home, and
his cries cannot be heard that distance. I will endeavor to
impress upon his mind, in the two days I shall engage him,
that Negro women are as sacred as his own, and that Negro
men will have to be reckoned with in the future when their
women are assaulted.''

''Abe, don't make a brute of yourself in this matter,'' said
Malcolm. ''What you propose to do will be a terrible punishment.''

''I mean for it to be terrible,'' answered Abe. ''I mean
for my first blow to strike terror to the hearts of these people.
Malcolm, you will see. But I must go and study the land at
the point I have in mind. I will ride Kate, if you do not
object.''

''Do not what?'' said Malcolm. ''You are getting mighty
careful all at once—asking for the use of a horse. I guess I
had better tell your dad that you want to use Kate, and where
you are going, and for what purpose.''

Both young men laughed as Abe rode away. He rode to
within fifty yards of the place, secured his horse, and proceeded to lay his plans. He first selected a sapling, bent it
to the ground at a point where bushes overhung the path, cut
the top out, and attached part of a plow line to it. Passing
the line through the bushes and once around a series of stakes,
driven in a circle on either side of the path, with their tops
leaning out, the plow line formed a loop into which the horse
would be sure to step, thus causing the line to leave the tops
of the stakes, release the sapling and thereby tighten the line
around the horse's leg. Should it be the foreleg, the horse
will be sure to go down in front. If the hind leg is caught, he
will plunge and kick, unseating the rider.

Abe expected to profit by the struggle that would follow the
springing of his trap. The afternoon of the Tuesday follow-

ing Abe noted Buck's departure, and immediately set out at a brisk run for the place at which he hoped to stop Buck and his horse. He had scarcely seated himself at an unobserved point, with his eyes on the path, when Buck came in sight, the horse sprung the trap with his forefoot and began rearing and plunging, tearing up the earth for yards. Buck fell heavily to the ground, and before he could recover himself Abe was upon him.

Buck was filled with terror. His teeth chattered; his lips were purple; his eyes bulged. Abe placed a small rope with a running noose about his neck, and ordered him to stand up and keep quiet, which he gladly did. Then, cutting the line which held the horse, he proceeded with it and Buck to a dense nearby thicket. Buck in his terror begged to be allowed to go home, saying:

"Mr. Overley, sah, yer knows I was always yer friend; 'deed I was. I'm yer friend now. What you treat yer friend this way fer? Mr. Oberley, if yer let me go home I will have my pappy send yer a dollar and a half; 'deed I will!"

Abe made the horse secure, after which he fastened the end of the rope that was about Buck's neck to a small sapling that was already bent to the ground, and when this sapling was released the rope tightened about Buck's neck with a suddenness that nearly lifted him off his feet. Buck grasped the rope and drew the sapling down to him, thus taking the strain off his neck. When he did this, Abe dealt him a blow which caused him to scream with pain and to release his hold on the rope, which again jerked him by the neck to his toes and held him there.

Up to this point Abe had not secured Buck's hands. He started toward him for that purpose. Buck seemed to divine his intention and pleaded:

"Mr. Overley, fer God's sake let me go home! My mammy——"

When Buck made this reference to his "mammy" Abe

sprang upon him, with a cry that resembled a wild beast, and
dealt him a blow on the crown of his head with the trace that,
but for the thickness of Buck's skull, would have crushed it.
Buck threw both of his hands into the air, and with a laugh
that appeared not to be human, as it echoed through the still
forest, sank to the ground. Abe stood looking at him for a
long time, as he lay prostrate and apparently lifeless. Suddenly he realized that Buck was getting black in the face; the
rope was slowly choking him to death.

He released Buck and sat down beside him. The shades of
night began to fall; the moonbeams and the shadows were
flirting in the gathering gloom. Buck, to all appearances,
was dead. Abe watched him as if he feared that even in death
Buck might escape him.. All night he lay motionless.

As the sun began to dispel the gloom of the forest Abe dis-
cerned a movement in him and reached forward to turn his
head that he might see his face, when Buck suddenly raised
himself to his elbow and their eyes met. Abe knew instinctively that he was facing a maniac. Buck, almost bereft of
reason, could see but one object, and that one hateful to him.
He bounded to his feet with the quickness of a wildcat, and
was upon Abe before he hardly realized Buck's intentions.
The struggle that ensued, spurred on as it was by a mortal
hatred on the one side and an unevenly balanced mind on the
other, was fierce, but of short duration. Buck, in his wild
rush, endeavored to grasp Abe about the middle, but failed,
and only succeeded in securing a hold on his shoulders, which
enabled Abe to more easily throw him. Buck fell with great
force, with Abe across his body. The small of his back struck
a stake, causing an injury to the spine which paralyzed him
from the waist down, rendering him totally helpless. Buck
never recovered. Abe, not knowing Buck's helpless condition,
belabored him with his horse trace, Buck at intervals bursting
forth in a laugh that resounded through the forest. When
Abe noticed Buck's condition he sat down to think how he
might get rid of his victim without killing him outright. He

finally concluded to take Buck back to the place where he was thrown from his horse, and where the ground showed a struggle, turn the horse loose, and leave Buck to be found by his friends. Abe was careful to cut the sapling which sprung the trap close to the ground and to remove all evidences that would tend to show that human hands were responsible for Buck's condition. The horse soon made its way back to the barn. Black Sue saw it and spread the alarm.

"I bet dat Abe Oberley knows sumfin' 'bout dis hos' an' 'bout dat chile," said Sue to herself. Soon a searching party was formed, which included some of the Overley Negroes, who were inspired by curiosity. When Buck's dogs were turned loose, they started for the swamp in full cry and soon had him located. Every man crowded about with an opinion, all finally agreeing that the horse must have kicked Buck in the back while his foot was hung in the stirrup.

When the Wardeman boys heard of Buck's mishap, Tim, who had become a local minister, concluded he would answer a call from a town in a Western territory. He left very suddenly. About two weeks later Abe learned that Rex Wardeman, the one who knocked his mother down in the cabin, breaking her jawbone, was riding three times a week into the next county to visit a lady whom it was rumored he would soon marry.

Abe set about to learn the truth. He was informed by his friends in the Wardeman home that such was the fact; that Rex seldom returned home earlier than 2 a. m., and that he traveled the same path night and day. Abe was also told that Rex was always heavily armed.

After an inspection of the path traveled, Abe found, at a point remote from any road or habitation, two trees, opposite each other, close to the path, to which wild grapevines were clinging. By pulling one of these vines nearer the earth it could be so arranged that a person riding horseback would be swept off his mount by it. Abe selected the following Wednesday night for his attempt, it being the dark of the moon.

CHAPTER XXV.

REX rode away from his lady's home whistling softly to himself. As he drew nearer and nearer Abe's trap he became drowsy and permitted his horse to make its own way along the path unaided, the bridle rein hanging loose. When the animal came upon the vine, as Abe had arranged it, it instinctively lowered its head and quickened its pace, and as it passed under the vine Rex was caught and lifted from the saddle.

Before he realized what had happened Abe was upon him. He seized Rex by the throat and pinioned him to the ground. Then began a desperate struggle for the possession of the pistol that Rex carried, and but for the strangle hold Abe had on Rex's throat the pistol would have been used with deadly effect upon Abe. As it was, Rex succeeded in getting his hand in his coat pocket, where the pistol was concealed, before Abe rendered him selpless.

Abe bound Rex and took him back into the marsh, where he had prepared for the vengeance that had mastered him. When Rex again gained consciousness and realized into whose hands he had fallen, his fear and abject cowardice were despicable. Abe sat by quietly waiting for the sun to dispel the darkness, that he might be better able to complete his work. Rex, true to his "cracker" nature, begged and promised Abe to make all amends possible.

"Fer God's sake, Mr. Abe, ain't yer got no heart in yer body?" he pleaded. "Yer knows my pappy has got a plenty money. 'Deed, sah, he'll pay yer lots—thirty, forty, fifty— only let me go home to my ole pappy!"

While making these supplications Rex raised himself upon his knees and drew closer to Abe, who dealt him a terrible blow on the head, which rendered him unconscious. The sun was high in the heavens when Rex again opened his eyes, and the sight that revealed itself to him caused him to tremble and close them again.

Abe, who had been watching him, observed that he had regained consciousness, and told him that his time had come; that he had five minutes to prepare to meet his Maker.

Rex, cringing, whining and pleading, dragged himself to Abe's feet, begging to be spared. Abe spurned him, refusing to say another word.

At the expiration of the alloted time Abe took his victim to a stump, to which, after stripping him of all clothing, he bound him, and proceeded to administer the trace to his bare back in a regular stroke.

Rex pleaded, yelled, threatened, cursed, and, finally, made a last frantic effort to break the thongs that bound him to his post of torture, exclaiming:

"I won't die! I'll see my po' mammy!"

This yell of Rex's seemed to arouse the half-slumbering demon in Abe.

"Your poor mammy? Curse you! Curse you for a cowardly hound! Beat my mother to death! Beat the flesh off the nude body of my sister! Curse you! Curse you! Your damnable crime is now being punished!" yelled Abe.

As Abe was delivering himself of these imprecations his fury seemed to redouble. He belabored Rex with both hands, until, in his mad frenzy, he fell exhausted beside the limp and lifeless body of his victim.

Had one of Rex's many friends happened upon the scene at this time Abe would have become his easy captive. When he recovered he stood for some moments seemingly appalled by the terrible crime he had committed.

The lifeless body of Rex hung to the post, torn and bleeding.

After his first fright, Abe concluded to hang a piece of the horse trace about the neck of his victim and leave him to be found by his friends or the vultures, and then made his way back to the Overley place. Upon his arrival Malcolm wanted to know where he had been and what he had been doing.

"Malcolm, suppose I tell you just what I have done, will that not make you a party to my crime, or whatever you may call it?" asked Abe. "No, Malcolm, I guess I had better not tell you."

After a moment Malcolm asked: "Why, Abe, can you not trust me?"

"Oh, that is not the point. I can trust you, but I do not want to draw you into this affair of mine."

While they were talking one of Black Sue's boys rode up to the gate on Rex's horse and asked if they knew the horse and to whom it belonged. When asked where it came from, the boy stated that he found it in the back lot on Nick Lashum's place. Nobody on that place seemed to know to whom the horse belonged. Malcolm did not know. As the boy left Malcolm turned to Abe with the inquiry: "Abe, who rode that horse to his death last night? Tell me; I want to know."

"Well," said Abe, " if you must know, Rex Vardeman fell from it last night about five miles back in the timber. When I left him this morning his soul was in Paradise."

"Abe, what have you done?"

"What I promised my poor mother I would do," replied Abe quickly.

When the boy on Rex's horse reached the main road he soon found persons who knew the animal and who directed him to take it to the Wardeman place. The Wardeman home was quiet, nothing having been thought of Rex's non-appearance. But, when the horse was brought in, the fear was expressed that he had been thrown and lay somewhere in the timber, hurt and helpless. The boy was questioned as to where he found the horse. He, of course, knew nothing. A searching party was soon formed and on its way to the timber to find Rex. They were not successful, however, returning as darkness came on. But the next morning with the returning sun a party of searchers rode away from the Wardeman place. This party, spread out over a large area of timber and soon came upon the mangled and lifeless body of Rex. At a glance it was apparent to all that human hands had brought about Rex's death. The opinions as to who committed the deed were numerous and varied. Si Weedels, who was ever present on occasions of this kind and ready with his advice, was of the opinion that the brothers of the girl whom Rex was visiting were the parties who took the young man's life. His decision may have been influenced by the fact that one of these boys had beaten him in a horse trade. It is strange, but not one of the assembled searchers thought of Abe. All agreed that some fiend among the whites was responsible for the killing.

Young Joe Wheatley, the Sheriff, who was present, said nothing, but listened to the story of each man, all the time firmly convinced that he knew the probable murderer. . After a coroner's jury had returned a verdict declaring that Rex's death was caused ''by a party or parties unknown to the jury,'' the clans of each county began to arm and to watch each other. Buck Lashum, not being in a condition physically to lead his clan, the leadership passed to Tom Smaly, who was known for his drunken brutality.

After a day's hard riding, following the hounds in a great fox hunt, Tom Smaly was not to be found among those who gathered at Goose Neck Inn to commemorate and celebrate the day's sport. His absence at first caused some comment, but mirth ran high, and rum flowed so freely that his absence was soon forgotten. It was not until next morning that his brother fully realized that Tom was missing. After an all-day search the body of Tom was found in the same condition and in the same place that Rex Wardeman's was not so long before.

When it became known that another white man had been killed in the same manner, at the same place, the wise people began to shake their heads. Some were in favor of calling on the Governor for a detective to ferret out the murderers; others were opposed to such a move, claiming that A—— County could look after its own affairs; that a county is the same as a State, inasmuch as it has the right to handle all matters that arise within its borders.

While these fiery arguments as to county rights were in full swing at Goose Neck Inn, one of Black Sue's boys, a worthless mixture of Black Sue and Nick Lashum, came forward with the story that he saw Abe riding away from the place where Tom Smaly was found.

CHAPTER XXVI.

THE next morning a self-appointed posse of citizens, good and true, soon formed for the purpose of finding Abe and lynching him. Within a very short time after the mob was in possession of this information Abe and the whole Overley plantation were warned. Messengers were sent out hurriedly for friends who could be depended on to aid in case of trouble. This mob, more or less liquorized, under the leadership of Si Weedles, mounted on a borrowed horse, he never having been able to recover from the disastrous horse trade mentioned above. swearing vengeance and promising great things, was soon on its way to the Overley plantation. As they drew near the place a discussion arose as to the gate they should enter. Some were for going through the big gate, while others favored the back cut.

"Ole Mal Overley is so d— funny," said their leader, in deciding to go in the back way, "that he might git mad and shoot somebody when he see so many of us comin' up his front way. It ain't proper fer no white man to git killed fer no 'nigger.'"

These people passed through the barnyard on their way to the veranda of the great house, where they found Malcolm Overley and a friend quietly smoking. When they lined up in front of him, off came their hats. Overley sat calmly surveying them, waiting for the leader to make known their business. As no one of them spoke, he demanded in an angry voice:

"What the h— do you d— meadow hogs want on my place?" at the same time thrusting his hand into his coat pocket, which movement caused them much uneasiness.

Si Weedles started up the steps of the veranda at the same time, saying: "Sah, Mr. Overley, we are on a——"

152

"Stand where you are," interrupted Malcolm Overley. "Who the h— told you your place was up here?"

Si moved back quickly to his comrades, with whom he held a short consultation, after which he again addressed Malcolm Overley, saying, as before: "Sah, Mr. Overley, we is here on a mission of law and order. We has hearn that your 'nigger' Abe is the one that is guilty of killing po' Tom Smaly and we came arter him; we wants to axe him about hit."

"Who the h— made the likes of you sheriff of this county? What the damnation business is it of yours who killed that d— hound? You d— meadow hogs dare to come to my place demanding my boy! You better get off this place, and never put foot on it again, or I will be found shooting the crumbs off you!"

When he delivered this speech he called to Malcolm to bring him his gun. Malcolm appeared at the door with a Winchester in his hands. At the same time windows suddenly opened and the muzzles of guns were to be seen. Si became very nervous. Three of his comrades left hurriedly. Si attempted to explain and excuse himself and friends, but was cut short by an order to leave, and leave "damn quick." At that moment the sound of clattering horse's hoofs were heard on the road leading to the house. Sheriff Wheatley and two Deputy Sheriffs dashed up.

"What is the matter here?" demanded the Sheriff of Si and four of his friends—all that were now left of the twenty who made the charge from Goose Neck Inn.

"We jes' camed here to axe Mr. Overley 'bout his 'nigger' Abe. We certainly didn't mean no harm. We is law'bidin' citizens, we is."

"You people get away from here, and remember that I am Sheriff of this county, and that it is not your business to arrest people. If you have any information that will lead to the capture of the man or men who killed Tom Smaly, give it to me. It is not your business to enforce the law. If I ever see or hear of anyone of you five men being on any man's place on such a mission as you are now engaged in, I will put you among the breakers. Now, go!''

"Yes, sah, Mr. Joe, we is goin'," answered Si Weedles, as they hurried back through the barnyard.

When Si and his companions had left the place Malcolm A. Overley, Sr., greeted the Sheriff very cordially, saying: "Joe, my boy, I am proud of you. You know better than any man in this county how to handle those 'crackers.' Come up and let me introduce you to my friend, a friend of my College days from Nova Scotia."

After some general conversation, the stranger said: "Sheriff, I heard Mr. Overley and you use some expressions to those men which they seemed to understand, but which I did not. Mr. Overley's expression was, 'shoot the crumbs off you.' What in the world do you mean by that?" This question brought forth a peal of laughter from all those present.

"Well," answered the Sheriff, "that is a slang phrase that should carry an insult with it. It means that the person so addressed is low and filthy. I am surprised that a fine old gentleman of Mr. Malcolm A. Overley's caliber should make use of such slang. Had it been just plain cuss words I would not have been a bit surprised. But what did I say?"

"Your expression was, 'I will put you among the breakers.' "

"That expression translated would read, 'I will put you in the chain gang to break stone,' " laughed the Sheriff.

"Well, well," said the stranger; "apt, indeed. I could but notice its effect on those men. We do not have that class of men in our section."

The Sheriff left, saying: "I am very glad to have met you. I hope you may learn to sight a rifle close enough to shoot the crumps off a 'cracker.' "

Two days later Black Sue's son was found hanging by the

neck to a young sapling that had been bent to the ground. He was dead, having strangled to death. Pinned to his breast was a card, upon which the following words were written:

"Let this be a warning to all 'niggers' who carry tales to the white people."

When the news of this young man's death reached Black Sue her grief and wrath were pitiable. This drunken, worthless scion, the most worthless of all her illegitimate brood, was her favorite. Black Sue reached the conclusion that Abe was responsible for her son's death. She, therefore, swore vengeance upon him. She, like all of her kind, was an adept in gathering and disseminating scandal. She instructed her pickaninnies to say that Abe injured Buck Lashum; that he killed Rex Wardeman; that he killed Tom Smaly; that he had now killed their brother. This story soon spread over the county. A demand was made upon the Sheriff for Abe's arrest. Sheriff Wheatley, however, refused, in the absence of facts, to arrest Abe. Feeling and excitement ran high. Those who felt the burden of the affairs of the county most heavily met every day at Goose Neck Inn, and their sessions continued until midnight, when the bar was closed. Si Weedels, always the busiest and most ragged citizen at these sessions, had undergone another change of heart with regard to Abe. Some of his friends were heartless enough to express the suspicion that the sight of the Winchesters at the Overley place were responsible for this sudden change. Si was loud in his protestations, and grew louder as the night grew shorter. He now insists that "no 'nigger' had the nerve to kill a white man like that. Whoever hearn of a 'nigger' doin' sich a thing! Black Sue and her pickaninnies has caused all the trouble in this hyre county for the past ten years. Them people was killed by some oncivilized critter in the next county." Thus Si talked and argued with kindred spirits, while the weeds grew up to his doorsill and the holes in his boots and pants grew larger.

CHAPTER XXVII.

TO DISCUSS the mysterious deaths noted in the previous chapter, and to devise ways and means by which these mysteries could be solved, Nick Lashum and his cronies met at their favorite nook, by the pig sty. Si Weedels was still of the opinion that some "oncivilized" white man from the next county had done the killing. Jack Smaly was of the opinion that Abe Overley did the deed, or that Burrell "nigger" did it. His cowardly conscience pointed out to him the real source of the calamities which had overtaken his brother and friends. He felt within himself that he would surely be called upon to answer for the part he played in the killing of Abe's mother and sister. Nick Lashum, Sr., could see no reason why any man in the next county should want to kill anybody in A—— County; neither could Casper Lashum.

"Si, yer is suttenly mistook. Who's in thet county thet has got nothin' 'gin anybody in this hyre county? Nobody's bin hurted by them people fer mor'n twenty yeirs. Not since Jeff Snooks took and killed Ollie Booker—and none of these boys 'long to them fam'lies. No, Sir, yer is mistook. We is got to look ferder'n thet. D—, ef I don't tek Black Sue's gess fer hit. Thet 'nigger' Abe done thet killin'. I'se axed my Buck mor'n onct who did thet job for him, but he don't seem ter understan'. By God! I would gin all I'se got ter know! Thet boy war a promisin' boy. He had his faults, but he was a promisin' boy. Now, look at him. Ef I thought thet thet Abe Overley hurted thet boy, I'l kill every d— 'nigger' in the county; thet I would."

"What good would that do, father?" asked Nick Lashum, Jr. "The other Negroes did not do it, nor are they responsible for what Abe has done."

"Thet is jes' lek yer. Forever takin' up fer them 'niggers'!" shouted Nick Lashum, Sr. "D— ef I knows who teached yer them sentiments. D— ef I did."

"No, you did not, father. Common sense taught me," answered the son, with some warmth. "It does seem to me that men grown would learn something as they pass through this life. When those two women were killed, did you feel that every white man in the county should be killed?"

"In course I did not. Who the h— ever hearn of white men bein' killed fer 'niggers'?" answered Nick, Sr. "Jes' sich talk as thet makes them 'niggers' think they is got the same rights as me and you is got. What right is they got to have one hundred and sixty acres and good horses and cattle— horses thet kin come down the road faster'n you kin? I tells yer, Mr. Nicholas Lashum, thet yer pappy don't want thet darn talk on his place. D— ef I does." This last remark aroused the quarrelsome 'cracker' blood in Nick, Jr., who answered hotly:

"No, I suppose not. Your whole bunch was so d— ignorant the day of the meeting here that you would not let white men talk who had as much right to talk as you had. Now, what is the result? Uncle Casper is out and all the offices are in the hands of the people opposed to you. Your friends are being killed under your very noses, and all you know and all you can say and all you can do is kill a 'nigger.' D— such ignorance! I have been with people of brains and standing long enough to learn that killing 'niggers' and burning their property is a mighty sorry way to control anything. While you and your friends were bellowing 'nigger,' these people used their brains and took the office of Sheriff away in one night. Now, your friends are being killed, and you are bellowing 'nigger,' instead of locating the murderer and bringing him to justice. I do not wonder that these people call you 'meadow hogs,' 'crackers,' and the devil knows what not. To h— with your d— brute ideas! I am cashier of the Pioneer

Savings Bank. I mingle with the best people of the State. Must I be forever and continually reminded that I belong to a family of murderers?"

"Yes, thet is very fine talk, but who the h— ever hearn of killin' 'niggers' bein' murder?" asked Nick, Sr.

"Your d—d ignorance is simply maddening," answered the son, with great wrath. "Can you give a 'nigger' life? Have you got a right to take that which you can't give? I don't care a d— for these 'niggers,' but I would like for my family name to stand for something besides brutal assaults and adulterous connection with 'niggers.' If this thing keeps up I shall leave the State and go where the curse of 'cracker' ignorance is unknown; go where I will not hear at every turn that Nick Lashum says this, and Nick Lashum says that, all of which bespeaks phenomenal ignorance and brutality. I am tired of it all."

"Yes, I suppose yer is. Yer an' Arabella is the only two thet tells ther ole pappy thet he is ig'rant and all these things," whined the old man. "Yer has al'ays been a good boy, Nick; but can't yer overlook them things thet I learnt when I was a boy?"

"Overlook h—!" yelled the son. "Are you never going to learn anything? Am I ever to be reminded that my father is different from the fathers I meet out in the world? Your whole bunch of d—d ignorant 'crackers' is despicable!" and Nick left with an oath applicable to them all.

When Nick, Jr., left the crowd began to melt away. Soon Jack Smaly, Nick, Sr., Si, and Casper Lashum were left to themselves. Casper said: "Nick, what did I tell yer when yer started thet boy to school twenty odd yeirs ago? I tole yer jes' what 'twud be. You never hearn my boys talk lek thet. Why? 'Cause I knows as much as they does. I took pains not ter let them go no longer than I did. Thet is what I done."

"Thet is so, Cas; I rec'on' I'se done wrong. But thet is a smart boy, an' Arabella is a smart chile. They do. both say a whole lot mor'n they has a right to," sighed Nick, Sr. "But what kin I do? They is learnt now."

"We kin git thet 'nigger' Abe and mek him tell," said Jack Smaly.

"I tells yer, Abe don't know nothin'," said Si; "an', 'sides, he is gone an' lef' now."

"Thet is so, Si; he is gone," said Nick, Sr.; "but if we should kill some 'niggers' the res' would git skeered and tell all they knows."

"Yes, thet is ef they knows," said Casper. "But sposen' they don't know, what 'scuse has yer got fer killin' 'em? Yer suttenly knows thet this county is not run now as it uster be. Joe Wheatley's dun swore thet he won't stan' fer no 'nigger' killin'. No, we'se got to go 'bout this thing lek them 'big bugs' does. Hire a detective and let him fin' out."

"Better gin thet job to Black Sue; she kin fin' out; I knows she kin," said Nick, Sr.

"Well, yer suit yerself," said Si; "but I says make Black Sue keep her d— mouth outen this whole matter. It's a white man's business."

"Yer is right, Si," said Casper; "no 'nigger' kin be trusted in this matter."

"Well, yer and Si do as yer d— please," said Nick. "I leaves the whole thing to yuens. But, one thing I tell yer, when thet mortgage on ole Mal's place comes due, I'll know what to do; yo'll see."

"Thet is so, Nick," said Casper; "I had mos' forgot thet mortgage. Yer will suttenly be a dumb fool if yer don't sell him out. I'll be right there to git the place when the sale comes off."

"No yer won't, by a d— sight!" said Nick. "What yer recon' I'se been holdin' them papers fer all these yeirs? To let yer come in and git what I wants? Youse a fine brother, yer is! Wan' ter rob yer own flesh and blood?''

"How's thet robbin' yer?" asked Casper, warmly. "Yer is sich a d— hog thet yer wants the best of everything. Yer tooked thet Burrell place from them 'nigger' chil'ren, which o'ny cos' yer one hundred and forty dollars, court cos's, an' yer promised to gin me eighty acres of thet lan' an' yer didn't do hit. I fixed thet deal fer yer, and yer keeps the whole hundred and sixty acres, an' I gits nothin'. Thet's the kin'er brother yer is. Then say I wants ter rob yer! Ter h— with thet talk!''

"Cas, yer and Nick's ferever cussin' at each other," said Si. "Is yer never goin' ter get ter act lek men when yer gits tergether? I wants yer both to do better, d— if I don't.''

Si's remark caused a laugh, accompanied as it was by an attitude of authority.

In spite of the suggestions offered, this assemblage broke up without reaching a definite conclusion as to the killings.

CHAPTER XXVIII.

IN THE meantime Abe had expressed his determination to Mr. Overley to quit the place, as the "crackers" were aroused to a point where it was likely they would fire the house and barn because of the fact that Mr. Overley protected him. The senior Overley, however, would not listen to Abe's protests, insisting that he was master on his own place. At this time Abe was approached by an Italian with whom he had been very friendly and who had worked for the Lashums for some time. He seemed to understand the whole situation and endeavored to persuade Abe to use bombs on the white people of the county.

"Abe, I maka de bomb. I learna in my country. I shoota one little birda. Da Counta de Costigni he beata me. I fixa de bomb under his door stepa. He comea. Buoy! Buoy! Ha! Ha! His heada go one waya, his feeta keep on running. I geta my revenga! I leava my country. I go backa some day rich mana. I liva and diea good mana. I makea you de bomb. No? Bah! No revenga?"

"No, Tony," said Abe, "I do not want your bombs. I have no quarrel with the whole county. Five men killed my mother. Two of them are dead. Three live. One worse than dead. He shall die, however. That leaves two more to be accounted for. Were I to use a bomb on the first white man that comes along, simply because he is a white man, I would commit a cowardly crime, for which I would deserve the worst punishment. This is not a question of race with me. But it is a step back to medieval days, when brothers avenged brothers' wrongs; when the State was not strong enough, as in this case, to right such wrongs. The time is now come when Negroes should kill the man or men who on the slightest provocation lynch or take the lives of their kinsmen. When they learn to do that, we will have fewer murders of

161

this character to mar our civilization. With me your bomb is impossible.''

"You say civilizationa. Thata for biga mana, not for poor mana and blacka mana. No. Civilizationa no gooda.''

Two years later it was announced in the *County Bulletin* that Cæsar Antonio Amato, of Reggio, Italy, had married Miss Josephine Walsh, a descendant of one of the oldest families of the State of Alabama. It is to be hoped that Amato "absorbed" the American idea to the point where he could understand the meaning of our civilization.

At this writing we do not understand the American civilization.

About this time Malcolm received a long letter from DeVaux and his Tennessee friend. They were spending the summer automobiling through the far West. It bore the post-mark of a small town in Nevada. That portion of the letter which was of most interest to us reads as follows:

Your section of the country certainly produces some queer characters, to say the least. I have just had the honor of meeting a preacher, an exhorter, a regular romping, roaring, raging, rambling backwoods parson of the kind who attracts attention by the use of his lungs, if nothing else. This man, together with his wife (?), whom he claims to be a mixed-breed Indian, but whose language would indicate that she is a mixed-breed Negro, has charge of the only church in this whole country. When we first called on him he was not quite steady enough for an interview; but when we saw him later, after his nap, he gave us his life's history. I was surprised to learn that he came from your county. He seems to be very well acquainted with Buck Lashum. He says Buck's horse crippled him. Such a pity. Have you a school of theology in your county? You have an advantage over me. You are living in an atmosphere of greatness. Rev. and Mrs. Timothy Wardeman are living evidences of greatness, and they hail from your county! How is your friend Abe bearing up? I hope he has done nothing rash. Will you and he return to College? Miss D. was in California this summer, so I am

informed. You may know that, however. With kindest
regards to Abe,

Yours,

DeVaux.

Abe sat silent for some moments after the reading of this
epistle, then said: "Again have those young men done me a
very great service; this time unconsciously. I have tried in
vain to locate Tim Wardeman. This letter, with its information, comes at a very opportune time. I had made up my
mind to go in search of him, which would have been a long,
tedious hunt. Now I can go direct. His wife! Black Sue's
girl Viney! She disappeared about the time Tim did, and
I have no doubt it is she who is with him. But we shall soon
know. Malcolm, when do you start for College?"

"When do I start for College?" asked Malcolm. "Have
you concluded not to go? We should start next Wednesday.
Dad said last night that we were to finish this year; that he is
very proud of the showing we have made. Have you talked
to your father about going?"

"Poor old dad! I had almost forgotten him. No, I have
not. I have had very little to say to him on any subject. He
will, of course, want me to finish my course; but I do not
feel that I should remain at College after what I have passed
through in the last two months. I shall leave here for Oberlin
when you do, however. I will then make my way out West.
I am sorry that I must leave Jack Smaly and Buck alive, but
I will return about Christmas."

Abe then went to his father, whom he found sitting silent
and alone, apparently weighted down by the burden of events
which have so rapidly succeeded the taking off of his loved
ones.

"Dad, you seem worried," said Abe. "What is the
trouble?"

"Yes, my son, I is worried," answered the father. "I'se
worried 'bout yo'. Two munts hab yo' been home an' yo' has

not spent two nights wid yo' ole dad. My son, my ole heart
tells me that all's not right wid yo'. When de Great Day dun
kum, an de question's axed yo' what yo' dun wid dem two
munts, what yo' goin' say? Oh, my po' boy, what kin yo'
say?''

The old man's head dropped to his breast, his whole body
quivered, tears ran down his careworn cheeks, his whole attitude was one of dejection, of despair. Abe stood for some
moments gazing intently at his father, whose age and helpless-
ness were apparent to him now as never before. He suddenly
realized what a blow his determination to live for revenge had
been to his old Christian father. His heart swelled with
remorse, but his purpose was not shaken for one moment. He
knelt before his father, whose hands he took in his own,
saying:

''Dad, why spend your last days worrying over a thing
which neither of us can remedy? You say this case can only
be settled at the bar of God. Dad, I sincerely regret that any
action of mine should cause you trouble, but my mother's
death calls for revenge.''

''My boy, does yo' 'member what de good Lawd say on dat
ıt? He say dat 'revenge is mine.' Does yo' feel yo'se'f
stronger dan He am? Does yo' feel dat you is on dis eart' to
do His work or His biddin'? Oh, my po' boy, what I teach
yo' when yo' a leetle boy at yo' po' mammy's knee? Did I
teach you to be 'vengeful? What has yo' lef' fo' de Lawd to
do in dis matter? My boy, it am yo' ole dad's wish dat yo'
goes ba'k to school and leve dese pussons in de han's of de
Lawd. If yo' does dat, yo' will tek yo' ole fodder's blessin'
wid yo'.''

As Abe's father spoke these words he laid his hands upon
his son's head, with a mental supplication to Almighty God
that He direct Abe anew.

''Father,'' answered Abe, ''I have come to you to say that

I will go with Malcolm next Wednesday when he leaves for school.''

The old man closed his eyes and murmured: ''Lawd, I thank Thee!''

Abe remained with his father listening to the old man's admonitions and advice, and when he finally left him Abe had promised, by implication at least, that he would do what his father wanted him to do. He went immediately to Malcolm, to whom he unburdened himself.

''Malcolm, for the first time in my whole life, I have lied to my father. I have promised him to do what I do not intend to do, and did not intend to do at the time I promised him. Oh, I have deceived him shamefully!''

''Abe, what have you promised?'' asked Malcolm.

''I have not promised anything in words, but by inference I have promised to leave Buck Lashum, Tim Wardeman and Jack Smaly in the hands of the Lord. I have led my father to believe that I am going to College with you and forget all about my promise to my mother that I would avenge her. God knows what effect it will have upon him when he learns the truth!''

''Abe, why did you not tell him the truth?'' asked Malcolm.

''Malcolm, I could not. If you had heard that confiding old man talk you would have done just as I did. The Lord will forgive me. I did it that dad may sleep in peace, at least until he learns the truth. I told him that I would go to College with you next Wednesday. That much is the truth.''

''Well, Abe, you are certainly in a very awkward position. You must tell my father before he makes arrangement for your tuition.''

''Malcolm, let us go to him at once. I want this thing settled now.''

They found the senior Overley dozing on the veranda, Old Abe being at the barn looking after the stock.

"Mr. Overley, I have come to talk to you about my going off to College with Malcolm next Wednesday," said Abe.

"You have, have you? Damnation! Do you think I want you to wake me up to talk about your d— school? Didn't I say go? How long have you been on this place that you haven't yet learned that I sleep at this hour? You did well last year. What the h— do you learn at school, that you don't know better than to disturb an old man during the hour he sleeps? You, both! Malcolm, I am displeased that you let Abe awaken me."

"Yes, dad, I'm sorry, but——"

"But?" interrupted the father, now thoroughly awakened; "what is the matter? What have you young devils hatched now?"

"Mr. Overley, I want to tell you how I am going to devote this school year. I hope you will bear with me."

Abe then related all that had passed between himself and his father; also his determination to find Tim Wardeman and wreak vengeance on him.

The senior Overley listened attentively. When Abe had finished he sat silent, with his eyes closed, apparently lost in thought. Neither Malcolm nor Abe dared speak.

"So, you want to go out West to kill somebody, do you? Well, if I thought you killed the two valuable citizens who were found dead back in the woods I would have you hanged, that I would. And you do not feel that you ought to go back to College? Why?"

"I do not know at what moment the hand of the law may reach me. I do not desire to bring disgrace upon the College by being arrested while there," answered Abe.

"Well, I never looked at this d— business in that light before," said Mr. Overley. "How are you going to live?"

"I have no fear along those lines," answered Abe. "I want to get back here by Christmas. I think that Jack Smaly would like to meet me about that time. I shall avail myself

of your kindness as far as Oberlin College, then I will drop
out of sight.''

''H——, boy, you are welcome to money to pay your way out
and back. I know that a good citizen would not let you have
this money, but——. I do not want you to walk that distance.''

''I thank you very much, Mr. Overley,'' said Abe; ''but I
cannot accept any assistance from you. I know it is needless
to ask it, but you will look after my father?''

''Look arter me?'' said a voice from the yard. ''Whose
been lookin' arter him dese sixty-five yeirs? How's he goin'
to look arter me?''

With the arrival of Old Abe the conversation turned to the
approaching departure of the boys. Abe's determination not
to attend College the ensuing year was not again mentioned
by Malcolm A. Overley, Sr.

CHAPTER XXIX.

THE day of their leaving came only too quickly, and the boys were on their way to Oberlin. It was agreed between them that upon their arrival Abe would call upon Miss Watson, see Dr. Finley, and leave the town immediately. He went from the station direct to Miss Watson's home. Their eyes met in a long, steadfast gaze, the one bearing the mute inquiry, "What have you done?" the other conveying the desired information. Miss Watson asked no questions. She seemed to know intuitively that Abe had kept his promise to the dead.

"Abe, will you finish your course this year?" she asked.

"No, Nancy; I am on my way out West," answered Abe. "I hope to be with you again just before Christmas. I have stopped in Oberlin to talk to you, also to pay my respects to your parents. I expect to visit Dr. Finley, Dean Sternly and Mr. Donewell, after which I shall leave the town."

By good fortune, Abe, after leaving the Watson home, found the three persons whom he most desired to see in the Doctor's office. He was greeted very cordially by them. The Doctor, assuming that Abe was back for the school year, immediately began to compliment him upon his determination to finish his College course. Abe's embarrassment was not at first apparent to the Doctor, who, when he did notice his confusion, asked for an explanation. Abe stated briefly that unforeseen circumstances had arisen that would not permit his attendance at College this year; that he had stopped in Oberlin to see his friends and say good-bye to them, and that he was going out West and might never return. Abe's vow to avenge the deaths of his mother and sister was known to the Doctor, Dean Sternly and Mr. Donewell, and they felt that that vow was the basic cause of his determination not to attend College this year. Dr. Finley arose from his seat greatly agitated. He walked over to Abe, placing his hand on his shoulder, saying:

"My son, may I not speak to you in God's name? Listen to me, an old man, who has passed the three-score-and-ten mark, and who firmly believes in the brotherhood of mankind. In God's name, do not leave this College; do not go on this errand to the West; do not begin this wreaking of vengeance; do not put yourself without the pale of the law; do not do that which will bring the wrath of God upon you. Leave this matter in His hands. I know that your provocation has been great. I know that you cannot invoke the aid of the law. I know that you feel, from your point of view, that revenge is the only course open to you. But, why take this matter in your own hands? Why take your own life in your own hands? Why leave off the building of a useful life, as you seem to have determined to do?"

"Doctor, my mother's death will then have been avenged," answered Abe.

"Avenged!" exclaimed the Doctor. "A false doctrine! To be avenged you would violate the law of the land; to be avenged you would take your own life in your hands; to be avenged you would forever put aside the building of a useful life, put aside the opportunities that are open to you, forever put aside, dwarf, deaden and transform into an agency for evil those faculties which God seldom bestows upon man in such abundance. My son, I repeat, you will do all these things to be avenged, *and after you have been avenged what have you accomplished?*"

Abe stood looking at the Doctor. His form seemed to heighten and expand. Finally he answered in slow and measured tones:

"Doctor, not being a Negro, you cannot understand nor can you appreciate my feelings in this matter. Taking your last argument first, granting that God has bestowed upon me in an unusual degree faculties that are susceptible to cultivation, must I not also be endowed with the accompanying sensibilities that would tend to make up the mentality of which you speak? Doctor, had your mother, YOUR MOTHER, mark you, been treated as mine was, though she was ten times guilty of what my mother was so wrongfully accused; had your sister been lashed upon her nude body until death relieved her sufferings, even though she had been guilty of murder—would you stifle in your breast your desire for vengeance when you knew that the processes of law were a farce and there was no such thing as justice? With no other means of redress but retaliation, and no remedy for the wrong except the torch, the knife or the club, would you refuse to hear the cry for vengeance from your dead mother and sister? Doctor, God may have endowed me as abundantly as you say, but the one gift from the great Jehovah for which I am truly thankful is this right arm of mine!"

As Abe spoke these words he raised his arm aloft in all the pride of youth and conscious strength of manhood. Then, with a sudden burst of passion, he exclaimed:

"Doctor, what do I now care for law, life or liberty? Could I go calmly through this life, trusting to a force which I can neither see nor feel, conscious that the brutes who foully murdered my loved ones, my poor old mother and my young sister, are enjoying liberty? Would I be a man? Would you, under such circumstances, bow your head, clasp your hands and trust in the Lord? Life is worth nothing to me now. I go forth from here with the deliberate determination to take the lives of those who murdered my poor mother."

When Abe had finished a silence fell upon the assemblage that was broken by Mr. Donewell, who invited Abe to walk to his home with him.

"Mr. Overley," said Dr. Donewell, "what do you expect to do after you have kept your vow? I have invited you to walk with me that I might ask you this question. I am not censuring you, mark you, but, as I place myself in your position, I can see nothing that I could do. My life would be a blank. Have you considered well the step you have taken?"

"Yes, Mr. Donewell, I have considered," answered Abe. "and if I do not forfeit my life in this attempt, the time allotted me from the consummation of my vow to eternity will be spent in the upbuilding of my people in some foreign land, perhaps. But I am frank to say that I feel that I have nothing for which to live. Why should I care to live? My poor old father, now on the very brink of the Great Beyond, is all that binds me to this earth."

"Why, Mr. Overley," asked Mr. Donewell, "I hoped there might be a young lady somewhere who would influence you to resume your course at this College?"

"Yes, yes," said Abe, "there is a young lady from whom I wrung a promise when the enormity of this crime was upon her, but who is too good, too pure, to have her life linked to one whose hands will be red with human blood. When I next see her I shall bid her forget me. I shall give back her promise. I shall then be an outcast, a homeless wanderer, an outlaw, maybe, with my hand raised against mankind and a price upon my head. God alone knows how it will end. But, no matter how it ends, no matter what I am forced to do, the dying cries of my poor mother and my outraged sister shall be answered by the dying cries of their brutal murderers. Though I face death at the fiery stake in this world, though I am sure to be engulfed in the fires of hell in the next world, my mother shall be avenged!"

As Abe uttered these words he stopped short, looked Mr. Donewell full in the face, and remarked: "Perhaps I had better not go further, sir; I am already a murderer."

Mr. Donewell gazed at Abe for some moments in silence. In spite of his conviction that Abe was wrong in his determination, he could not but admire him. The thought ran through his mind that here is a splendid life wrecked, one of God's rare creations, one of nature's noblemen, made wretched and reckless by the wanton killing of his mother and sister—a killing directly traceable to lust and drunken brutality. After some moments' silence, Mr. Donewell took Abe by the arm, resuming their walk.

"Mr. Overley, I feel for you. My heart is with you, but my reason tells me that you are wrong. I would to God that I might be of some service to you, that I could say or do something that might help you to the right course! What can I do to help you?"

"Mr. Donewell, I know of nothing you can do for me; but away down in the State of Alabama there are two old men who are dear to me, who have made great sacrifices for me. I wish there were some way in which you could look after them and help them to spend their last days in peace on the old plantation. Mr. Donewell, do this, and you will surely be rewarded in heaven. I will leave you now, sir."

As Abe extended his hand to his friend, his eyes filled with tears. He said simply: "Good-bye, Mr. Donewell; I may never see you again."

"Good-bye, my boy," was all that Mr. Donewell could say.

CHAPTER XXX.

WHEN left to himself, Dr. Donewell recalled Abe's words, "see that they spend their last days in peace on the old plantation." After some thought he recalled Dr. Finley's remarks concerning the conditions under which Malcolm and Abe entered the College. He determined to have a thorough investigation made at once, which investigation resulted in the disclosure that the mortgage on the Overley place was about to be foreclosed; that some of Malcolm A. Overley's friends were pooling their money to buy the place in for him.

Mr. Donewell instructed his solicitor to buy the place in at any cost. When the day of sale came, Nick, being precluded from bidding, left that duty to Casper. The bidding started slowly, and it seemed at first as if the probable price brought would not pay the mortgage. Soon a stranger raised the last bid of Casper's one thousand dollars. Casper stood aghast. He raised the bid one hundred dollars, however. The stranger bid one thousand dollars more. Casper yelled, "Five hundred dollars mor'n thet last bid!" The stranger calmly bid one thousand dollars more. Neither Nick Lashum nor his cohorts could understand this move. They consulted together, after which, at the request of the auctioneer, they bid one hundred dollars more.

The stranger, who was seated in a public carry-all, arose, remarking in a loud voice: "Mr. Auctioneer, I propose to have this place, if it costs me a half million. I bid twenty-five hundred dollars more!"

"Mr. Casper Lashum, will you let this grand old place get away from you for seventeen thousand five hundred dollars? Do I hear a bid of one hundred dollars more? Seventeen thousand five hundred dollars for property which is worth

more than fifty thousand dollars! Mr. Zeph Smaly, do I
hear one hundred dollars more? Seventeen thousand five
hundred dollars—going! "Five hundred dollars more," said
Smaly. At this point Malcolm A. Overley, with tears in his
eyes, supported by Old Abe, made a mute appeal to Big Joe
Wheatley and Jack Connors. Big Joe Wheatley, with his
clinched hand aloft, pushed himself through the crowd close
to the auctioneer, shouting: "May I forever be damned, if I
permit this place to get away from my old friend Overley. I
bid——"

Before he could offer his bid, the stranger, who was beside
him, held his hand up to his gaze. In the palm was a card,
upon which was engraved in red the words, "Life Brother."
Big Joe Wheatley immediately withdrew, making his way to
Malcolm A. Overley, to whom he whispered: "He is one of
us; 'Life Brother' is in his hand."

All eyes were now centered upon the stranger. What would
he do next? "I bid two thousand dollars more," he said.
What could he mean by such bidding? Was he trying to put
somebody in a hole? How did he silence Big Joe Wheatley
so easily? "A trap," Si Weedels whispered to Casper
Lashum.

"I don't give a d—! I wants thet place, and I'se goin' ter
have hit. I bids five hundred dollars more," said Casper.

"Well, you will have to pay for it if you get it," said the
stranger. "You will give dollar for dollar. I bid five thousand dollars more."

Casper Lashum again consulted with his friends. They
concluded that the stranger could not stand another raise of
one thousand dollars. So, with a great flourish, he bid one
thousand dollars more. The bid was scarcely made before the
stranger cried: "I bid five thousand dollars more!"

Nick Lashum, Sr., and his friends, not being accustomed to
such, to them, reckless use of money, stood aghast, not knowing
what to do. Nick Lashum, Jr., explained to his father that

the last bid took the selling price up to thirty-one thousand five hundred dollars, all the place was worth, and if the stranger refused to bid again he (Nick) would have more than twenty-five thousand dollars cash to raise over and above his mortgage; that this stranger was setting a trap to break him. But Nick, Sr., whose cupidity was now thoroughly aroused, whispered to Casper to bid one thousand dollars more.

"Naw!" exclaimed Casper; "who the h—'s goin' ter git they money together? 'Bid one thousand dollars more, Casper.' When my home's gone yo'll gin me one lek you did them eighty acres. Yer put yer own head in the trap. Yer is a nice——"

"Thirty-one thousand five hundred dollars! Going! Going!" yelled the auctioneer, now thoroughly satisfied with his prospective fee. "Going—once! Mr. Zeph Smaly, do you bid one thousand dollars more? Mr. Casper Lashum, are you done. Do I hear one hundred dollars more? This property is worth fifty thousand dollars, if it is worth one cent. Going—twice! Thirty-one thousand five hundred dollars! Make it one thousand more, Mr. Wardeman? Will you let this opportunity pass? Are you all done? Going! Going! Gone! This gentleman here gets the place for thirty-one thousand five hundred dollars. The bargain of his life. Mr.——"

"John K. Evers is my name," said the stranger.

"Mr. John K. Evers, the terms of this sale, of course, are known to you. One thousand dollars at time of sale, balance in thirty days."

"Yes," said Mr. Evers; "I am prepared to comply with the terms here and now."

"It is not necessary to go into details here in the road, sir," said Nick Lashum, Jr. "We will drive to the bank, where we can arrange all matters and where the papers are to be found."

This was satisfactory to Mr. Evers, who made the deposit and promised to come to the bank next day at 2 p. m. and make the final payment. He then drove to the Overley place. He found Malcolm A. Overley seated on his veranda, surrounded by his friends. As he drew near the group, they asked each other who can he be.

"He is surely one of us," said Big Joe Wheatley. "He gave the sign known only to the inner circle amongst us. But we will see."

Mr. Evers advanced to Malcolm A. Overley and extended hand, saying in a low voice, 'Life Brother,' with the accompanying grip.

"I am, indeed, more than glad to meet you, Mr. Evers," said Malcolm A. Overley; "but you have put it out of my power to ever gain possession of my home. Oh, my God! Six generations of Overleys have lived on this place, and now we must go!"

"Say not so, sir," said Mr. Evers; "I bid this place up to show those 'crackers' that they may never expect to obtain possession of any of our ancestral homes. I would have bid indefinitely, as I have the means at my disposal. Now, you, of course, understand that the amount over and above the mortgage goes to you. I do not want your home; nor do the people whom I represent. This is December 10th. December 25th, Christmas day, the real owner will present himself and settle matters with you. You will be satisfied. That is all that I can say at present. I am very glad to have had the honor of meeting these gentlemen, of whom I heard so much before I came to your end of the State," added Mr. Evers, when introduced to the gentlemen present. After a few more unimportant remarks, he took his departure. A few days later Mr. Evers sent a full statement to Mr. Donewell concerning this transaction.

By way of explanation, it may be here mentioned that al' the old aristocratic families in this State are oath-bound for mutual protection, 'Life Brother' being their password.

CHAPTER XXXI.

MALCOLM left Abe at the station, and went directly to Miss Mabel Donewell's home, where he was very warmly greeted.

"Malcolm, why did you not wire me that you were coming?" asked Miss Donewell. "I would have had some friends here to welcome you. Where is your friend, Abe?"

"Why ask for Abe? Where am *I*? Did I not hurry from the station to find the girl whom I love? Where would you be likely to find him? And you have not even offered me your hand! I know Abe's little girl has done better than that."

"Well, Mr. Overley, do you expect me to offer you my hand?"

"I am going to take it, whether you offer it or not," laughed Malcolm, as he attempted to seize her hands.

At this point Mrs. Donewell appeared at the door and remarked: "Why, Mabel! What does this mean?"

"It means, mother, that Mr. Overley is trying to take my hand. He finds fault with me for not offering it to him."

"Mrs. Donewell, I did think that, after several months' absence, Miss Donewell would at least shake hands with me. I was endeavoring to instruct her as to how she should conduct herself toward the best of friends," answered Malcolm.

"I suppose, Mr. Overley, you mean to infer that her mother has been derelict in that respect?" said Mrs. Donewell.

"Oh, no; by no means," answered Malcolm quickly. "I would not presume for a moment to even insinuate that Miss Mabel's training has not been all that could be desired. I can testify that with this single exception her conduct has always been above criticism."

"You have been very observant, Mr. Overley," remarked Miss Donewell; "one would conclude from your remarks that you are competent and willing to set up a standard of deportment for the young ladies of your acquaintance."

"Mrs. Donewell, do you not think your daughter a little severe in her comments?" asked Malcolm.

Before Mrs. Donewell could answer Malcolm's query, Mr. Donewell came into the room.

"Mr. Overley, I am very glad to see you; very glad that you are back to finish your course."

"I am very glad to be back," answered Malcolm. "This old College is very dear to me. We form ties at College that should never be severed."

"Father, what is the matter?" asked Mrs. Donewell. "You look as solemn as a judge who is about to pronounce a death sentence upon some person whom he does not believe guilty."

"Well, I feel just as you express it," said Mr. Donewell. "I have just passed sentence upon a young man whom I admire and respect. My heart tells me he is right in his determination to take the law in his own hands. His is a position calculated to try the strongest. I would——"

"You have seen my friends, Abe, Mr. Donewell," interrupted Malcolm. "What has he told you he means to do?"

"He insists that his vow must be kept," said Mr. Donewell. "His only concern is for two old men in Alabama who seem to have made great sacrifices for him. His concern is that they spend their last days quietly on the old plantation. What can he mean by that remark? I tried to persuade him to remain at the College with us this year, but he would not. He has a mission to perform in the West, he says. I hope something unforeseen will prevent the fulfillment of that mission."

"Mr. Donewell, nothing but death will stop Abe," said Malcolm. "I have not tried to dissuade him for the reason that I know it would be useless. He will surely keep his vow."

"Mr. Overley, what vow has your friend Abe made?" asked Miss Donewell. "Do you refer to his vow to avenge his mother's death? I thought those men were arrested at the time. Released! Do you mean to tell me that the men who committed such a dastardly crime were released? Then, I do not blame Abe. I would take the law in my own hands, mother dear, were you to meet a like fate. How can such crimes be overlooked under a civilized government?''

''Miss Donewell, you do not understand the sentiment that prevails in the land of my birth,'' answered Malcolm. ''That sentiment does not pronounce it a punishable crime to kill Negroes, either men, women or children. We do not believe in that doctrine; but it prevails, nevertheless. The unwritten law is that no white man, no matter how low and depraved, shall die or be deprived of his liberty for the mere killing or maiming of a Negro man, woman or child. Abe knows this. He acts accordingly. I do not blame him. He is doing no different than other persons classed as good citizens have done.''

''Is it possible that men live and worship God who commit such crimes and see no harm in them?'' asked Mrs. Donewell.

''Mother, what Mr. Overley says is only too true,'' said Mr. Donewell. ''It is to be hoped that the influence of brotherly love may change all this some day.''

''Mr. Donewell, you do not understand the nature of this 'cracker' blood, if you think that anything short of an infusion of new blood will change this sentiment. This blood asserts itself, no matter where you find it—in the United States Senate, in the House of Representatives, in the Governor's chair, in the pulpit, on the rostrum, on a Pullman dining car—anywhere this 'cracker' blood predominates, there you find a bloodthirsty sentiment toward the Negro. These people have had access to the Bible and Biblical teachings for centuries, but have they learned the Ten Commandments? No, and they never will, not until God Almighty injects into their veins a newer and purer blood—a blood that will bring about a complete change of natural instincts. We people of the South who believe that every man has a right to life, liberty and happiness, have studied these people, and have come to the conclusion that new blood injected into the 'cracker' is all that will save the Southland. These people are non-progressive. They produce little and consume much. The Negroes are outstripping them at every turn, and let me say that herein lies the trouble. The 'cracker' will not do himself, and resents with great fierceness the progress made by his black neighbor. But where is this new blood to come from? Some States have agents soliciting emigrants, contracting for them abroad, in violation of the laws of the United States. When they come here they look the 'cracker' over, turn from him to the better class of Negroes, or leave the country. They will have none of the 'cracker.' And the birth rate of the mulattoes goes on and on. Where will it end? We have men in public life who have Negro blood in their veins. These men are fiercest in their denunciation of the Negro. In a few more generations, in some sections of the South, the line will be obliterated, much as some of us may deplore it.''

''Mr. Overley, you draw a gloomy picture of the future of the South,'' said Mr. Donewell. ''Can you see no light of hope, no gleam away in the far distant future, that would indicate an awakening in this 'cracker' element?''

''No, I can see nothing in them,'' answered Malcolm; ''they are today where they have been for generations, with an exception here and there. Where one has reached the United States Senate, he stands even there for those things which have disgraced the South. In the Governor's chair, some low-bred 'cracker' has brought disgrace upon the State. There is nothing you can do with them. As a whole, they are intractable, unteachable and incapable of cultivation. They simply multiply like the germs of a contagion, fighting ever at the vitals of the body politic. But where has Abe gone, Mr. Donewell?''

"Your friend has gone to say good-bye to Miss Watson," answered Mr. Donewell, "after which he will see you, then leave for the West."

CHAPTER XXXII.

ABE, after leaving Mr. Donewell, went to Miss Watson's home and took his final leave of the family, saying that he would return the week before Christmas. He then went to Malcolm's room to await his arrival. Malcolm soon came into the room, fully persuaded to try to show Abe the error of his way. He found Abe seated by the table, gazing at a little homespun jacket which he held, as the great teardrops fell like rain upon the garment. Malcolm stood for amoment as one suddenly awakened from a dream.

"Abe, where did you get that little jumper?" he asked. "Oh, Mammy Rinda made that for me years ago! Let me see it. Yes, this is one of mine. Here is the family coat of arms she sewed on the collar. Sh! Poor old Mammy Rinda! How I would love to see you now! Abe, do you remember——"

"Do I remember? My God! Malcolm, how can you ask——"

"Now, Abe, be reasonable," said Malcolm. "I want to ask you about the good things Mammy Rinda used to fix for us. I remember her as the only woman who nursed me, who sang me to sleep, to whom I told the story of my sufferings, and who always comforted me and soothed my pains. Now she is gone, and by the hands of murderers! Curses on them! Abe, when do you start for the West? I will go with you. Those hellhounds must surely die!" Malcolm forgot for a moment the fine resolutions he had made to persuade Abe to stay at school. He remembered nothing but that that old black woman, the mother of his childhood, had been foully murdered. The little garment took him back to the days and acts of her kindness and love never to be forgotten.

Malcolm sat with his face in his hands for several moments.

He finally said: "Abe, I want to help you. God knows I do.
But in what way? How can I help you most? Poor old
Mammy Rinda! The only mother I ever knew!"

Malcolm arose and walked to Abe, placing his hand upon
his shoulder, saying: "Abe, you are my brother. The
brother of my childhood. Why did God Almighty make you
black and me white? Make us to love and revere the same
things? Alike in all respects but color? And this world
holds you responsible for your color! Abe," continued Malcolm, as they clasped hands, "what can I do now to help
you?"

"Malcolm, you can best serve me by not becoming involved
in these crimes I am committing," answered Abe. "While
I appreciate your feelings in the matter, and believe you are
willing to avenge my mother, it is not right that you should
do so. You should not stain your hands with human blood.
You cannot justify yourself before man or God. This is my
affair and mine alone. I have come to say good-bye to you,
Malcolm. I am going to find Tim Wardeman. He shall not
escape me. But I feel that I am leaving my brother, if not in
blood, in unity of soul. Malcolm, brother, look after my old
father. See that he wants nothing. If I never return and he
should learn the truth, tell him what I have confessed to you—
that I lied to him that he might not suffer the anguish the
knowledge of my errand would bring to him. If I ever
return, I pray God that it will not break his heart. Can there
be a God, Malcolm? Is there a God that directs and shapes
the courses and destinies of nations alike? Why, my brother,
are we brothers, yet as far apart as the poles, north and south,
and held apart because I am black and you are white?
DeVaux and his friend, ready and willing with their money
and their blood to defend me, would not sleep under the same
roof that sheltered me, because they are white and I am black.
This must be the God that Rev. Dr. Snell down home preached
about. You have no conception, Malcolm—you can have no

conception—of the terribly humiliating effect of this undefinable something that makes me an object of scorn, of derision, something to be shunned, to be ever set apart from other men, not because I am not decent, clean and orderly, but because God made me black; a something that white men with the Christian love for their fellow men in their hearts, and millions of money in their pockets, have not the moral courage to stand up before the world and combat. Though the Sermon on the Mount is against this unbrotherly feeling, they are unwilling, though professed followers of Christ, to say, 'this black man is my brother and has a man's rights.' They cannot take a black man into their religious institutions, even when he is weak and exhausted by the toils and disappointments and diseases of this world, and say, 'Rest here in peace, brother; God will show you the way.' That Christian spirit of brotherhood is reserved for all nations and races of the earth save the American Negro. In all civilized communities the Negro, even the American Negro, is welcome and welcomed, save in such communities as are protected by the Star Spangled Banner, the emblem of the land of the free and the home of the brave. I leave you now, Malcolm; but I feel that God has made some white men after His own image. I feel that, should I never come back, my good name will not suffer in your keeping. Good-bye, my brother!"

"Good-bye, old boy," said Malcolm, as their hands doubled over each other—and Abe was gone.

As Malcolm stood listening to Abe's receding footsteps he suddenly remembered that Abe had no money. Taking all he had (forty dollars), he wrapped it in his handkerchief, well knowing that Abe would not accept it if given openly, and called to Abe, saying that he wanted him to take this handkerchief, as that was all he had to give him. Abe placed the handkerchief in his inside pocket, remarking that he would keep it always.

After Abe's departure, Malcolm soliloquized: "Why was Abe not made white the same as I am? Why should a man of his fine intellect and sensibilities be placed in this world where he is looked down upon even by the most ignorant of white men? What, indeed, must be his feelings as he meets that sentiment at every turn. But Tim Wardeman will surely die. Abe will come back as he said he would and go South with me and finish the rest. Poor old Mammy Rinda! My old black mother! I nursed at that breast, drew my life from her care. Father has told me time and again that but for Mammy Rinda's care I would not have lived. Now she is dead. Am I not a craven that I do not avenge her? Is she not the only mother that I ever knew? Beaten to death! My God! And I have not struck a blow in her defense, nor have I uttered one word in protest! Shame! Shame! And I am a white man! I shall go back home, and when Abe returns he will find nothing to be done. I shall finish where he left off. I shall see Mabel and go tomorrow."

With this determination uppermost in his mind, Malcolm sought the sleep which, try as he would, was denied him.

CHAPTER XXXIII.

ABE, after leaving Malcolm, went direct to the station, catching the Chicago express. While thinking over the events of the day Malcolm's gift presented itself to his mind. Upon examining the handkerchief he discovered the money which Malcolm had concealed in it. His first impulse was to return it to Malcolm when he arrived in Chicago. He concluded, after much thought, however, that to send the money back to Malcolm would be an offense which would wound his feelings. He felt that Malcolm had made a sacrifice for him which he should appreciate. His mind turned to the working out of some plan by which he could accomplish his mission without detection. Abe found that his money amounted to sixty dollars, all told, and that he must find employment to procure funds to pay his passage to St. Louis. While searching about the docks for a job, he fell in with a person who interested him a great deal. His new friend was a young white man, apparently thirty years of age, well educated, but a slave to drink, who said his name was "Draper." He could not be induced to talk further about himself. He appeared to "take" to Abe at sight. "Draper" worked upon the docks when he felt so disposed, seeming always to have a job at his disposal. He procured a job for Abe. The second day after they met, while waiting for a boat, Abe asked him why he did not let liquor alone, get himself together and go back to his home and friends.

"Draper, you are a bright man; you are College bred; you come of good stock; you have no excuse in the world for living as you do. Now, I am not trying to lecture to you; I simply hate to see you in this condition. Come, old man, tell me why you are throwing your life away?"

"Black" (this is the name he gave Abe when they first

met), "I do not acknowledge your right to ask me such questions. But your motive is a good one, and I will tell you what I have never told my own brother, the last of my blood living. You say that I come from good stock; you are right. I come from the best in the State of Louisiana. My brother and myself are the only survivors, however. I came through Oberlin College. My brother is there now and will finish this school year, I think. I have a letter from him in which he begs me to come to see him or let him know where he can see me. Black, what would you do? Send for the kid or go to him? Do you think I would look good at College in these togs? Well, I guess not. We have money between us, plenty of it. What do I care?"

"Yes, yes," said Abe; "but Draper you have not told me why you do not care. What makes you so reckless?"

"Black," he said; "I have been grossly deceived by a woman. I loved her beyond all reason. She deceived me; married another man, inferior to me in all respects, and——"

"Say, Draper, does he keep sober?" laughingly inquired Abe.

"Why do you laugh, Black?" asked Draper.

"I did not intend to offend you, but you assume that you are superior to somebody," answered Abe. "Look at yourself. May not this young lady have seen your weak point and been afraid to trust her future in your hands? Do you think that being deceived by a woman is a sufficient excuse for your doing those things which would break your mother's heart, were she living? No, Draper, you are showing a weakness that this young lady may have discovered, and you are simply justifying her. Cut the booze out, old man. See your brother. Go home and be a man."

"Black, you are certainly taking great liberty in telling me what to do. I did not ask you for your advice, did I? But, I'll think this thing over."

"Come on, Draper; there is our boat. We can get seven
hours off her; that will take us up to dark. Then we can go
to the Y. M. C. A."

"Y. M. C. A.?" asked Draper; "what put that into your
head? I have not been inside of one for two years. Then
they drove me out. But we will go."

That night Abe and his friend made their way to the
Y. M. C. A. building—a large and commodious place, given
over to the reformation and upbuilding of the men along the
docks. The building was filled with all the conveniences need-
ful for such work. The dormitory was a model in itself.
After hearing a long and very instructive lecture by a local
preacher, without a charge, Abe and his friend betook themselves to the library. They had been seated but a short time
when a gong sounded and the inmates of the library arose and
began to file out of the room. Abe and his friend sat still.
Soon the Superintendent came to them, remarking that he
observed they were strangers. He also remarked that the
gong had sounded for bedtime. Turning to Draper, he asked:
"Do you expect to tarry with us tonight?"

"Yes, that is what we came for," answered Draper.

"Well, er—you might—but, er—your friend—he, er——"
stammered the good man.

"He, er—hell! What is the matter with my friend?"
asked Draper.

The chargeless minister, who had just been discoursing so
eloquently on the brotherhood of mankind, together with two
other persons who were evidently Christian workers, joined the
group. "Well, er—the fact of the matter is, our rules forbid
the sleeping of colored men here; we will do all else we can
for them," said the Superintendent.

"Oh, I see! Dagoes, Sheenies—any old nation—is welcome
but the American Negro," said Draper. "Come, Black, let's
go back to Con McNulty's. We can get a room over his booze
joint, but you cannot get one in this Christian institution.

Black, I promise you not to touch a drop tonight." Then
turning to the minister, he remarked: "Doctor, how can you
reconcile the turning out into the streets of this man, at this
hour of night, with the doctrine you labored with so eloquently
for one and one-half hours this evening? The rules of your
Y. M. C. A. are paramount to the teachings of Christ, it
appears."

Before the man of God could answer Abe and Draper had
passed out into the street.

"Black, don't let a little thing like that worry you," said
Draper; "we are not far from a bed, and we have the price.
These Biblebacks are something awful; they don't have to
save the soul of an American-born Negro, but they will take
your money and go away off to Africa and hunt up some
heathen who does not understand their love for him nor their
talk nor their tracts. Here is Mac's place."

"Mac, we want two rooms."

"Sure! Dannie, me bye! Sixteen and seventeen. Show
the gintlemen up," said McNulty, without a moment's hesitation.

Several weeks after the Y. M. C. A. episode, while on their
way to the docks, Abe suddenly asked Draper what his brother's name was, saying that he had some friends at Oberlin
College.

"Black, you ask too many questions," said Draper; "but
I will tell you. That kid's name is Leon DeVaux. He is
the——

"Why, Black, what is the matter?"

Abe had grasped Draper by the shoulder and stood looking
at him in a way that was puzzling to his new friend.

"Leon DeVaux! And what is your name?" asked Abe.

"My name? What the h— do you want to know that for?
You are the most persistent black man I ever saw. Let go,
you are hurting me. Are you crazy?" said Draper, all in
one breath. "Well, I will tell you. My name is Napoleon

DeVaux. I am the ninth DeVaux of that name. But why do you ask?"

Abe was about to unburden himself, but wanted one more proof that this friend was what he seemed to be.

"One more question," said Abe. "What nickname has your brother?"

"We called him Onnie when he was a boy, and they called me Nips. Now, are you satisfied?" asked Draper.

"Yes, my friend, perfectly. Tonight, after work, I will tell you something that may interest you. I will say now, however, that I know your brother. And a man is he! DeVaux, I will never call you 'Draper' again. This is my last day on the docks. I am going to leave the city tomorrow. I have saved the amount of money that I needed, and more. I am going to the far West."

"Black, I am sorry to hear that. You have been an inspiration to me. Your disinterested friendship has kept me sober for three weeks. I have never before come in contact with a black man like you. I feel like a new man. We need not work today. Let us talk. I want to hear your story."

"Well," said Abe, after some thought, "let us hire a boat and go fishing. This is my last day with you, and we may as well spend it in pleasure. I want to say something to you which I hope you will appreciate."

Abe and his friend were soon out on the lake at the end of a deserted pier.

"Black, tell me about my brother," said DeVaux. "I am anxious to hear about him. I have not seen him for seven years. He was a kid when I left home."

"He is no kid now. He has been very kind to me," answered Abe. Abe then told DeVaux the part his brother played in his troubles, of how his brother believed in him, when he was accused of stealing Malcolm's pipe, of DeVaux's sending men down to Alabama to investigate the killing of his mother and sister; of the fact that he offered to go with him to his home to avenge the killings; of how his letter put him on the track of Tim Wardeman, and ended by saying that there was nothing in the world he would not do for him and that he would never be able to return his kindness.

"Abe, you have paid him. You have saved his brother from a drunkard's grave," said DeVaux. "When I first saw you I knew that you were a different kind of black man from any that I ever met. I liked you at sight. But when you began to point out to me my worthless life, I began to sober up. I felt the shame that only a Southern man of my blood can feel when his shortcoming are pointed out to him by a Negro. I felt at first that even this Negro feels himself above me. I know you better now. You are a man, although you are black. You are my friend. I am proud of that fact. You have awakened the DeVaux blood in me. You have done what the Y. M. C. A. failed with their rot and tracts to do. I also shall leave tomorrow. I go to Oberlin to see Onnie; then I shall go home, a new man. Abe, listen; this is on the word of a DeVaux. If you ever need a friend, if you need help on this errand of yours, whatever it may be, if you need money, no matter what amount, I will come or will send it. I care not to what part of the world I may have to go or send. That stands until death."

"DeVaux, I appreciate your offer. But I cannot draw any man into this affair of mine," said Abe. "You certainly make me feel proud when you say I have persuaded you to join your brother. Tell him that I shall always remember him. Tell him when he is Governor of his State to deal leniently with the misguided ones of my race who appeal to him. We had better go ashore now; it is getting dark."

"Abe, we will have a farewell supper tonight; then we part, maybe forever," said DeVaux.

These two men parted the next day, one bent upon beginning life anew, with the world open to him, notwithstanding his downfall; the other to seek the men who had ruined his life by murdering his mother.

They never met again.

CHAPTER XXXIV.

ABE left Chicago, going direct to St. Louis; he then made his way, as a laborer, to Nevada, entering the country in which he hoped to find Tim Wardeman. After a short search he located his man in a small mining camp where Wardeman was known by his loose habits and hard preaching. His wife (?) was also known to all the miners in that section. Abe set about to learn something of Tim's habits, and found that Tim spent much time fishing. Abe determined to surprise him while engaged in his pastime. While loitering about Tim's cabin, Abe heard him call to his "wife," saying: "Vinnie, I am goin' fishin'. I believe them fish'll bite better'n they did yestiddy."

"Goin' fishin'," cried Vinnie, "yer is always goin' fishin'." I never hears you say yer is goin' to chop wood ner tote a pail er water. Yer better tak dis chile out in der sun, ef yer don't wat hit ter die."

"I got no time to nus yer kid," growled Tim.

"No, in course yer haint." snapped Vinnie, "but yer had time to bring hit hyre. Yer ain't no man, yer know dat."

Tim shouldered his poles and walked away without further comment. Soon he was seated on the edge of a mountain pool, singing softly to himself:

"Camptown race track five miles long,
            Du a du a do,
Camptown ladies sing this song,
            Du a du a do,
Gwine to run all night,
Gwine to run all day,
I bet my money on the bobtail nag,
Some one take and bet on de bay."

Suddenly there was a movement behind him. Looking up

192

he found Abe Overley standing over him with a horse trace in his hand. Tim collapsed, and would have fallen into the water had not Abe caught him and pulled him away from the bank. When he recovered, he looked at Abe with bulging eyes, and fear and guilt were stamped on his every feature. Their eyes met. Tim felt that his time had come. His craven heart manifested itself. His one endeavor was to get away. He bounded to his feet in a vain attempt to escape, but was felled to the ground by a terrific blow on the top of the head that rendered him unconscious. When he regained his senses, he found himself stripped of clothing, bound to a stump, and Abe standing over him with a horse trace ready in his hand to administer the terrible blows that Tim felt were sure to come. He began to plead.

"Mr. Abe, would yer?"

"Did you ever see this horse trace before?" asked Abe, holding the trace before Tim's eyes.

"How kin I tell, I'se seed so many?" answered Tim.

"How many have you used on helpless old women?" demanded Abe.

"Deed, Mr. Abe, I never did sich a think in my whole life," was Tim's answer.

"Liar!" hissed Abe, at the same time bringing the trace down on Tim's shoulders with a force that split the skin. "Take that, and that,—maybe you can remember an old woman whom you beat to death with this very trace. Curse you, I am now going to treat you as you served her. I am going to beat you to death."

"My God! Mr. Abe, spare me," he pleaded. "Think of my wife and chile. They will suttenly starve without me to find for them."

"Your wife and child? They will suffer! Did my poor old mother suffer? Did my sister suffer when you brutes were tearing her garments from her back?" thundered Abe.

"Take that, you cursed brute, and that, and that. Yell, you dog. Did my mother's cries stop you? Yell, curse you. Your cries are what I have come to hear. Ha! ha! Yell! Yell! Damn you, yell!"

Abe stood over Tim and belabored him with the trace, first with an even stroke that was cruel and diabolical in its sameness of contact with Tim's body, each stroke cutting deeper and deeper into the flesh. Abe's temper arose with Tim's cries. He soon began to wield the trace with both hands, regardless of where the blows fell, until he stopped from exhaustion, dropping down beside his victim, who was unconscious.

Abe waited for Tim to recover, thinking then to finish his work. It was nightfall before Tim recovered, although Abe had repeatedly deluged him with water.

Tim's first cry was, "Spare me, Mr. Abe! Spare me fer my ole father!"

"Spare you for your old father!" yelled Abe. Did you spare my sister for her old father?"

"Mr. Abe, my po' ole mother, she——" With a cry that was beastly in its fierceness, Abe sprung upon Tim, dealing him a shower of blows that soon rendered him lifeless. Tim, as the life left his body, gave vent to one cry which was heard by two miners who, together with Vinnie, were in search of Tim. They immediately returned to their cabins, the miners leaving Vinnie in great haste.

When Abe discovered that Tim was dead, he cut a piece of the trace and hung it about his neck, after which he made his way to the cabin where he found Vinnie cowering in great fear, the cry which she heard having completely unnerved her. When Abe strode into the room, she instinctively knew what had happened, but when she saw the blood-stained horse trace in Abe's hand her terror rendered her helpless. Abe stood in the gloom of the poorly lighted room, gazing

intently at her. Vinnie was held transfixed by his gaze,
her eyes bulging, her tongue refusing to move. At last she
whispered in a voice, uncertain and weak, "Abe Overley?"

"Yes," said Abe, "I have come to tell you not to move out
of this cabin, not to let any person in, nor to tell any person
on earth that you ever saw me in this country. If you do,
the voice that you heard on the hill an hour ago will call you
to that door. Do you understand?

"Yes, Abe, I does, an' will do jus' as yer says," was her
trembling reply. "But Abe, yer is goin' 'way. Don't leave
me here. We was chillen togedder, yer tooked me ter Sunday school many a time; tek me back ter the ole place. Abe,
I'll be yer wife. I swears ter yer, Abe, I never had a 'nigger'
man in all my life. Ise always been a good woman. I——"

"Been a good woman?" was Abe's contemptuous reply.
"What do you call that?" pointing to the child. "Be my
wife! Move out of this cabin before twelve o'clock tomorrow night and you will join Tim Wardeman in hell." With
this remark, Abe left Vinnie, as he had a distance of ten
miles to walk to catch the Overland express to Utah City.
Abe reached that city in safety. He then went to San
Francisco, from which city he shipped on a coastwise
steamer plying between San Francisco and Vancouver.
From Vancouver Abe made his way to Windsor, Canada,
from which point he wrote Malcolm, asking whether it was
advisable for him to come to Oberlin. Malcolm wrote him
that he might come in perfect safety, and Abe left Windsor,
arriving in Oberlin ten days before Christmas.

When he left Vinnie, she sat for a long time trying to
think what was best to do. Suddenly she thought of a miner
by the name of Hutchins who had been very friendly to her
in Tim's absence. She arose and looked out of the door,
remarking that surely it was after twelve o'clock. In reality
it was little past sunrise. Vinnie determined, however, to

make her way to Hutchins' cabin, the location of which she knew very well.

"Hutch, I'se come ter ax yer what I am ter do. Tim ain't come back, an' me an' Ben an' Jim Waters her'n sick a yell when we was lookin' fer him thet we was feared to go any furder."

"Well, Vinnie, I am sure I don't know," answered Hutchins, "where did this yell come from?"

"Over by the pool in Devil's Holler," said Vinnie.

"Vinnie, you stay here; I will take Jim and Ben and see if I can find the parson. Was he drunk or sober when he left home?"

"He was sober. He hain't been drunk now for mor'n a week. Hutch, I'll stay right here 'till yer comes back and longer, too, ef yer says so."

After several hours' hunt, this trio of Tim's members found their parson bound to a stump, dead; his body covered with cuts and bruises and a small piece of horse trace on a string tied about his neck. Hutchins hastened back to Vinnie to break the sorrowful news, while Jim and Ben went in search of a team to convey the body to the parsonage.

"Vinnie," said Hutchins as he entered the cabin in great haste, "you are free. The parson is dead. We found his body. Now, ah, what did you say when I left, about staying here?"

"I said I would stay here if yer said so," answered Vinnie.

"Yes, but what are you going to do with that child? That is the parson's child; I don't want it."

"No it ain't his'n, its your'n," answered Vinnie.

"Mine? No, it is not mine. You cannot put that on me," said Hutchins.

"Well it's as much your'n as its his'n, yer knows thet, don't yer?"

Hutchins agreed to take Vinnie to himself. Three years later he struck a very rich vein of ore and left the mining camp, taking his family of three children and his half-breed Indian wife with him. It is not known whether Vinnie ever saw her mother and brothers again. It is to be hoped that their new life and new surroundings will be an inspiration to them. Parson Tim was taken to the parsonage by his members and prepared for burial. In the absence of either undertaker or preacher, the preparation and burial were not of long duration. Tim died as he had lived—a miserable wretch.

CHAPTER XXXV.

UPON Abe's arrival in Oberlin he proceeded at once to Miss Watson's home. After a short wait Miss Watson came into the room, greeting him with a smile, saying:

"So you have arrived? How long have you been in town? I have been——."

"I have been in town just thirteen minutes," said Abe, so solemnly that Miss Watson gazed at him in wonderment. "I came to you direct from the station. There is something I want to say to you and then I shall leave Oberlin immediately — without seeing another person. Nancy, I have been thinking of your promise, that you would some day be my wife. I have come to the conclusion that I should not hold you to that promise, and that I should not expect you to marry me after I have steeped my hands in human blood. Nancy, I give—I release—I insist that you cast me off, for your own good. You should not marry me, in simple justice to yourself. You would always think of me as a murderer. Our children would have a murderer for a father. As you pressed your child to your breast you would be oppressed with the feeling that its father is a murderer. I cannot bring you to this. God alone knows where or how my life will end. I therefore do not feel that I am showing my love for you by dragging you into the mire with me."

"Abe, listen to me," said Miss Watson, earnestly. "I understand and appreciate all that you have said. I thought of those things before I gave you my promise. My father has since spoken to be along the same lines, but I see no reason why I should change toward you. I will keep my promise!"

"Nancy, your confidence in me gives me strength and I

love you more for it," said Abe, implanting a fervent kiss upon her forehead.

"Abe, what do you propose to do now?" asked Miss Watson.

"I am going home to settle accounts with Jack Smaly and Buck Lashum," answered Abe.

"Abe, when all this is ended, what will you do the rest of your life?" inquired Miss Watson.

"I do not know, Nancy. I shall do something that will gain us a livelihood," was Abe's reply.

"When are you going home? When do you start?" was Miss Watson's next query.

"I will leave here tomorrow at midnight. I want to join Jack Smaly in his Christmas festivities." answered Abe. "But before leaving I want to see Mr. Donewell. I will leave you now. May I return later?"

"I will inform you when you return whether or not you may remain," laughed Miss Watson.

Abe went immediately to Malcom's room, where he found the latter hard at work.

"Hello, Malcolm! How are you? Are you still in the lead in your classes? You look well. Hard study and good company seem to agree with you. Why, what is that you are reading? For what are those clothes being aired? I never saw those full dress clothes before. What's coming off? Going to a ball? Don't let my coming stop you. I want to see——"

"Abe Overley!" interrupted Malcolm. "I have been looking for you for several days. You are hurting my hand. How can I answer all those questions? I am not going to a ball. I am going to be married."

"Be what!" exclaimed Abe. "Be married? Will your father be present? When will the event take place? To-night! Want me to stand with you? Malcolm, are you crazy? That would never do. Tell me about it."

Malcolm told Abe that he and Miss Mabel Donewell were to be quietly married that evening and were to start immediately for Cleveland and New York, leaving New York in time to reach home Christmas day. Abe was also informed by Malcolm that he had not consulted his father,—that the whole thing was intended to surprise him.

"I have no doubt that it will surprise him," said Abe. "You have my word for it that what he will say will also surprise your bride."

"Be that as it may, I want you to stand with me,—to give me away," laughed Malcolm.

"I have no clothes," said Abe, "nor do I think it proper for me to join the company in which I would find myself should I accede to your request."

"I have had several full dress suits brought here for you to select one from," said Malcolm. "It is out of the question for you not to be present at my marriage. You are my only friend at this College. Would you desert me at this time?"

"No, Malcolm, of course not. I will wear those clothes and try to look happy for your sake," said Abe. "But, Malcolm, this is very sudden, is it not?"

"Yes, it is sudden," answered Malcolm.

DeVaux soon came into the room in company with his friend from Tennessee; they, together with Rattles and Forbes, having promised to stand by Malcolm, and make all the trouble possible for him. They had bribed the Negro coachman to drive them out toward Lake Erie, to within a short distance of a road house kept by Joe Hilton, where he would be met by those young men, who would stop the carriage, relieve them of their baggage and valuables, detach the horses, and leave the bride and groom to find their way, as best they could, to the road house. Abe learned of the plot and determined to frustrate their plans. The driver was again bribed, this time by Abe, to let him (Abe) drive in his stead. After the ceremony and while the couple held an impromptu reception, Abe slipped out of the house, donned the driver's livery, and took his seat upon the box. DeVaux came out and asked the driver if everything was all right, Abe said: "Yes, sah," then added: "Boss, can't yo' gin de ole man another ten; I'se lierble to git fired fo' dis."

"Here's the money, old man; now keep your head and drive fast."

"I'll sho' drive fas', sah," said the driver, with a broad grin.

DeVaux did not recognize Abe in the darkness. Soon Malcolm and his bride came out followed by the throng of mischief makers. They put the bridal couple in their carriage, remarking to the driver that he had just seven minutes to catch the midnight express.

"I'll git thar, sah," said Abe.

DeVaux and his friends got into their carriage motioning Abe to proceed, the whole party moving off at a terrific rate. At the second corner Abe turned toward the station. The occupants of the other carriages noticed this move. Then began a race to the station that was fast and furious, but of short duration. Abe dashed up to the platform just at the express was pulling in. He jumped off the box and opened the door, saying:

"Quick, Malcolm, run for the train." Noting Malcolm's hesitation, for he did not recognize Abe in his livery, Abe grasped him by the arm and pulled him out of the carriage.

"Run for the train, I tell you; they are coming."

Malcolm did not need a second warning, but hurried aboard. Abe grasped the baggage and was soon on the train. They were not seated, however, before Malcolm's friends were also in the coach. They started for the supposed coachman, but recognized Abe. The trick was apparent and the joke was on them. Abe relieved himself of his livery, passing it out to the Negro coachman, forgetting at the same time that he had placed DeVaux's ten-dollar bill in the pocket of the coat, where it was found by the Negro driver.

DeVaux extended his hand to Abe, saying: "Abe, in consideration of what you did for my brother in Chicago, I forgive you this trick."

Abe laughingly replied that he appreciated his goodness of heart and as an evidence of that good will DeVaux might call on Miss Watson and explain Abe's sudden departure. Soon the train was on its way to Cleveland.

"Abe, tell me about this escapade. What had those fellows planned to do?" asked Malcolm.

"Mr. Overley, do tell us. From their disappointed looks I know they had planned something that would have annoyed us very much," said Mrs. Overley.

"Yes," said Abe, they had planned to delay your departure. You were to be driven out on the road toward Lake Erie, held up by highwaymen, robbed of bag and baggage, the horses detached from your carriage, and you were to be left to the tender mercies of the storm."

"I would not have cared, would you, Malcolm?" asked Mrs. Overley, as she nestled close to him.

"Cared! Of course I would. Suppose you had become chilled and caught cold? I would never have forgiven those fellows," said Malcolm. "Abe, how did you manage to frustrate them?"

Abe then related his connection with the affair, also stating that DeVaux had given him a ten-dollar bill which he put in the pocket of the coachman's coat and forgot it when the coat was returned.

"Abe, where are you going now?" suddenly asked Malcolm.

"Why, Malcolm, do you think you can get along without my care?" laughed Abe.

"I will be glad if you will stay with us," said Malcolm, "but as you have said nothing of your intentions, I, of course, do not know what to expect."

"Malcolm, I am going home. I want to arrive at night. I will have ten miles to walk across the country. My plans must all be arranged before Christmas day. I will have but two days in which to perfect them. So you may expect me to leave you in Cleveland," said Abe.

When the train bearing Mr. and Mrs. Malcolm A. Overley, Jr., reached Cleveland, Abe took his leave of them and they betook themselves to a hotel.

CHAPTER XXXVI.

MALCOLM made known to Mr. Donewell his love for the latter's daughter, Mabel; his desire to marry her and take her to his home to spend the Christmas holidays with his father. Mr. Donewell gave his consent, seeing therein an opportunity to release the Overley estate without seeming to be doing an act of charity. When it became known at the College that Malcolm and Miss Mabel were to be married the presents and congratulations were numerous. Mr. Donewell concluded to make up a large party and visit the bride and groom on the Overley plantation. Dean Stearnly, Professors Smirchum and Narrows, together with several others agreed to join the party. It was not convenient for Dr. Finley to leave the College at this time.

Dean Stearnly was a native-born Southern man, with all the peculiarities of the upper-class Southern people; open, honest, frank, having a thorough knowledge of Southern conditions, gleaned by personal observations and early environment. Professors Smirchum and Narrows had made a study of Southern life from books, newspapers and magazine articles. The primary object of this trip was to study conditions in the South. Mr. Donewell's party proceeded to Mobile, Alabama, direct, where it was arranged they would be joined by Malcolm and his bride.

The arrival of such a distinguished party of Northern visitors created quite a little excitement among the hospitable Southerners, and they vied with each other in showing courtesies to Mr. Donewell's party. Mr. Donewell himself had traveled extensively throughout the South, and his large business interests made him well known to many of Mobile's leading citizens and merchants. The second night of their stay in Mobile was enlivened by a banquet given in their honor, at which Southern wit and impulsiveness were pitted against Northern brains and caution.

Among the Southerners was a former United States Senator who was "disingenuous" enough to assume that he, too, like other United States Senators, could annex the public domain to his private belongings while bellowing "wolf!" on the floor of the United States Senate. This distinguished Senator's doctrine as to the ultimate results of the education of the American Negro is sound, for he predicts what will surely happen as a result of the education of the Negro—his ascendency over the "cracker."

In this assemblage was a Governor, of questionable lineage, who was notorious as the apostle of the doctrine of arson for Negro schools, colleges and churches, and no State appropriation for Negro education. The good people of his State, however, appear later to have swept him and his doctrine into oblivion. We also find around the banquet table Southern men of wealth, culture and influence, whose ideas are always sound on the policies of State and Government. The speeches that brought out the sentiments of the banqueters were made by Dean Stearnly, who made the final speech, Professors Smirchum and Narrows, the former Senator and the Governor just mentioned. John K. Evers presided as toastmaster.

In response to the toast, "Education in the South," the former Senator said, as he slowly arose to his feet:

"Mr. Toastmaster and Gentlemen: I guess you all know who I am, and knowing me, you know my sentiments on this troublesome question. We need education in our Southland; I mean education in its broad sense, and I mean education for the white man. Gentlemen, you cannot discuss this question and leave the 'nigger' out." This last remark was brought forth by murmurs of disapproval when the drift of the Senator's talk was noted. "Up in my State there is an agitation now on foot for compulsory education. They don't seem to understand what that means. It means that 'niggers' must be educated, the same as white men. It means that in a few more years 'niggers' will be able to qualify to vote the same as white men. Do you want that?" Cries of "Yes," and cries of "No," were heard from different parts of the hall. It could not be determined which sentiment prevailed. There were enough cries of "Yes," however, to encourage those who believe that the Southland has reached its awakening day. The Senator resumed, saying: "I know that education increases intelligence, increases the usefulness and value of the citizen. I——."

"Then why not educate these 'niggers?'" asked a voice to the Senator's left.

"Because education makes them too 'damn smart.' Have you ever come in contact with an educated 'nigger?'" the Senator asked.

"Yes, hundreds of them. Does not education make him a better citizen?"

"Can a 'nigger' be a good citizen, when he is out of his sphere?" was the Senator's reply. "I know the 'nigger's' place, and it is not in the schools, nor is it at the polls, where he is dictating to white men. His business is to do the white man's bidding. This is a white man's country. I tell you if you persist in this fool idea of educating those 'niggers,' in one more generation they will have their feet on our necks; they will rule us instead of our ruling them. I——"

"Why, Senator, can these ignorant Negroes overcome your race in one generation? Are your people at a standstill? Are you retrograding?" asked a Northern man.

"Overcome! Standstill! Retrograding! Hell, no! My people are the finest in the world. Before they will be overcome they will shoot every damn 'nigger' off the face of the

earth. Standstill! Retrograde! White men cannot retrograde. We are burdened with this 'nigger' load. If there
were no 'niggers' in- —.''

"Yes, but that does not answer my question," persisted
the Northerner. "How, under a compulsory education law,
can one part of a community outstrip another, all things
being equal? If your people are superior to these people,
and I assume that they are, wherein lies the danger? Would
not their education be a positive benefit? Would——.''

"You are entering into a discussion of a matter that
Northern men cannot understand; only Southern men are
capable of understanding this question, of explaining it in
its proper light," was the Senator's peevish reply.

"Yes, I suppose so," was the snappish rejoinder. Cries of
"order" came from all parts of the hall.

"Mr. Toastmaster," continued the Senator, "I have been
interrupted. I had not contemplated a discussion of this
'nigger' question. In conclusion, let me say, and to this I
stick, that the only possible way for us to maintain our suprem-
acy is not to educate these 'niggers.' By their education
we are only hastening the day of conflict between the races."

When the Senator resumed his seat he seemed a bit surprised that his sentiments fell flat upon all his hearers, save
the Governor.

Professor Smirchum responded to the toast: "The College
as it Shapes the Destinies of Nations." The Professor en-
larged on the beauties of College life. The ties of friendship
that are formed at Colleges and never severed. The many
great men that have gone forth from them who have made
the world better by their teachings. That the College is
the great beacon light which attracts all men. That the
great God of the Universe had put it into the hearts of men
of means to endow Colleges in large sums of money that
their usefulness to all mankind might be perpetuated.

"But," added the Professor, "there is one element of our society, the Negro, which is not contemplated in the organization of our Colleges, who has become so persistent that we cannot keep him out, and who is creating no end of trouble. We should keep the Negro out of our Colleges."

"Why?" came the question in a chorus of voices.

"Well, because we should," answered the Professor.

"An excellent reason," laughed a questioner.

"Have you ever taught a Negro?' asked the Professor.

"Oh, yes; I have been teaching them all my life," was the response. "I played with them when a child. I have eaten, drank, slept, and shared my roof with these people, as all Southern men of the old families have, and will do again. But, Professor, I am interested in your remarks. The great God of the Universe is the head of all Northern Colleges, is he not?"

"I do not care to enter into a discussion of that question with the gentleman. Suffice it to say, this Negro element is causing a great deal of trouble in our Colleges." The Professor seated himself, not wholly satisfied that his tirade had struck a popular chord.

In response to the toast: "The State" the Governor gave his experience as Governor. He spoke of the great trials and burdens that a governor has to bear, how perplexing it is, at times, to determine what course to pursue. He thanked God, however, that he always knew what course to take when it came to 'niggers.'

"I cut off our money that was appropriated for 'nigger' normal schools. I would rather see this money burned than be used for such a purpose," shouted the Governor, making this last statement in a loud voice as the climax to his speech. As he took his seat he wondered what had come over these Southern people that such sentiments failed to arouse them. The Governor failed to see, as some of his Southern brethren for years had failed to see, that the world is moving forward and not backward, and that even the South must move on or stand a desert country in a land of plenty.

Professor Narrows was called upon to respond to the toast, "The Ladies," though none were present. He did justice to his subject, not once referring to Negroes. It would have been very bad form, indeed, to have referred to a Negro while speaking to the toast, "The Ladies."

The Professor seemed to be aware of this rule of Southern etiquette.

When Dean Sternly arose to respond to the toast. "Mankind," there was a momentary silence, a stillness that was broken only by a greeting of hand-clapping which was accorded no other speaker of the evening. His eyes sought those of the former Senator. The difference betwen these men was very marked. The former Senator was of the mushroom variety. His family had never been heard of beyond the limits of his native county, until his advent into politics. His general air, his table manners, his deportment, did not bespeak the cultured gentleman. His whole appearance gave unmistakable evidence that he was born of no gentlewoman, but was undeniably a scion of that "cracker" element that a turn of the wheel of fortune had suddenly tossed into prominence.

"Mr. Toastmaster and Gentlemen," said Dean Sternly, "I did not expect to be called upon to discuss the Negro, when I accepted your invitation to respond to the toast 'Mankind.' But it appears to me, from the remarks of the gentlemen who have preceded me, that they consider him, at least, a part of mankind. That, to me, is very encouraging.

"It may be proper at this point to state that I am a native of this State, of this county, of this city. My ancestors were among the first settlers here, when Alabama was a trackless forest, inhabited only by the aborigines and wild animals.

My ancestral home across the river can still be seen from the windows in this hall. There, ten generations of Stearnlys have lived and contributed in no small degree to the property, the strength, the intelligence of our dear old State. I make mention of these facts that you may all know not only that my training was received here, my sympathies are here, but that this Negro question is nothing new to me. I have known the Negro all my life. I have lived with him on those dear old hills across the river, and I have loved him for his simple faith, his unquestioning devotion, his unselfish service to me and mine.

"Mr. Toastmaster and Gentlemen, I am going to say some plain, unvarnished things to you. Let me say, first of all, that I am thoroughly aware of the fact that it is not popular in this section of the country to tell men of their faults, particularly when those faults have relation to their treatment of the Negro. The world would be better off, mankind would suffer less from chicanery and deceit, there would be less heartache, if we would frankly tell our brothers, in love and not in anger, of their faults. I feel perfectly justified tonight because of my ancestry and my relations in talking frankly upon this Negro question, which has been so unfairly and so unjustly handled here tonight.

"When he states that it is better to keep white children in ignorance and not force them by legislative enactment to attend school, for fear that the same law will force Negro children to attend school, the Senator lays down a most remarkable doctrine. It is preposterous that the relative education of the Negroes and the whites will result in the domination of the whites by the blacks. For us to believe that the shotgun and the torch are the necessary sequels of a compulsory education law is to admit that the Negro is the superior race, and ours the inferior one, and that we fear the loss by force of the position we now hold by fraud. It is no compliment to the intelligence and standing of the gentlemen who are present tonight for such sentiments as we have heard here to be heralded to the whole country as the opinion of the sober-minded and better-thinking whites of the South I do not subscribe to such sentiments and wish most emphatically to be put on record as expressing my disapproval of them. Such ideas are in contravention of the spirit of the Constitution of the United States, which every good citizen is pledged to uphold and support. They are opposed to the doctrines of Christianity, which teaches the Fatherhood of God and the Brotherhood of Man. They violate the spirit of our American civilization, which declares for equal rights for all and special privileges for none.

"If we are not patriotic enough to uphold our Constitution; or, if we do not accept the Christian doctrine of Brotherhood; or, if we do not believe in the theory of equal rights, as business men we ought to seek the Negro's elevation politically, socially, and economically; because the more we elevate him and increase his earning power, his saving power, and his intelligent appreciation of his relation to his community, the more valuable he is to us. He becomes a land owner and must need money which he will invest in our stocks and deposit in our banks. As he earns more he spends more. Intelligence and education increase his needs and wants, which we alone can supply. It is worse than suicidal for us to restrain and restrict the development of such an element in our community.

"The rural Negroes in this county earn on the average eight dollars per month. Nearly every dollar of it comes back to us through our stores and business people. Suppose in some way we could increase their earning power to twenty, thirty, or fifty dollars per month; their additional earnings would still come to us. If you had a piece of poor land, would you keep it poor? Would you use every effort to prevent the improvement of the land or would you fertilize and cultivate it so as to increase its productive power? Of course you would improve it. Why not pursue the same course toward the Negro. If schools improve the earning power and civic value of the whites, they will do the same for the Negro. If kindness and brotherly love and opportunity make the white man a better citizen, they will make the black man more useful and more valuable. Whenever a citizen is made better the community is made richer. It would seem therefore that this attitude of repression and proscription toward the Negro is not only un-American, un-Christian, and unjust, but it is positively impairing the very communities we are pretending to serve.

"Again, it is impossible to practice such injustices upon our weaker brother without directly injuring and preventing the right development of our own moral natures. To cultivate unreasoning prejudice, to concoct schemes which are aimed at the peace, happiness or welfare of another is to set in motion influences that sap out the sweetness and beauty of our souls. This sort of an attitude embitters our own lives, handicaps our children, spoils our women, degrades our homes and undermines our civilization. I cannot understand and have never understood why we commit ourselves to this unwise and un-Christian policy.

"For myself, there is no right or privilege which I enjoy or which I seek for my family that I am not willing to accord to the humblest Negro in the land, and I believe that it is in this spirit that the proper solution of this vexed question must come.

"We must realize and accept the fact that we cannot keep among us and treat as aliens a race of people who are worshiping the same God, reading the same Bible, attending the same school system, serving under the same flag, forming a part of the same civilization. We must accept them as a part of our homogeneous population and treat all alike, or we must get rid of them entirely. Since the latter is impossible, the former is clearly our duty.

"Let me urge you to educate the Negro to see political issues as you do; to treat him politically as you do other races of mankind that have come among you.

"Your legislature has just enacted a State-wide prohibition law. In Mobile it is enforced strictly against the Negro. The Negro dens and saloons have been closed up and it is well-nigh impossible for Negroes to obtain intoxicating liquors, a thing for which the better class of Negroes are truly thankful, while the low and vicious whites have free access to it. Your prohibition law, so far as it is enforced, is similar to your educational qualifications as to the franchise. You place before these people an incentive, an obstacle to overcome, which you do not place before the ignorant of your own race. Illiteracy among the poor whites is not decreasing as rapidly as it is among the Negroes. The poor whites have practically the same percentage of illiteracy now as they had fifty years ago. You say to the Negro, educate your children. You leave the ignorant white man to flounder on and on, upon the theory that because he is a white man, that will suffice. It does seem to me that the folly of such a policy should be apparent to all men.

"Gentlemen, do you know what these Negroes are doing? Do you know that they control just a few thousand less than five hundred million dollars worth of farm property in this country? Do you know that they own and operate farms valued at six millions of dollars more than the total of all capital invested in manufactories in the twelve Southern States in eighteen sixty? This farm land that they own and operate if put acre to acre would make a strip of land five miles wide that would reach from New York City to San Francisco. If by nineteen forty, as predicted by the United

States Census Bureau, the illiteracy of the Negro disappears and the ratio of their increasing wealth continues, what will you do? You will have forced him to qualify for the ballot, both educationally and financially, and by this course will have made a man of him, as it were, at the same time leaving the poor white where he has been for generations. You have kept the Negroes out of your lives, politically. You have not taught him to believe in your political creed; but you have taught him that your creed means disfranchisement and oppression for him and his children. You will have educated him up to the white man's standard and that standard set by yourselves. He will be an American citizen, thanks to your foresight. What will you do with him?

"Gentlemen, there is but one way to solve this question. That is, to prove the superiority of your race. Treat these people, as you do all other peoples who come among you; educate them up to your way of thinking; make your interests their interests. Bind them to you by kindness and consideration and make them feel that their interests lie with the men who are native to the soil. I beg that you gentlemen will bear with me for confining myself wholly to the Negro question; but it seems that this is the all-absorbing topic in most Southern gatherings of the day, and unless we take a more rational view of it we will lay the foundation of trouble for the generations to come."

When Dean Stearnley had finished a silence filled the hall. Many gentlemen left their seats to congratulate him. This line of argument, so different from that usually advanced by Southern men, caused considerable adverse comment from those who hoped to profit, politically, by keeping up a strife between the races; but it was plain that with a majority of those present Dean Stearnley had advanced a line of thought that struck responsive chords in their hearts. They were, many of them, tired of the everlasting flaunting of the Negro bugaboo for political purposes and were sincerely desirous of devoting their time and their talents to the best interests of the South; and they welcomed this new doctrine as sane and safe.

The Senator and his followers who had profited by preaching "nigger," "nigger," all the time, did not dare assail Dean Stearnley's arguments, which were so plainly true and unanswerable, but waited until they were among the class of whites who are always ready and willing to listen to this senseless babble.

After spending some time in after dinner conversation, Dean Stearnley's party, which now included Malcolm and his bride, left the hall and resumed their journey to the Overley plantation, in A—— County.

CHAPTER XXXVII.

WHEN Abe left Malcolm and his bride he proceeded at once to the County of C——, nine miles below the Overley plantation. He arrived near midnight, walking across the county to Cleo's cabin, where he rested during the day, while gathering the news of the neighborhood. Abe learned that Buck Lashum could be seen any fine morning in a glass inclosure, which his father had built on his front porch. His chair is rolled into this retreat where he is left for hours at a time.

Abe concluded to visit him in this place. When he saw Buck in his helpless condition, noticed his look of recognition, and that, although he could neither move nor speak, his face bore a look of terror, he concluded to leave him as he was, feeling that his punishment would be greater if left in that condition. Abe succeeded in regaining the Overley plantation without having been seen. Early Christmas morning, Abe, mounted on Ben, the Overley horse mentioned in a previous chapter, was riding through the back woods, when suddenly he came upon a horseman, who, upon seeing him, wheeled his horse and fled into the woods. Abe recognized Jack Smaly in the fleeing horseman.

"Go, Ben! Go!" cried Abe. The old racer seemed to understand that he was to make the effort of his life. Away he dashed along the cow path over which Jack was racing. Abe noticed that Jack was well mounted. His horse seemed scarcely to touch the earth, so quick was she in her movements.

"Ben, go! Are you going to fail me now? On! On! I tell you!" Abe had his horse trace buckled about his waist; he raised it above his head to deal old Ben a blow, but lowered his hand, muttering: "No, this is not for you.

216

Never will I disgrace you, old horse, by a blow with this blood-stained lash. This is for murderers."

The old horse, now thoroughly aroused, increased his pace, rapidly closing in on Jack, who seemed to know that he was being overhauled. A few more bounds brought them to a clearing, across which their course led. Jack turned in his saddle, with a pistol in his right hand, which he leveled and fired at Abe twice in rapid succession. Abe swung his horse to Jack's left, making it impossible for him to turn far enough in his saddle to get his range without unseating himself. Jack's movements were fatal to him, as they caused his horse to slacken her pace. At the same time his shots went wide of their mark. As old Ben came along side of Jack's horse, Abe dealt Smaly a blow upon the head which knocked him to the ground. Jack fell upon his head, the force of the fall breaking his neck.

Abe dismounted and hastened to his victim, thinking to lash him as he had his brother; but he found Jack dead, and concluded to leave him where he had fallen knowing that his friends would soon find him. Abe then went to his father's cabin, where he found the old man at breakfast, which had been prepared by one of Cleo's girls. After greeting his father, Abe greeted the girl just as if he had not seen her before. He remained until, by the confusion at the big house, he knew Malcolm and his bride and friends had arrived. Abe found them as Malcolm was introducing Mrs. Overley to his father.

"What is that you say, boy?" exclaimed the father. "Your wife? Who the ——? What the ——? How in the ——? You have disobeyed me, Sir. Abe, tell me what my Abe has done. Got married? Didn't he tell me that? Not one word, sir. You have disobeyed me. Abe," he cried, addressing Old Abe, "I have asked that boy of yours to tell me what my Abe has done. He does not obey me. Those devils still hang together and defy me. That boy has been married.''

Old Abe seemed to take in the whole situation at a glance. He went to Mrs. Overley, looking at her long and searchingly, then said: "Yo'll suttenly be welcome on dis heah place. Dem is Miss Miranda's eyes. Mr. Overley, Miss Miranda sent dat chile heah to look arter yo' in yo' ole days.''

There was a long silence, during which the old man looked first at Malcolm, then at the bride, and then at the assembled friends. Finally he extended a hand to Mabel, drawing her close to him, and as he did so he implanted a kiss upon her forehead. A great tear stole down his cheek, his lips trembled, he whispered in a voice scarcely audible, "Rinda," the name by which he always addressed Malcolm's mother. This act, simple and courteous in itself, revealed the true heart of this Southern gentleman.

Old Abe in a voice rich and melodious, one of those voices around which sweet memories of plantation life still cling, broke forth in the good old hymn:

> "Blest be the tie that binds
> Our hearts in sacred love;
> The fellowship of kindred minds
> Is like to that above.''

Old Abe's happy selection inspired the most cordial feelings among all the company.

Mr. John K. Evers, who had joined the party in Mobile, said to Malcolm A. Overley, Sr.:

"Mr. Overley, I wish to call your attention to the fact that it is now 12 o'clock, noon, December 25.''

He then produced the title deeds to the Overley estate which he had purchased at the auction. Mr. Evers delivered the deeds to Mr. Overley, who saw, as he hastily read them, that he still held title to his family estates. When the old man fully realized that the burden of his mortgage was lifted from him he staggered to a chair, where he remained several moments in deep thought. Finally he said:

"To whom am I indebted for this? Gentlemen, something has been done in this matter that I cannot accept. Somebody has paid by debts without my consent. Mr. Evers, I ask for a full explanation of this matter."

"Mr. Donewell here may be able to enlighten you," said Mr. Evers.

"This is Mr. Donewell, the father of your daughter-in-law, Mr. ——."

"Why, Malcolm, you have not introduced your friends to me. Why——."

"Dad, if you will only give me a chance I will be glad to do so," laughed Malcolm. Then followed a general introduction. After which Mr. Overley again asked the question as to how the mortgage on his place had been paid. Addressing himself to Mr. Donewell, he said: "I have been told, sir, that you can explain this matter. Who did this, and why was it done?"

"Mr. Overley, you are giving this affair too much consideration. I straightened the thing out. I felt that I had as much right to provide for my daughter as you had to provide for your son," laughed Mr. Donewell. "We concluded to keep this place in your family, provided we are permitted to live upon it at times."

"At times!" cried the old man. "If you are willing to take that disobedient boy of mine in exchange for this sweet girl, I am willing. I am glad enough to be rid of him. He has caused me no end of worry. But——. Come here, boy," addressing Malcolm. Malcolm A. Overley, Sr., placed his hands upon the head of the young couple remarking, "I give you both a father's blessing."

"Amen, I jes knowed yo' would," broke in Old Abe.

Messengers were sent out and soon the house was filled with
the friends and well-wishers of the Overleys, young and old.
A Christmas dinner was served amid wit and humor, the
kind only known to those who have enjoyed the hospitality
of the old plantations of the South.   Speech, song, and
laughter resounded through the rafters of the famous old
dining room until early morning. Abe's thoughts and feelings not being of the kind that held sway at the big house,
he had stolen quietly away and made his way to his mother's
grave. He cast himself upon the cold ground beneath which
she lay still and motionless.

"Mother, I have avenged thee. Thy murderers now lie
cold in death. Their jeers and curses are stilled forever.
Their pleadings and cries will be answered by the imps of
torment. Oh, great God! Where art Thou? Mother, my
work is done. What wilt thou have me do? The land of my
birth, the land of the morning of my life, the land that knows
all the sweetness of my childhood, the land that knows thy
motherly care, is accursed to me now. By the gods!" he
exclaimed, as he sprang to his feet, "I would that I could
kill each one of them over again. Oh, mother, guide me
anew. What wilt thou have me do?"

While Abe stood looking down upon his mother's grave
his father approached him and said: "My boy, come wid me,
I wants to talk to yo'."

Abe went to the old man's cabin, where he listened to plans
for the future. Abe did not divulge the secrets of his life
to his father.

Jack Smaly, after his horse had made its way home, was
found by his friends where he had fallen. The verdict of
the coroner's jury was, that he came to his death by a "fall
off his horse, which broke his neck." Jack's well-known
habit of riding through the woods to his home after his
nightly carousals paved the way for this verdict. Abe was
not mentioned in connection with his death.

CHAPTER XXXVIII.

NEW YEAR'S day came only too soon. Malcolm was reminded of the fact that he still had his course at Oberlin College to finish. His father insisted that the bride stay with him for a short time only. It was finally agreed that she would stay on the plantation until Easter time, when she, and the·Senior Overley, would visit Oberlin. At the end of the school year the Donewells and Overleys would make an extended tour of Canada and Europe. The party finally left. Abe bade farewell to his friends, the mates of his boyhood days, knowing that he would never return.

His farewell to his mother's grave was taken in silence. He approached the mound in company with his father, Messrs. Overley and Donewell, Dean Sternly and Professor Smirchum. This old woman's grave nestled among the graves of seven generations of Overleys, and was marked by a granite stone upon which was inscribed "Mammy 'Rinda," a term of endearment fully understood only by those who knew and appreciated her. As the party stood with uncovered heads different thoughts and feelings surged through their breasts.

Abe's sorrow was of the kind that wrings men's hearts. He was a strong man bowed with grief, a strong heart bursting with a sense of injustice. His whole being strained to the bursting point, with no outlet. Dry eyes, twitching mouth, clinched hands, rigid form, marked his terrible sufferings. All eyes were turned upon him. Professor Smirchum, who seemed to be greatly affected by Abe's mute agony, took his hand and said in a kindly voice:

"Mr. Overley, I am sorry, indeed, to see the extent of your sorrow. Your mother must have been a grand woman to

221

have deserved the respect she seems to have commanded. What can I do to help you?"

"Nothing, sir; I must begin life anew, and amid new scenes, new environments. From now on my success or my failure will depend upon my personal efforts."

Professor Smirchum drew to one side soliloquizing: "How could I have been so blind as to believe that these people are different from any other people. This trip reveals to me what they are doing, what they have done, in what respect vast numbers of them are held by the better class of whites. I am now convinced that the great howl and cry sent up by this Governor is a fear of what they are doing and not what they are not doing. He vetoed the bill appropriating money for a colored normal school. At the same time he was forced, as Governor, to sign charters for twelve Negro banks. Then these people raise thousands of dollars among themselves to carry on their school. What an object-lesson! Could there be a more convincing argument as to the energy that lies dormant in this race? What in the name of God will be the future of this people? If my Southern brothers do not bestir themselves, do not awaken their 'cracker' brother, these Negro people will own this fair Southland." Thus this new convert reasoned within himself.

"Abe, my boy," said Malcolm A. Overley, Sr., "I am still your friend in the full sense of that word. Whatever you do when you leave school, remember that I am entitled to know."

"Mr. Overley, I shall always remember you," answered Abe. "I shall always keep in touch with you. Your kindness to me is the one bright spot in my memory that binds me to this old plantation." As Abe finished Mr. Overley placed his hand upon his shoulder, saying with intense earnestness.

"My boy, that mound of earth covers one of the noblest

women that it has ever been my lot to meet. I can never forget that she took my Abe to her breast, a puny, sickly child, nursed him day and night, put new life in him, guided his footsteps, was a mother to him, indeed, until he is now the man of whom I am proud. That old woman was your mother. She was a slave in name, but never in fact. Boy, there is nothing I will not do for you so long as you are true to her teachings. Your old father has ever been my companion. We shall continue our journey of life together.''

''I thank you, Mr. Overley,'' said Abe, as they clasped hands.

Professor Smirchum had been a close observer of all that was transpiring. He had never dreamed of such friendships among the people of the South.

When the party turned to leave Abe put his arm about his father and said: ''Dad, I leave with Malcolm tomorrow. I have three more years in school in which time I hope to have finished a course in civil engineering; then, if God has been merciful to us, I will send for you to spend your last days with me and mine.''

The old man raised his eyes to heaven and said: ''Lawd, watch over my boy. Thy will be done.''

As the sun went down the next day, the Donewell car, with Abe aboard, crossed the Alabama line, bearing him away from scenes and faces which he was destined never to see again.

CHAPTER XXXIX.

WHEN the Donewell party arrived in Oberlin Abe took his leave of them, explaining that he would go to New York City and prepare himself for entrance to the College which he had selected. After tramping about the city for several days he procured a job as assistant janitor to an old Negro, who had charge of a flat building, at ten dollars per month and board. Abe soon made himself felt by his willingness to work. The owner of the flat, who was a prosperous Jew, watched Abe very closely. Noting his studious habits and general deportment, he concluded he would offer Abe a better job.

"Young man I haf noticed dot you never goes out. You haf always a book. What for you reads all of the time?"

"I am trying to prepare myself for College. I want to take a course in civil engineering," answered Abe.

"Vell, dot is very goot. I likes to see a young man dot is trying to help himself. I needs a goot man in a goot job. But you haf no vife. You gets yourself a goot vife, and I finds you a good job."

"Mr. Goldenheimer, your suggestion makes it well nigh impossible for me to accept," said Abe. "I am sure I do not know where I will find this good woman. What will this job pay?"

"Vell, for you and a vife I pays seventy-five dollars a month and rent free. Dot is very goot vages. I works for three dollars a week for two years onct. Vot you think of dot?"

"When do you want me to go to work?" asked Abe.

"I needs a man right avay," answered Mr. Goldenheimer. "But vy you axe ven I vants you?" Abe was silent for some moments. He was considering the advisability of explaining his love affair to Mr. Goldenheimer. Finally he said:

224

"Mr. Goldenheimer, I am engaged to a girl who is college bred, who has always had a good home, has never done work of any kind, save that which would naturally fall to her about her father's home. We are to be married when I finish my course. I do not feel that I should offer her this home, being so different from that to which she has been accustomed. But I am sure, sir, I can do your work as well without a wife, as I can with one."

"Young man, I pelebes you can. I make it a rule to hire no mans dot has not a vife," said Mr. Goldenheimer. "But I say dot if dot young lady ish a goot one she vill come. I vates two weeks. Nine hundred dollars a year. You mind dot?"

"What must I do? Will Nancy think me a fool if I make this suggestion to her? I will ask Uncle Joe and Aunt Jane what they think. I will also write Malcolm. Mr. Donewell ought to be able to write me what is best to do. Mr. Overley —but he is too far away. My father would be compelled to get some person to write for him." Thus Abe reasoned with himself. He finally concluded to write Miss Watson and explain the matter to her.

He wrote her as follows:

NEW YORK CITY, February —, 18—.

DEAR NANCY:

The contents of this note may not please you, but read it carefully and answer by return mail, as I have but two weeks to consider. Mr. Goldenheimer, for whom you will remember I am working, has offered me a position as janitor of a building at nine hundred dollars per year and house rent, light, and fuel free, provided I get a wife. Nancy, can you help me out in this matter?"

Yours, as ever,

ABE.

P. S.—Answer by return mail.

ABE.

P. S.—This offer is open to me for two weeks. Answer soon.

ABE.

When the letter reached Miss Watson she smiled to herself thinking that Abe must have been a bit agitated when he wrote. She, however, went immediately to her mother and put the letter in her hands. After reading the note several times, the mother said:

"Daughter, what do you want to do?"

"Go," was the daughter's brief reply.

"But will your father consent? This is so sudden," answered the mother.

Mr. Watson was called into the room and given the note. He, too, smiled when he read it.

"Daughter, this is a very sudden proposal. I am not prepared to give my consent. I will communicate with my friends in New York City. I have had dealings for years with a Goldenheimer, of that city. I wonder if this is he? However, daughter, I will not keep him waiting very long."

Mr. Watson called Mr. Goldenheimer, who was a wholesale grocer, over the long-distance telephone. He appeared to be satisfied with what he learned, but said nothing to his wife, preferring to wait for Abe's next note.

Abe received the following in reply to his urgent letter:

OBERLIN, OHIO, February —, 18—.

MR. ABRAHAM OVERLEY:

DEAR SIR—Your brief and ambiguous note has reached me. I am at a loss to understand just what you want. Can I "help you out?" Do you want me to look up some woman to be your wife? Two weeks is a very short time in which to undertake such an important matter. I will consult my mother. Maybe she can "help you out." In the meantime you write my father and ask his assistance. I will be glad to have your plans more in detail.

Your friend,

NANCY WATSON.

When Abe read Miss Watson's note he immediately forworded to her a full statement of his plans, laying great stress upon the fact that he could have his old father with him should he be able to obtain this position. He also wrote Mr. Watson, explaining the situation. Before the letter reached Mr. Watson, however, one from Mr. Goldenheimer had reached him in which he was told Abe would be carefully looked after and that so long as he did his work in a proper manner this job or something better was open to him. Ten days later we find Abe installed in his new home, a four-room flat which had been furnished by Mr. Goldenheimer as a present to the bride-elect.

Abe was the proudest man in all New York City. Miss Watson and her father were due in the city at 2 p. m., but we find Abe at the station before 1 o'clock, scanning the faces of the passengers as they pass out from the trains. Mr. Goldenheimer happened to notice Abe as he passed in with some friends, and said with a merry twinkle in his eye:

"My poy, vat you do here now? Your train ish not due for ein hour yet. You think dot girl vill go mit some fellow?" passing on before Abe could answer. At last Abe's vigil is ended. Miss Watson and her parents appear at the gates. The party was joined by several of Mr. Watson's friends, men of means, two of whom were real estate dealers, the third an undertaker. The party went immediately to the home of the editor of a well-known newspaper, where it had been arranged the marriage ceremony would be performed.

The eventful night of March 4, 18—, came. The wedding guests filled the editor's home to overflowing, elaborate gowns were conspicuous by their absence, it being understood that the bride would be attired in street costume. The Rev. Dr. C—— officiated. After the ceremony Mr. and Mrs. Overley received the congratulations of their friends after

which they quietly drove to their new home in company with
the bride's parents. Abe had written a long letter to his
father and Mr. Overley, explaining the situation, and received
their hearty consent and approval in return. Within six
months Mr. Goldenheimer raised Abe's salary to one hundred
dollars per month, saying that he considered the work more
than one man could do, and in view of the further fact that
the flat was filled and several prospective tenants were on
the waiting list. Abe's management of the building made it
a very desirable place in which to live. When he entered
College he was astonished to find that the two Japanese,
whom he had known at Oberlin College, had also entered
upon the same course which he had undertaken. Abe saw a
great deal of these men. They seemed to be very familiar
with certain facts connected with his past. At the end of
the first school year Abe found himself marked thirtieth in
a class of forty-four. He seemed very much disappointed at
his rating.

Mr. Goldenheimer said to him a few days later: "Vell, my
poy you pass. You do very well mit all dot vork to do.
I makes you my head janitor. You gets one hundred dollars
a month and rent free. You haf more time. You pass high.
How dot suit you?"

Mr. Goldenheimer, I scarcely know how to thank you,
I——."

"No; dot is beseness," interrupted Mr. Goldenheimer.
"You do my vork vell. You keep my house full all the time.
Now, you keep ten houses full and I pays you more. You
buys everything dot goes in dose houses. You keeps my
house account. Now, vat you say to dot?"

"I will do my best, sir," answered Abe.

"Vell, dot is beseness; ven you not do dot I pays you and
gets somepody," said Mr. Goldenheimer.

CHAPTER XL.

ABE now had more time to devote to his lectures, and with his wife's assistance he brought his rating at the end of his second school year up to sixth in a class of forty-nine. His wife was delighted with this improvement, though Abe insisted that but for her assistance he would surely have failed. At the end of his third year, when it was known that he was one of the first three of his class, now numbering forty, the Japanese approached him with a proposal which at first was very hard for Abe to resist. They called Abe's attention to the political conditions in the East, which were changing very rapidly. Japan was determined to be mistress of the Pacific, and in the near future he might hear the roar of Japanese guns off the Western Coast of the United States. They told him that he had no reason to love nor fight for a flag that was no protection to him; that the Japanese Government wanted educated American Negroes in her service, where his race would be no bar against his advancement. They explained to him further that they were princes of the blood Royal and were commissioned by the Mikado to enlist or commission recruits as they saw fit. They also stated that they had commissioned the three Negroes, who would graduate with them, Second Lieutenants in the Engineer Corps of the Japanese Army at a salary of sixteen hundred dollars per year, and they were frank to state that they wanted Abe because they felt that he would be of great service to Japan, should a conflict come on between the two countries. The wily Jap then pictured the lynching of Abe's mother and sister in such colors that the demon in him, which had lain dormant for three years, was aroused and took flaming hold on him once more. His blood took on the fire that arouses men to kill. He was in the full height of a consuming passion when the vision of Nancy and her child came before him. His passion was subdued. His calm reason regained its sway. Abe was himself again. He promised the Japanese that after he had consulted his wife he would give them a definite answer. When Abe arrived at home that night he found Nancy in a dimly lighted room, quietly rocking his little son, who seemed fretful. Nancy noticed by Abe's demeanor that something unusual had happened. Motioning him to a seat by her side she asked what was troubling him. Abe told her of the offer made him by the envoys of Japan laying particular stress upon the commission, but he said, speaking as if in a dream. "Can I renounce forever, the allegiance I owe my country because of personal wrongs, because of the crimes of murderers; can I renounce forever the land that gave my mother birth, the land in which she now lies buried; can I renounce forever, the land that my fathers knew, the land which I now know as my country, my home; can I renounce forever, the land of my few friends, the land in which they are daily appearing; can I renounce forever that which I know, and embark in a foreign land in that which is problematical; can I——?"

He suddenly sprang to his feet, saying:

"Nancy, my mother appeared to me in my thoughts. She held the Stars and Stripes proudly above her head while her other hand was extended to me. My mother wills that I shall defend the flag of my country."

Two days later the Japanese called upon Abe to obtain his final answer. He said: "Gentlemen, I have considered your proposition very carefully and conclude that, although the Stars and Stripes afford me little protection, although the laws of this land are interpreted against me, although the machinery of the law is too weak to bring the murderers of my mother to justice, in spite of these things and in spite of attempts at every turn to humiliate me, in spite of what may seem strange to you, that one part of a nation can and does hate another, I must decline your offer. Will you fight the land of the Rising Sun? No! Nor will I fight the land of my birth, over which the sun is now rising. I am proud that I am an American!"

The Japanese were astounded. They, like hundreds of thousands of other people, American citizens, too, never imagined that a Negro's heart was governed by the same honorable impulses that other men's are; that his soul is alive to the touch that stirs other men; in short, that a Negro is a Man.

Two weeks before Abe's commencement, Mr. Golden-heimer died very suddenly. Abe was notified that his services as superintendent would be dispensed with, but that he could have the choice of the care of any one of the flats, that now numbered thirteen, at seventy-five dollars per month. Abe immediately severed all connections with the estate. His wife, who handled his finances, showed him deposits to the amount of twenty-five hundred dollars, and Abe concluded to embark in the practice of his profession.

Abe's commencement day was June 1st, 18—. May 31st a long, legal envelope was handed Mrs. Overley by the postman. It proved to contain a very important document. It appears that Leon DeVaux had been making yearly trips to New York, and had kept in close touch with Abe's progress, through Mr. Goldenheimer, and knew his standing in the college. DeVaux's brother was the head of a large corporation that was reclaiming land in the lower counties of the State of Louisiana, and building a narrow-gauge railroad to the coast. This envelope contained a contract guaranteeing him employment for five years, at twelve hundred dollars the first year, twenty-four hundred dollars the second year, three thousand dollars the third year and thereafter. His

salary to commence June 1st, 18—. It also contained a draft
for five hundred dollars. When Abe came home his little
son came up to him and handed him these papers. Abe paid
no attention to them, but simply cast them upon the table,
and took the boy in his arms, remarking:

"Nancy, is it my turn to feed this young wolf of yours?"
For an answer the young mother handed the papers to the
child, who again handed them to his father. Abe's eye
caught sight of the check which had fallen to the floor. Upon
examining it he was amazed to find that it was drawn by
Napoleon DeVaux. He hastily examined the contract, noting
that he was not expected in New Orleans until the September
following.

"Nancy, you have certainly brought success to me. 'In
three years and thereafter' I will surely be earning three
thousand dollars per year. What shall we do with the four
months I have on my hands before September, when my
labors must begin?"

"Let us go to Oberlin and read up on Louisiana Geology,"
answered Mrs. Overley. "We can send for your father
again; maybe he will come to spend a few months with us;
he would not leave the plantation to live. It seems queer
that he should feel bound to stay on that place with Mr.
Overley until one of them dies. Malcolm is down there now,
and they do not need him."

"Nancy, you do not understand these old men. They love
each other as brothers love. Neither would live long without
the other. They have known each other and lived on the
same place in peace for seventy-eight years. Three-quarters
of a century; just think of it! They must live out the rest
of their lives together. Abe sent for his father, who came to
Oberlin and spent two months with him, promising to join
him and his wife in Louisiana should be outlive Mr. Overley.

At the end of three years the company began paying Abe

AS WE SEE IT.

three thousand dollars per year, he having come up to their full expectations.

We leave him on his plantation in the full enjoyment of home life, surrounded by his father and growing family, his wealth and usefulness increasing as the years speed by, increasing as the wealth and usefulness of many Negroes before him, and as the wealth and usefulness of many Negroes who come after him will increase.

And to a woman's love, a woman's implicit faith under most peculiar circumstances, a woman's tenderness, Abraham Overley gives all the credit for his success in life, and when the night is come, and the boy kneels beside them, Abe whispers to his sweetheart: "God grant, Nancy, that he loves you as I loved my mother."

THE END